HAPPINESS IS POSSIBLE

HAPPINESS
IS POSSIBLE

A NOVEL OF OUR TIME

Oleg Zaionchkovsky

Translated by Andrew Bromfield

Introduction by AD Miller

First published in English in 2012 by
And Other Stories, 91 Tadros Court, High Wycombe, Bucks, HP13 7GF

www.andotherstories.org

Originally published as Shchaste Vozmozhno
© Oleg Zaionchkovsky 2010
Agreement by www.nibbe-wiedling.com

English language translation © Andrew Bromfield, 2012

ISBN No. 978-1-908276-09-4

A catalogue record for this book is available from the British Library.

Supported by the National Lottery through Arts Council England.
The publication was effected under the auspices of the
Mikhail Prokhorov Foundation TRANSCRIPT Programme to
Support Translations of Russian Literature.

CONTENTS

INTRODUCTION

Moscow is a monster. The real Moscow – not the Chekhovian ideal or the inverse romanticism of espionage on Red Square – is a place of brutal roads, daunting architecture and icy steps on which, in winter, 'old ladies tumble like ninepins'. Moscow sometimes seems to have been designed without reference to the needs or convenience of actual human beings; it is overseen by corrupt, capricious bureaucrats and threatening policemen, who hover at the margins of Oleg Zaionchkovsky's novel. Often cruel, always indifferent, Moscow will 'find a replacement . . . in a minute or two' when one of its innumerable, anonymous petty functionaries drops dead. Ordinary Muscovites are 'brazen and timorous at the same time', and 'suspicious of everything'.

Yet few cities inspire such devotion – however caustic and ironic, as the love for Moscow that permeates *Happiness is Possible* often feels. But it is love all the same. Moscow, to its residents and would-be residents, is still the imperial capital, still sucking in money, ambitious people and their ideas from across the defunct empire: almost, these days, an overstimulating, infinite empire in itself.

So fierce is the devotion, so coveted Moscow's pleasures and privileges, that the fight for the right and space to live there is intense. The quest for a Moscow residence permit and apartment, or at least a room in a *kommunalka*, has for decades been one of the defining missions of many Russians' lives, both before and after the fall of the Soviet Union. (The continuities between Soviet times and afterwards are one of the minor themes of this book. These days, 'the shortage of gourmet delicacies and the lack of reliable information about what was happening in the world', as Zaionchkovsky's narrator summarises the old privations, are less severe; Moscow now has more glitz, more neon and more sports utility vehicles. But while they might be less lurid, the continuities can be just as striking, in this novel and in the real city it hymns.)

Now, as before, and as in *Happiness is Possible*, the urge to find and keep a place to live in Moscow dictates where and how people choose to work. And the same need can determine who they live with and for how long – as seems to be the case for the feuding mother and daughter with whom the novel opens, and for the succession of its characters who sacrifice a portion of their happiness to their permit. The housing question also governs the narrator's courtship, marriage and divorce with his beloved Tamara.

This tension – between romance and the city, between love of people and love of Moscow – is one of a triangle of relationships that are the backbone of this novel. Or, rather than relationships, it might be better to talk about the struggles between the city and romance. It is a contest that the city – 'the arbiter of our destinies and the master of our wills' – seems likely to win. 'Never argue with the city,' the narrator concludes. Although that is only halfway through his story. In a quiet but powerful way, children, or to be precise childlessness, are also at the subtle centre of this book.

Rivalling the theme of love and the city is that of the city and storytelling. Vast and volatile, Moscow is a natural factory of fables and fabulists, such as Zaionchkovsky's narrator, a flâneur who records or paraphrases or imagines the stories of his relatives, neighbours, chance acquaintances or non-acquaintances. There are a lot of novels about novelists, perhaps too many. But few writers use their avatars quite so originally. As the narrator's extrapolations spiral zanily into pure invention, Zaionchkovsky brings to life the miniature dramas, often tragedies, which populate the city. (In a place whose daily obstacles, whether climatic or bureaucratic, can often seem insuperable, 'drama' is an unusually fitting term for the business of everyday living.) More than that, though, Zaionchkovsky shows how lonely and isolating cities can be. After all, the real versions of the lives he describes are being lived right next to the narrator's, and right next to ours. Imagining them is a reminder that, outside the novel, we tend to know and care little about our metro attendants and street-sweepers.

The third and final side of the triangle is the link between storytelling and love. Both, in the narrator's account, involve passion and prevarication, long spells of timidity and sudden leaps of daring. Both, here, involve dreams and idealisation, and the creation of something that didn't exist until it did, which can just as instantly vanish. Yet both love and fiction are also, to some extent, formulaic and scripted, shaped by rules and expectations that comfort yet constrain. One of the book's beguiling subtleties is the way its Ovidian twists and connections keep leading, from dogs or funerals or some humdrum Soviet indignity, through some grimy Moscow street, back to Tamara.

Relatively few post-Soviet Russian novels have been translated into English; of those that have, many have been fantasies, fairy tales or historical detective stories. If you come to *Happiness is Possible* from the expansive realism of 19th-century Russian literature, the intimate, claustrophobic scale might surprise you. It's almost all Moscow, with a few visits to a *dacha* outside the city (a retreat that is also, in a way, part of the city: the *dacha* is the antithesis of Moscow, as much a place in the imagination as a real one, meaningful only in relation to the metropolis). There is also a very funny fishing trip, during which an expensive car gets stuck in the mud, as they often seem to in Russia.

But when you finish *Happiness is Possible*, and realise how much cleverer it is than it first appears, at least some of the expectations bequeathed by the Russian canon will have been met. Zaionchkovsky has an identifiably Russian, dark sense of humour. His writing is rewardingly risky, his slow-burn structure even more so. And I expect that, as it did for me, his novel will continue to make you think after you've finished it: about love, storytelling and Moscow.

One final observation. Readers may well find a few of the references to ethnic minorities made by the narrator to be unsavoury. It's worth pointing out that epithets and social attitudes that are now considered unacceptable in London or New York are indeed still common in Moscow, for all its sophistication.

AD Miller
London, January 2012

I'LL KILL YOU

'I'll kill you, you cow!' It's like a voice in a telephone receiver, only louder.

The air vent in the kitchen of my flat works like one of those old wired-in Soviet radio speakers that you can't switch off: it starts talking and goes silent whenever it feels like it. Unfortunately, it broadcasts the same old performance all year round. Even so, I still don't know the characters by name, because they address each other exclusively as: 'cow', 'slut', 'bitch', 'whore' ... There are too many epithets to list them all, far more than the number of *dramatis personae*, and I used to get confused at first about who was who. That's a problem I have in general: when I read other people's novels or watch 'heavy' movies, they're almost over by the time I start to figure out who's called what. It can be quite disappointing – I've only just settled in and got to know the characters, and it's the end of the movie already. But the ventilation system show is different, it doesn't have an ending, so like it or not,

1

eventually you start recognising the characters from their voices and their selection of epithets. The TV has assimilated this genre now as well, especially for dunces like me. But I think the censor spoils it all for them: if they've decided to show something, why blank out the most expressive parts of the dialogue with that hypocritical beeping? There isn't any censor in my kitchen. I could try stopping the voluble vent's mouth, of course, but then I'd be left with no air to breathe.

I don't know their names, I don't know what they look like, but I think about them a lot. When my own text – the one that's my vocation, the one I'm paid money for – when that text betrays me, then my weary thought mingles with my cigarette smoke and streams out through the air vent.

So who are they, these mysterious, familiar strangers, living in my ventilation system? They are two women, apparently mother and daughter. The young one is more often called 'bitch' and 'whore', and the one who's older is referred to as 'cow' and 'stinking slut', although sometimes they swap epithets and perhaps even roles. Occasionally the voices of some men or other reach me through the grille, but these male characters are clearly transient, and for them one epithet fits all: 'asshole'.

Living in the ventilation system – that's a joke, of course. In actual fact they live in the flat above mine, a fact that is easily confirmed by correlating the most vivid passages of their dialogue with the blows on my ceiling. 'I'll kill you, you cow!' – and immediately a loud crash overhead sets all the lights in my flat blinking. Whitewash dust sprinkles down onto the computer and my timorous thought takes flight, fluttering this way and that haphazardly, but up above they seem as right as rain. Still alive, despite all the threats, pursuing their interminable combat with even greater gusto. I don't know what weapons they use, perhaps they even pour water on each other, because sometimes after one of their battles royal the upper left corner of my kitchen turns damp. Incidentally, that's a good excuse for going upstairs and getting to know these dear ladies a bit better. I ought to do that, but every time the damp patch dries out before I can pluck up the courage.

I hear broadcasts from below when I open the little cupboard under the sink, where I keep the rubbish bucket. They come up through the hole in the floor that the drain and water pipes disappear into. Fortunately, the people who live down there are quite meek, no one ever kills anyone, and their contentiousness peaks over the issue of soup that isn't salty enough. I'd gladly swap floors with this good-natured family below me, but unfortunately that's an idea from fantasyland. Flat swaps are a sore point with me in general – but we'll get round to that later.

The people living below me and the turbulent couple above are unaware of each other's existence. I'm the only connecting link between them. That's the way things work in our high-rise: we live in layers and only play neighbours on the horizontal plane. And the one thing that obliges us to be neighbourly is our joint zone of responsibility and defence: the secure common hallway between the stairway and the flats. We call each other by name here as we argue about the felt boots left outside someone's door and whose turn it is to sweep out our small piece of communal territory. I don't mean by this that residents who live on different floors don't recognise each other at all. Ultimately, we all share another common line of defence: our ironclad entrance door. We can spot outsiders – complete and total strangers – and we eye them severely, not to say suspiciously. But nonetheless, to each other we people of different levels remain a closed book behind seven seals. And I myself, when I encounter that young woman with the tired-looking face in the lift yet again, think: could she be the bitch who irrigates the corner of my kitchen? Or that respectable-looking man in spectacles: could he be the captious soup-lover who speaks from under my kitchen sink?

Sometimes my position seems strange even to me. There they are, knowing nothing about each other, and probably not even wanting to, but I know or, rather, I have invented so much about them. I'm stuck in the middle, I am – pardon the comparison – like a sanitary towel, absorbing other people's intimacies. Now why would I want that? Perhaps it's the reflex response of my authorial gland, secreting away compulsively even when I am overcome by the sleep of reason? Ah, if only that gland always functioned to good purpose . . .

And meanwhile, I have absolutely no response to offer my neighbours, nothing to entertain them with while they're on pause. I am mute: my own soap opera has been a silent one since my wife left me. Only one thing betrays the fact that I'm still alive: the infrequent smell of bachelor-style home cooking seeping out under my door into the hallway.

'I'll kill you, you cow!'

No, Tamara and I never sank to the level of expressions like that. Even during the most difficult periods of our relationship, neither of us wished the other would croak or anything of that kind. And the point here is not that even in emotional extremis, cultured individuals always bear in mind the ease with which domestic sounds travel in a building. It was simply that we hadn't really anticipated getting rid of each other just yet. 'I'm so tired of you!' – that was what Tamara used to shout and then, after darting a rapid glance at the air vent, she would add the unquotable part of the phrase in an undertone. As befits a well-educated Moscow girl, she could be quite robust of tongue but, I assure you, she never made any threats against my person.

We lived as a married couple for many long years. Sometimes I recall those years with a radiant sadness, sometimes I want to lead as healthy a life as possible, so that my longevity will compensate for wasted time. The fact is, however, that when I ceased to be my wife's husband, the scales seemed to fall from my eyes. The plugs seemed to drop out of my ears and the cotton wool out of my nose . . . Newly orphaned, I was adopted by the entire world, taken under its wing. Sounds forgotten since my childhood thronged around me once again. A little tree stirred by the wind, a fly buzzing past, even that kitchen air vent: they all started speaking to me, prattling away in thousands of voices, purveying some significant babble of their own. And I started wondering what the fly was buzzing about, and what the 'cow' on the next floor up had done to earn her death sentence.

I used to spend long periods smoking on the balcony, bemused and bewildered, swamped by the sounds of existence. A previously inaudible aeroplane sang in the sky; a little dog tethered outside a shop wept inconsolably; children twittered in sparrow's voices ... The immense noise of the city, formerly echoed in my cranium only as a persistent, wearisome, drone, had now resolved itself into a multitude of small, distinct musical parts. And it seemed to me that if I investigated each one of these parts separately after only a very little while I would comprehend the total symphony of the universe ... But the cigarette burned out, and the little dog would still be crying. The little dog cried and nobody came to untie it. The flies buzzed, the trees rustled their leaves, the city droned on and on and the 'cow' on the next floor up was still being killed. And then one day I realised that nothing would change, the symphony of the universe would not come together, if I remained a mere listener. What the symphony lacked was my own voice: that was what the leaves were murmuring to me. And so for the first time I became fully aware of the purpose of my writer's calling and, having once grasped that, I started spending less time on the balcony and more time working. And this entire revolution took place when my wife left me.

Standing on the balcony is good for the nerves, by the way. Gazing at the generally peaceful, teeming bustle of humanity down below fills you with a benevolent, epic kind of calm. It's so convenient to love humanity from the height of the ninth floor.

'Filthy slut! Lousy skunk!'

The battle's roar is even more distinctly audible out here; the window above me must be open. What if someone – the mother or the daughter – suddenly falls out of it? What if one of the two skunks tumbles out and goes flying past my balcony, flailing her legs? And then, a couple of seconds later, thwacks down onto the asphalt, falling silent forever. But no, while I'm on the balcony it won't happen, no matter how much I dream about it. And it would be hard for her to thwack down onto the asphalt. The vast number of cars parked in our yard doesn't leave enough space for an apple to fall, let alone a human being. Most likely she would land on one of their polished roofs, which would give me additional pleasure. I must confess that for some time now I have regarded automobiles with profound animosity. When my wife left me, cars became my major source of irritation (apart, that is, from the turbulent couple heretofore described). Automobiles are the root of all evil in Moscow. Scuttling about insolently all over the city, breathing our air and polluting the environment. Creeping into every chink they can squeeze their fat bodies into. But, worst of all, at night the cars crowd into the yards of the buildings and perform hideous caterwauling concerts. Automobiles acquired their vocal apparatus as a means of defence against robbers. There was a time when cars used to have their windscreen wipers, mirrors, wheels and even windscreens stolen without complaining, because they were unable to appeal for help. I don't think anyone steals parts from them nowadays, but the alarm signal has developed into an independent form of musical art. I, however, am no fan of this music.

Lying in bed at night, listening to the demoniacal wailing, trilling and whistling, I call to mind other times, now long past. A nightingale nested quite close to us then; it wove its nocturnal melodies while Tamara snuffled peacefully in her sleep beside me. And though the car thieves were up to their tricks in the meantime, nothing they did ever disturbed the peace of the night.

Now the cigarette's finished. What do I do? Launch the butt downwards along the flight-path of the neighbour who didn't go zooming past? No way. I can't remember a single occasion when I've thrown anything off the balcony. I have no wish to resemble the individuals who do that – and there are, by the way, quite a few such individuals in our block. The flat roof of the shop that is located below us has a scattering of assorted garbage. Gusts of wind, especially before a thunderstorm, stir up the lighter items and bear them off, but the empty beer cans, which can't fly away, roll backwards and forwards across the roof, adding their own tinny thunder to the general aura of alarm at such moments. Today, however, the cans are lying still, because the troposphere is serenely becalmed. I don't know how the geomagnetic background's doing – I've never been sensitive to it – but the sky above the city is cloudless and tranquil. It's the same colour as a woman's eyes that you describe as blue while you're trying to win her favour. Today the gauzy veil of Moscow's habitual exhalations is so thin that the moon is actually peeping through it. So that's how it amuses itself: spying on us during the day, while we go about our business.

Business . . . I mention that word without any specific

reference to myself. For me personally, all the business of the day is over, thanks to the two skunks upstairs. Now I'm entitled to relax, which basically means I can put on my sandals and go for a walk. Beneath the moon or in tandem with it: I shall go spying on people too. There are lots of interesting things to see in the city.

Yes, I think that's what I'll do. Walking is better for the nerves than watching TV. Of course Philip . . . haven't I mentioned him yet? Philip's my current flatmate. Of course, Philip will want to come with me, but I'll ask him to stay at home. Because it's only a manner of speaking to say that he comes with me, everything actually turns out the other way round. It has to be one thing or the other: a walk with Philip or a stroll with the moon . . .

'I'll kill you, you cow!'

Damn! Where have my sandals got to?

THE WALK

I'd have liked to change the subject, only there's a problem. I still can't find my sandals. Or rather, one of them. Philip rarely steals the complete pair; even he has enough brains to realise I can't escape from him in just one. I've looked for it in the front hall, and in the kitchen, and under the sofa in the room – but all in vain. The sandal's not in any of the places where it ought to be. Even the kidnapper himself is confused. He'd be only too glad to help me now: Phil's intuition tells him I've already given up the idea of going out on my own and I'm willing to take him along with me. We'll go for a stroll together, the pair of us inseparable, as ever, if only the other half of my pair of sandals shows up. But where is it? Phil can't remember. And it seems like only a moment ago he had it in his teeth. . .

This time he's really outdone himself: he buried it in our bed! Of course, that same sandal is immediately applied to his backside. But then, the question could be raised of why, sandal or no sandal, the bed is still unmade. Except that there isn't anyone to raise it: the solitary life has its own bitter privileges. The snag is that I'm not entirely solitary. If I wish to retreat into genuine solitude, Philip imposes his company on me, and when I get the urge to commune with him, it turns out that he's not really a person after all.

Well, things can just carry on the way they are, it's no great disaster if not everything goes the way I'd like it to. It's about time I got used to it. Especially since there are occasional happy coincidences – for instance, the good weather and my desire to go for a walk. When I think about it, there are lots of these coincidences. Say, we get into the lift and there's a sweet little bitch already riding down in it. That's for Phil, of course, but at least I can feel glad for him.

To be honest, though, I prefer reliable pleasures, without any coincidences. For instance, our Tajik doorman is an unfailingly pleasant individual, come rain or shine.

'Hello, Nasir!'

See, he gave me a little wave. It isn't a holiday today, or Nasir would certainly have congratulated me on it. He congratulates me on all the Orthodox holidays and Russia Day. I only congratulate him on the end of Ramadan, because that's the only Muslim holiday I know. Incidentally, there's someone who's familiar with our entire stairwell from top to bottom. If I weren't so shy, I'd have complained to him about my contentious neighbours long ago. I've noticed lots of people do that: they take all their little woes to Nasir, and he decides who merely deserves his sympathy and whose problem merits a call to the emergency services or the militia.

Which means that in the person of Nasir we have another coincidence, in this case of the pleasant with the useful.

Phil and I walk outside and immediately meet another Tajik sweeping the pavement. But this is no coincidence, it's merely the norm. A Tajik and a broom in summer, a Tajik and an ice pick in winter, a Tajik and a lawnmower – these are all integral concepts of Moscow life. True, I have heard that in the business-class neighbourhood to which my ex-wife has moved, the sweeping is done by Ukrainians, but it's not yet clear who does the job better. I've got no complaints about the Tajiks; I don't know how they feel about me.

I look around, adjusting to the dense air at ground level while I wait for Phil to relieve himself quickly in the bushes by the entrance. I've learned not to feel ashamed of this habit of his. Now we're ready to set off, I just have to note the time. I like to keep track of time, not only when I'm boiling an egg or something else, but whatever I'm doing. I don't actually know which ancestors I inherited this meticulous approach from. I raise my wrist to my eyes, but there's no watch on it – I forgot to put it on when I was looking for my sandals. All right, it's no disaster. The sun is stuck in the south, between blocks 24 and 26B, and it seems to me that it will be hanging there for a long time yet. We have lots of time, time already past and time still to squander. As the true descendant of that anonymous meticulous ancestor I have, of course, planned out the route of our walk in advance, and we can easily cover it in the time available. We'll manage it all right, if Phil doesn't give every single bush a thorough sniffing and I don't analyse every single Tajik that we meet.

My plans involve walking all the way to a genuine, large park. This is a realistic goal, we only have to walk past two neighbourhoods of seventeen-storey buildings exactly like mine, past another neighbourhood of buildings a bit older and lower, cross a couple of streets with traffic and one major road and then walk two hundred yards along that road. Not far by Moscow standards. In theory, about twenty minutes' walking; in practice – that is, with Philip – forty. But since I don't have a watch with me, that doesn't matter anyway.

So, we go to the park but, naturally, not to the gates that were erected by the municipal authorities, where there's always a militiaman hanging about, yawning. We infiltrate the territory of the park illegally, via a shorter path, known only to me and Philip and another two or three hundred thousand Muscovites. This inconspicuous path runs between the brick wall of a factory and an old abandoned sports ground. Although the sports ground isn't entirely abandoned. Drinking and sleeping on the remains of the stands are tramps (aka Individuals of No Fixed Abode) and several aboriginal Muscovites who have latched onto them. And some young guys are screeching belligerently as they kick up their feet clad in high boots and smash bricks against their shaven heads. While the Tajiks sweep the streets, *they* are honing their martial arts skills. The young guys look terrifying, but Philip and I have nothing to fear. My ancestors' twisted strands of DNA could not possibly have endowed me more clearly with the features of the titular ethnic group, while Philip's rather more complicated genome has moulded him into a purebred mongrel. And anyway, the skinheads are so busy smashing bricks, they're not likely to notice any-one else nearby. I don't think they can see anything but stars right now.

Our secret point of access is masked by a heap of rub-bish – broken bricks and all sorts of dubious garbage that gets dumped by the tramps. Not everybody would even guess that this is the entrance to a genuine big park.

Blessed be the fences of Russia! We have so many of them, but there's a secret way through every one. Knowledge of these gaps is what makes us free men and women. Like any arcane knowledge, it gives us a sense of elite superior-ity. Probably the first thing Russians do when they get to the next world is seek out the loose planks in the fence enclosing the Pastures of Heaven. They seek them out in order to wan-der to and fro at will, bypassing the apostolic face-control. The knowledge of passable gaps is a prerogative of the local population. In our provincial towns, only the locals can move about without sinking knee-deep in mud, and every native Muscovite is naturally endowed at birth with knowledge of the metro system map. Although I wasn't born in Moscow, I regard myself as a local too, because I have mastered this loophole. Tamara, my ex-wife, is a native Muscovite, and it feels good to know that since she left me I have by no means lost my way in the big city.

Once in the park, the first thing I do, to our great mutual satisfaction, is unleash myself from Phil. Even for creatures who are very close, it's good sometimes to sepa-rate, to lose sight of each other. To go running off, but not very far and only for a short while, and then, when that momentary pang of orphanhood strikes, you can stand up on your back legs in the grass and see: Yes, there it is, my own kindred creature. Of course, when I let Phil go, I don't abandon my responsibility for him. If a mounted militiaman were suddenly to appear and ask whose dog that is running around, I should be obliged to admit that it is mine. For that, the militiaman could reprimand me and prohibit further off-the-leash dog walking, or he could simply nod and proceed majestically on his way. I don't know what he would do, because so far not a single militiaman, either mounted or on foot, has ever shown up in this remote corner of the park. There isn't really anything here for the militia to patrol: no one can disturb the public peace, for lack of any public, and no one can damage public property for lack of any such item. That's what's so wonderful about a genuine big park – the authorities aren't able to put it all in good order. The authorities don't have enough benches, lamps, paving slabs and militiamen – and that's just the way we like it. Phil and I both prefer paths that lurk in the unmown grass and trees that haven't grown according to a plan from the department of landscaping, but simply where the parental seed happened to fall. Perhaps that's because, after all, both he and I are only first-generation urbanites?

But this is not yet the final point on our itinerary. We go further. The faint, narrow track is hidden, as I have already said, in the unmown grass, which is actually mostly old, vicious nettles that sting even through trousers. Then we have to clamber down a steep slope that would be easier to slide down on my backside. At the bottom there's a permanently soggy little meadow that squishes underfoot. We cross it, gathering burrs along the way, surrounded by bees and dragonflies that shoot up around us in alarm. Just a little bit further, and we shall arrive at our destination. 'But what kind of destination is it,' you ask, 'if it takes such a great effort to reach?' A moment's patience, please. We force our way through a barrage of tenacious little bushes, and there it is before us, the goal of our journey. And that goal is the River Moscow.

The Moscow, greenish and not very wide, washing against a bank reinforced with boulders. Like any river, it serves as a natural barrier, a dividing line and border. Here on the riverbank the park ends. And somewhere in the navigable channel – perhaps where that pyramidal buoy is bobbing about – lies the border of my municipal district. If I were to take it into my head to swim across that border, I would emerge onto the far bank as a second-class citizen. If I were to lodge a complaint with the local council, they wouldn't even bother to register it, they'd send me back across the river.

'There is no land for us beyond the Moscow,' I remark jokingly to Phil.

But he's quite happy on his own native riverbank. After a quick slurp of the Moscow's dubious water, he sets off on his usual duck hunt and I sit down on a rock and take out a cigarette. Phil has his interests and I have mine. I smoke and gaze at the river, anticipating the appearance of some little ship. But the Moscow waterway is surprisingly deserted. I can't understand how there can be almost no pulse beating in the aquatic artery of such an immense city. Especially at a time when life is seething so exuberantly on dry land. And seething with particular intensity in that district beyond the river where my complaints have no validity. Over there, white-and-pink business-class apartment blocks rise up into the air one behind the other. On the twenty-fourth floor of one of them my ex-wife lives her bright, sparkling new life. I know the building, I can even see it from my little rock. If I had a pair of binoculars, I could examine Tamara's windows from here.

I sit there, waiting for a little ship and thinking how strangely everything has turned out. Tamara and I never used to go for walks in this part of the park, because it's impossible to walk in high heels here, but now I trudge all this way as if I were coming to visit her.

THEY DRIVE TO THE *DACHA*

Summer. Saturday morning. A self-assured Geländewagen in the stream of cars rushing out of the city. Dmitry Pavlovich and Tamara are driving to the *dacha* in their jeep. Tamara is Dmitry Pavlovich's second wife and Dmitry Pavlovich is Tamara's second husband. I don't know who Dmitry Pavlovich's first wife was; he doesn't associate with her anymore. But I was Tamara's first husband and they're driving to my *dacha*. They actually have a country house of their own, but since Tamara introduced me and Dmitry Pavlovich, they've started visiting me regularly. Dmitry Pavlovich and I are on a friendly footing, as they say. I address him simply, by his abbreviated patronymic – Pavlich – the same way as his driver does. I've seen the driver a couple of times; he is Pavlich's namesake, another Dmitry, so to avoid confusing them, everybody calls him Little Dima. Little Dima is six feet seven inches tall.

Dmitry Pavlovich has several reasons for travelling to Vaskovo, sixty kilometres from the centre of Moscow, to visit me several times this summer. Firstly, it does no harm for his Geländewagen to remember occasionally that it's an SUV. Secondly, Dmitry Pavlovich claims he thinks my shish kebab is absolutely wonderful. And thirdly, for some reason he finds it necessary to share his observations on life with me. Dmitry Pavlovich himself is a man of business, these observations are of no use to him, but I'm the only writer among his acquaintances. He thinks factual material is very important for me, so that I won't have to 'suck it all out of my finger', as he puts it. I'll tell you later what his material's like and where he sucks it out of.

It's harder to understand why Toma comes to my place. If I ask her, she'll answer without a second thought: 'What do you mean, why? I have to make sure you're alive and well. And someone has to water your vegetable patch'. But it's worth remembering that if a woman answers without a second thought, it means she's lying. She never watered the vegetable patch, even when we were married. I suspect she doesn't water the patch at their new country seat either, if there is one. It seems more likely to me that she comes here to convince herself once again that she hasn't fallen back in love with me. And at the same time to compare me, the slob, with her Dima; just look how clever and observant he is, he could quite easily have been a man of letters too, if only he wasn't so busy with business and knew how to write.

So on Saturday morning this couple are driving to my *dacha*. It being the weekend, Dmitry Pavlovich is driving the car himself. He swings the wheel left and right and Moscow turns first one side of itself, and then another, to the windows of the Geländewagen. The car radio is playing. Seven speakers, hidden in various places, create full surround sound, so the DJ's squawking is sometimes here, sometimes there, like an escaped parrot fluttering around the interior. When Dmitry Pavlovich is at the wheel, he prefers the sounds the radio makes to the sounds that Tamara would make. She knows this and keeps quiet.

Meanwhile, the cityscape outside the windows changes. At the present moment the highway is lined with concrete warehouse terminals that look like immense shoe boxes. They alternate with concrete high rises that look like warehouse terminals. This is the Moscow periphery. Soon there'll be the orbital highway, and beyond that . . . There's actually nothing very terrible beyond it, it's just that it's this psychological frontier: the MOH or Moscow Orbital Highway. As it approaches, Tamara starts showing signs of anxiety and eventually breaks her silence.

'It's the ring road soon,' she announces.

'Well, so?' Dmitry Pavlovich responds.

'Are you going to stop to get some food?'

'Dammit!' he exclaims in annoyance. 'Why didn't you say anything earlier?'

'Sure, it's always me who has to think of everything!'

Dmitry Pavlovich slows down and watches the sides of the road.

'Just try finding a decent shop round here . . .' he mutters with a frown.

There are shops here all right, but they lack impressive brand names: just plain 'Delicatessen' and 'Groceries'. Eventually Tamara spies a big, spanking new supermarket up ahead.

'There,' she says, pointing. 'See it – on the left?'

'I can see it's on the left,' Dmitry Pavlovich responds sullenly. 'The question is, where do I find a place for a U-turn?'

He pulls up at the verge, but doesn't get out of the car, just carries on sitting there with his arms round the steering wheel.

'What are you thinking about, Dima?' Tamara asks him.

'I'm wondering where I can make a U-turn,' Dima answers. 'We'll have to drive to the ring road.'

Tamara has been married before; she knows how to exercise self-restraint.

'We're here,' she says in a calm voice, 'and the shop's over there. All we have to do is cross the road. There's no point in looking for a place to turn.'

Don't get the idea that Dmitry Pavlovich is slightly dimwitted. He's no more dim-witted than other men, and in his own area, according to Tamara, he's quite the creative individual. It's just that he's a territorial creature, and his creative capacity decreases proportionally as he moves further away from the city centre. But now Tamara takes control of things. She manages to persuade Dmitry Pavlovich to stroll across to the other side of the road, since there happens to be a pedestrian underpass not far from the spot where they have stopped. Every cloud has its silver lining. By stretching his legs for a few minutes, Dmitry Pavlovich will augment his stock of observations on life and avoid arriving empty-handed to visit a writer.

And so our couple abandon the Geländewagen and set off to the supermarket for provisions to bring to Vaskovo. Meanwhile in Vaskovo, preparations to receive them are already under way. The old stocks of provisions have been audited: some have been extracted from the fridge, some have been scraped off the frying pan. Everything that might offend Tamara with its appearance and smell has been thrown into the compost pit. The garland of freshly washed socks has been removed from the kitchen as an excessively pathetic symbol of the bachelor life. The small double bed I share with Phil has been made up. Phil himself has been brushed more or less clean. Even the sky above Vaskovo some-how looks especially clean and well-scrubbed today – but that's not due to my efforts.

The blue of the sky, the green of the gardens – a delight-ful rural district scene. I smoke on the porch, enlivening the composition with a patch of bright red: I'm wearing a scarlet Finnish t-shirt that Tamara once bought for me. In years of wearing, it hasn't faded – when I've got it on, insects come flying up to investigate whether there's any nectar on me: even little beetles are suckers for something foreign. But what do they need nectar for, when the air here is so pure and delicious? 'It's really great to have a *dacha* in Vaskovo,' I think complacently between drags. 'I wouldn't swap it for anything.' But in reality, I did that already a long time ago: swapped Vaskovo for Moscow. Because – I'll tell you a secret – the *dacha* isn't really a *dacha* at all, it's my very first home. Yes, dear people, I was born here, but I later abandoned my native parts. I used to play on this porch as a child. My father and mother lived out their lives in this little house. And it was Tamara who taught me to call this place a *dacha*.

Something stirs on the nearby church bell tower – the human clock is about to chime the hour. . . Should I shout and ask if they can see an approaching Geländewagen from up there?

'Bong-ng-ng!'

It's coming. I can feel it in my heart. And there it is, bowling slowly along my street, crunching the stone chips and feeling out the potholes with its broad tyres. Show more spunk, automobile, you're an off-roader! The encounter is now assured: Misty, Philip's friend who doubles as the local town crier, runs out in front of the Geländewagen like a paparazzo in front of some movie diva, choking on his ecstatic barking as he bites at its wheel. And now my neighbours have stuck their heads out from behind their fences, like puppets peering round screens. Only this time they're not giving the performance, but gaping at the car. All right, let them decide if the sight was worth abandoning their vegetable gardens for.

The Geländewagen is still moving, but conflict has already arisen in the welcoming committee: in their excitement Philip and Misty have got into a scuffle. I settle the incident with a few well-aimed kicks, but the general air of tension persists. And now ready, get set – the automobile has stopped outside my gate. The doors on both sides of it swing open and two quite different feet appear below them; on the left, a woman's foot in a light shoe; on the right, a man's foot in a long-nosed ankle boot. They both step down onto the soil of Vaskovo rather uncertainly . . . and basically that's it: the arrival has taken place. After that come the hugs, the tickling of dogs behind the ears and the unloading of the boot. Three or four minutes later, the stage is already deserted, apart from Misty and the Geländewagen. The Geländewagen, however, has played its part for today; its heart stopped beating even before the gate closed behind its master, it barely even had time to whistle in farewell. To Misty it is now no more than a cooling heap of metal. Quite indifferently, purely for form's sake, the little dog sprinkles a motionless tyre and trots off about his business. The performance is over.

But is it really over? If we move backstage, we'll see the show is still going on, out of sight of prying eyes.

'A great place you've got here!' Dmitry Pavlovich booms in his deep voice, drawing the air in noisily through his nose. 'You know, kind of cosy . . .'

He says that to be magnanimous, and I disagree to be modest.

'What's so very cosy . . . ? The country's the country.'

'Oh, come on,' Dmitry Pavlovich protests. 'I see you've got apples over there.'

'Big deal, apples . . . Apples grow at your hacienda, don't they, Pavlich?'

'Na-ah . . . Tomka grows those whatsits there . . . orchids. And they smell of shit.'

He casts a sidelong glance at Tamara, and he's not wrong – she admonishes him.

'I don't like it when you talk like that. It's not becoming to a man.'

Tamara wants her Dima to appear *comme il faut* in my company.

'And incidentally,' she continues in a defiant tone, 'while we're on the subject, it smells of that round here without any orchids. And his apples are only good for compote.'

'Well, compote's something at least ...' Dmitry Pavlovich is squinting sideways at me now. 'And as for the stench, Bunny, you're wrong there – there's no smell like that ...' – and, deliberately taking another deep breath, he unexpectedly sucks in a midge and gives a shrill sneeze.

To put an end to their quarrel, I invite both 'bunnies' inside. But even here the theatricals continue. Tamara assumes an air of no-nonsense solicitude and checks the cleanliness of my kitchen. Dmitry Pavlovich demonstrates his relaxed amiability and common touch by taking a seat in Phil's armchair without being asked. I don't drive him off: let his expensive trousers collect a good thick coating of dog hair. The only reason Phil doesn't growl at him is because he's already investigated the bags that arrived with the visitors and now he's pretending to be a cute little doggy, in hopes of rich pickings. An understandable motive, if not very pretty. But just why I am pretending to be a cute and affectionate relative is something I can't explain.

The day passes in the way that a summer day at the *dacha* should: in glorious idleness. So that it will be remembered for nothing but this state of drowsy, delightful drifting. The scene in my garden is a kind of orgy in reverse, with the four of us relaxing in the style of a pride of lions. Philip sprawls in the shade under a bush. Tamara sunbathes on the grass, displaying her lack of cellulite. Dmitry Pavlovich, as the dominant male, reclines in the hammock with a newspaper. And I am also installed rather comfortably in an old wicker armchair. To avoid dozing off completely, Dmitry Pavlovich and I do the crossword as a team. The division of labour is as follows: I give the answers and he writes them in with a pencil.

'A composer beginning with G.'

'Gounod,' I reply.

'Doesn't fit. Five letters'

'Gluck, then.'

'Well done, the writer . . . Right, next . . . A condition of an insurance contract . . . ten letters, starting with D . . . Oh, that's deductible!'

'That's my great brain!' Tamara purrs from the grass.

I thought she wasn't listening to us. That's the first word her Dima has guessed.

'Damage,' Dmitry Pavlovich continues.

'Injury,' I reply.

'No, only four letters.'

'Loss, then.'

'Loss, loss . . . Right . . .'

Dmitry Pavlovich suddenly jerked his head up and swayed in the hammock.

'Listen, today Tomka and I saw this little scene – it might come in handy to you as a writer. This tramp and his lady tramp are swearing at each other in an underground passage. He hits her, and she yells at him: "Do you want to lose me?".'

A pause.

'Is that it?'

'Well yes . . . "Do you want to lose me?" – it's hilarious.'

'I don't see anything funny about it,' Tamara puts in.

I agree with her.

VASKOVO-MOSCOW

Have you ever found yourself in the Central Administrative District of Moscow on a fine Sunday in summer? Probably not, because, like all normal people, you spend days like that at the *dacha*. I would be out at Vaskovo too, and wouldn't have a clue about what's going on here in the CAD, if not for a certain important circumstance. Which is that today I have been invited to do a radio interview. Generally speaking, I'm not very fond of interviews of any sort. They say some writers have a yen for publicity that is even more powerful than their sex drive, but that's not me. However, if I have to give an interview, I prefer it to be on radio. On TV they always start powdering your nose just before you go on, and the trouble with a newspaper is that print immortalises all the stupid things you've said, augmented by the interviewer's own inanities. So radio is best: it doesn't matter what you look like and anything you happen to blurt out will simply evaporate into the ether and be forgotten, even before the next programme starts.

I have been invited by a radio station that is small but reputable. Its studio is tucked away somewhere round here, not far from the centre of Moscow, in a flat in one the buildings. If I can find it, and you can hook this particular station out of the FM ocean, in half an hour you'll be able to hear my muttering going out live. I still don't know what we're going to talk about, but that doesn't matter anyway. The important thing about a radio interview is not to lisp, blow your nose or leave any long pauses. If everything goes well, the interviewer will give me a thumbs-up, but you, the listeners, won't be able to see it.

Such is the serious reason I have for being here now, right smack in the middle of Moscow on this hot summer noon. As I walk along, I have to stick to the shady side of the street, and let me tell all of you out there at your *dachas* that you wouldn't recognise your city at this moment. Imagine a whale, cast up on the seashore and drying out in the sun. All those who sailed on it, who inhabited the folds of its vast skin, have scattered, creeping off to save their own little lives. Where are the usual crowds of people? Where are the legendary Moscow traffic jams? The streets are as empty as a writer's head before an interview. Only a small number of the megalopolis' most devoted parasites remain in its skin, those who are fated to live and – if it comes to the crunch – to die with it. Who are they, these most urban of urbanites? For the most part, they are Individuals of No Fixed Abode and various kinds of beggars. The Abodeless Individuals sleep or wander wherever the mood takes them – today they are as free as the cockroaches in the kitchen when we go out. But the beggars have a simple way of amusing themselves – to keep their skills well-honed, they cadge handouts from each other. There aren't many other people about: apart from writers who have come to be interviewed, most are probably burglars, plying their trade in the flats that you, dear *dacha*-lovers, have abandoned.

I don't know this area very well, but I can sense that I'm going in the right direction. I have never once lost my way in Moscow while in a sober state, and if I'm feeling slightly squiffy at the moment, it's only because of the sultry heat. As I wander through the unfamiliar side streets, an angel flies ahead of me, showing me the way. And right now he prompts me to turn left, then right, then jump over a section of subsidence or, perhaps, excavation, and I find myself . . . yes indeed, I find myself in the courtyard that I need. Every-thing's right: the street name, the number of the building and, most important of all, the sign with the name of my radio station by the entrance. Only the time is wrong: I was told to arrive twenty minutes later. As you already realise, this is very un-Muscovite, arriving somewhere ahead of time. The girls in the office will have to give me coffee and make idle conversation with me. And every now and then they'll go running off on some urgent matter or other, leaving me alone with my own embarrassment. And apart from that, in our Moscow editorial offices you never know beforehand whether you can smoke or you have to go out onto the stairs.

All these considerations are expounded to me by my

other angel – the angel of reason. I take his advice and decide to spend my last few non-public minutes sitting on a bench in the courtyard. I sit down, light up a cigarette and, for want of anything better to do, start gazing around. It's a normal Moscow courtyard, the standard four walls. Except that the item standing at the centre of it is not a transformer shed or a pumping station, but a large cubic structure with gill slits in its sides. Warm, insistent winds blow out of these slits in all four directions with a steady drone, saturating the courtyard in an aroma well known to every inhabitant of the capital. I don't even need to summon the angel of reason to know that this structure is a Moscow Metro blowhole. Apart from that, everything is the way it should be in an ordinary courtyard: children's swings, sandpits, benches for those who wish to sit. And all this is empty just at the moment – not because of the currents of suffocating air emerging from the blowhole, but because, let me remind you, it is a Sunday in summer.

Although ... I beg your pardon, I didn't spot the old woman sitting diagonally across from me in the shadow of a tree. Perhaps she was left behind by someone when they were packing their things for the *dacha* ... She isn't smoking, or feeding the pigeons, or reading a book. Just sitting on a bench, with the wind from the metro stirring her grey locks. 'She's probably not right in the head,' I think. 'These Moscow grannies can be very weird.' We're sitting a long way apart, so I can't make out her face. In five minutes' time I'll go to tell the listeners about myself and my art. I'll forget about the old woman and never discover that she and I are actually very, very old acquaintances.

Her name is Marina Mikhailovna and she's not entirely a Moscow granny. At least, her pre-dotage years were not spent here in the Central Administrative District but on suburban trains on the Vaskovo route: sixty kilometres in each direction; for forty-five years and a few months. Aunty Marina lived in the little house next to ours and, of course, she also had a plot of land – the standard 400 square metres – but it was my mother who had to cultivate it, because Aunty Marina herself had no time. She worked in the Moscow Metro. To thank us for helping her, she used to bring us sweets from the Babaev Confectionery Factory and she once took me to Moscow for a children's New Year party. I remember her always being dressed in good taste, with a beret on her head, but she never found happiness as a woman. How could she possibly organise any kind of happiness, when she spent half her life travelling? Of course, lots of men walk by in the metro, but who, can you tell me, is going to stop and flirt with the woman operating the escalator? My mother and I once happened to be at Aunty Marina's station during her shift. When my mother recognised her, she was delighted, but Aunty Marina merely nodded to us severely and turned back to her microphone: 'Move along, citizens, don't crowd at the turnstiles!'

It wasn't as if it was difficult to find a job in Vaskovo in those days. The chemical plant was smoking away like billy-o, not to mention the reinforced concrete and timber-processing plants. My parents just couldn't understand why our neighbour put herself through the torment of that daily journey to Moscow. It couldn't be just so that she could eat sausages and Babaev chocolates every day. My father, a blunt man, said it straight out: 'That Marina's not all there'. 'But where else could she be?' I wondered to myself. 'There aren't two of her are there?'

In those years, naturally enough, I was under my father's influence, but in my heart I liked Aunty Marina's metropolitan style. I didn't know then that in a few years' time I would come down with her ailment and discover for myself what love is. For me, it wasn't Moscow in general, but only one of its inhabitants, who cast her spell on me, made me love her and ruined my life. But that's a different story.

Moscow remained indifferent to Marina's selfless love. This woman paid for her brief trysts with the city with arduous shifts deep underground. She walked with the stride of a Muscovite, she dressed like a Muscovite and she bought sausages at the delicatessen – a nicely judged three hundred grams. But it was all in vain. In the evenings Marina saw the warm glow appear in the windows of the Moscow high-rises, but not a single window belonged to her. In all this vast and magnificent agglomeration of living space, there was not a single square metre for Marina. The trams clanged invitingly as they bore off the genuine Muscovites to their legally registered addresses, but her way led back to the railway station. The dirty, smoke-filled suburban electric train, crammed with other non-residents like herself, screeched like a sick rooster as it carried Marina off and away into the dark and cold.

And so it went on, year after year. It's a commonplace to compare human life with a journey, but in Aunty Marina's case, the route was very specific: Vaskovo-Moscow, followed by Moscow-Vaskovo. I don't know if there were ever any occurrences or events worthy of note on this route of hers. She and my mother occasionally whispered together about something or other, but my father and I were not in the habit of listening to women's talk. Practically nothing changed in Aunty Marina's life until she retired. And when her professional journey came to an end and she was obliged to settle down in Vaskovo, we all thought she had reached the end of her line. There were no more sausages and Babaev sweets, and it saddened us to see how quickly our neighbour grew old when she was separated from the object of her undivided passion.

Naturally, her plot of land was the most neglected on our street. She hated the chickens that she had bought on my mother's advice; in fact she was afraid of them. They responded in kind and ran away whenever an opportunity arose. We were the only people she spoke to, because the other neighbours disliked her and referred to her derisively as 'the Moscow woman'. A headscarf and knitted cardie certainly didn't suit Marina Mikhailovna, but now she deliberately went around all got-up for days at a time, as if she was expressing her contempt for our entire wretched village.

However hard Marina Mikhailovna's previous life might have been, those years were the most joyless for her. What could be sadder than a lonely old age? Just sitting there, fading away, and if you go scampering after a chicken, the thought of how the sprint might end is terrifying. How would it all have ended for Marina Mikhailovna? Most likely in a stroke or a heart attack. The answer to this question seemed close at hand already . . . but, as things turned out, it was unexpectedly postponed.

My own good parents were instrumental in bringing about a surprising and fortunate turning point in Marina Mikhailovna's fate. Her happiness came knocking at our gate first, in the form of a polite little old man who enquired if he could rent a room from us for the summer. In those days, that was all in the order of things: Muscovites rented *dachas* from the local residents instead of building their own. At first, for a moment, my mother was delighted. A household can always do with more money, and her son's room (that is, mine) was free, because he (that is, I) was living in Moscow then. The son, however, sometimes came home for a good feed, or simply for the weekend, and when he saw that his room was occupied, he might take offence, who could tell? But on the other hand the son was no pampered toff and the house had a veranda where he could be accommodated quite easily . . . Basically, my mother was in urgent need of my father's advice. My father listened to all her reasoning, then went outside to take a look at the old man. The two of them chatted for about ten minutes, then my father came back into the house to speak to my mother – so that the visitor wouldn't hear:

'He's no good for us. Far too tedious. You know what . . . fix him up with Marina the Moscow Woman.'

And he went off again to watch the television. There was no point in arguing with him, so my mother took the lodger to our neighbour's house. It was easy enough to see why my father hadn't taken a shine to the old man: if a man doesn't drink at all, doesn't smoke and doesn't play chess, it's simply not possible to live under the same roof with him, even if he is paying for it.

But, strangely enough, the old man settled in well at Aunty Marina's house. Or perhaps she had her eye on him right from the start – women are great strategists in such matters. However that may be, this granddad not only stayed with her for the whole summer, paying punctually, but at the end of the season he offered her his heart and his hand. Exactly how Marina Mikhailovna had captivated the old Muscovite is a secret that he took with him to the grave, but we don't even need to ask why she accepted his proposal. The young couple didn't have a grand wedding, but they completed all the due procedures at the register office.

Of course, you've already guessed what happened after that. The little old non-smoker, whose name we can't even recall now, died soon afterwards – they say he ran after a chicken. And Marina Mikhailovna didn't think for too long before selling her 'country estate' and taking up residence in his Moscow flat.

Many years have passed since then. Possibly Marina Mikhailovna herself has forgotten the name of her transient spouse, but that's not important. She's happy; she'll live for a long time yet ... but I don't have time to invent that life right now, I have to go to my meeting with the radio girls and you ... When Marina Mikhailovna eventually does die, Moscow – the love of her life – won't even notice.

HAPPINESS IS POSSIBLE

Night. Patchy with cloud, the yellow-white sky sags down over the city like a slack cinema screen. Streaks and patches of light ramble across it, and the glow-worms of various flying-machines add to the interest with their slow, soundless movement. But there's no film tonight or, rather, this is the only one on the bill, a free psychedelic show for the inhabitants of Moscow's high-rises. Not exactly an action movie, it must be admitted, but strangely enough this final performance attracts quite a lot of viewers. All the seats here are economy class and smokers are welcome.

On the balcony I breathe life into my little spark, and similar sparks glimmer on the balconies and loggias of the buildings nearby. Every year, until the frosty weather sets in, we nocturnal smokers broadcast our indecipherable light signals to each other and the sky. We ourselves cannot be seen

– we're like that dark cosmic matter, the existence of which can only be inferred indirectly. Who are you, my nocturnal fellows, lurking in the crepuscular cavities of your loggias? What philosophical and metaphysical heights have you scaled while gazing at the Moscow sky? Perhaps some of you have far outstripped me in your intellectual development . . .

An aeroplane probes the air with its searchlight like a feeler as it topples towards the airport. These days all the airlines are economising on fuel, so the landing will be precipitous, but even so the passengers will fight off their nausea and applaud. The cigarette butt that flew past my nose only a second ago will land sooner than that and without any applause; the anonymous smoker who lives somewhere above me clearly does not belong to any advanced civilisation.

The cigarette butt lands on the ground and slowly fades. It could have landed on the roof of a car parked for the night or the head of a teenager drinking beer, but it lies there on the asphalt, dying slowly without disturbing anyone – and there's another one! Asphalt is the basic ground of the city and deposits like this accumulate on it. I don't know exactly what asphalt is brewed out of, or how, but I have heard that its substance is organic in origin. That gives me pause for thought. I certainly know people are wrong when they claim that nothing grows on asphalt. There's a group of youngsters bawling away below me at this very moment, exuberant growth that has sprung up on asphalt. And I grew on it too, as a person and as a writer.

I wouldn't wish to sound like some kind of urban idealist, but life in a city really is rather comfortable. Sleeping to its quiet clamour at night and hearing the refuse truck churring considerately in the morning as it assists your building's collective intestinal tract to void itself. Passing the day swaddled in urgent concerns, with breaks for nourishment, and in the evening enjoying a well-earned dose of relaxation, according to your own taste. What could possibly be better? You're afraid of the dark, but in the city it's never dark, even at night. You're afraid of the distant stars and outer space, but you won't see them here. And if you should wish to give your nerves a subtle *frisson* before bed, you can watch the news of the city on TV.

I enjoy watching the Moscow news sometimes – especially the crime news. Especially the news about scores being settled in the upper echelons of power and business, and about celebrities' limousines being stolen. At moments like that it feels good to know that you are poor and obscure. There is no better defence than being small and unimportant. A tiny creature can hide more easily and it doesn't hurt itself when it falls over. Say what you will, it feels good to be inconspicuous, and what else, if not the city, can bestow this snug, secure feeling upon us?

Of course, we little people also weep, and there is drama in our life too. Our life has all sorts of amusing twists, never mind that they don't make it into the news bulletins and are immediately consigned to oblivion or, in the very best case, are assimilated by second-rate novelists. Actually, before you fall asleep, I just wanted to tell you a story about a woman I know, a perfectly ordinary city-dweller. In fact, she's a schoolfriend of my ex-wife, but a close acquaintance of mine too.

Her name is Lida Surkova. That is, her first name is Lida and Surkova is her school name. I won't say maiden name because that's an archaic and imprecise term these days. After Surkova she bore the surname Lyubokhiner (only very briefly), and then Barbotkina. There's nothing unusual about this; with the dynamic pace of modern life everything wears out very quickly. And every now and then, women have to change their surname or – to use the contemporary term – rebrand themselves. Lida was rather unfortunate in this respect, but that's not so unusual either. Her story remains fairly typical overall, with the possible exception of the happy ending.

And so, from the beginning. Once upon a time there was a girl called Lida with the (nominally) maiden name of Surkova. A quite normal young woman, a good student, rather attractive. They say she had a pleasant singing voice too. And she had the simple, maidenly fears that everyone understands: she was afraid of thunder and lightning, abortion, unhappy marriage and getting fat. In other words, she was afraid of the inevitable. One summer Zhora Lyubokhiner, the son of a student friend of Lida's father, was staying at their home. Zhora had come from Dnepropetrovsk and he intended – or was pretending that he intended – to enrol in some college or other. Then one day, when Lida's parents were not at home but Lida and Zhora were, an appalling thunderstorm broke out over Moscow. Frightened to death, Lida sought salvation by flinging herself on Zhora's breast. Manfully maintaining his composure, the youth covered her with his body in order to protect her more effectively. And then, casting caution aside, the girl conceived to the accompaniment of thunder and lightning. When Lida's father discovered what had happened, he gnashed his teeth and wanted to throw the rascally sponger out immediately. But Lida and her mother exclaimed in chorus: 'Anything but an abortion!' Preparations for a wedding were set in motion. A host of Lyubokhiners and their relatives arrived from Dnepropetrovsk, all speaking Russian with a fricative 'g'. The young couple drove to the register office in a Chaika automobile, but a bus (manufactured in Lvov) had to be hired for the relatives. These vehicles delivered everyone to the cafe where tables were laid for the wedding feast, and there the Chaika was let go, while the bus drove round the corner and halted to await the eventual conclusion of the festivities. The refreshments were adequate. Some of the Lyubokhiners might possibly have been expecting more, but many of the invited guests and, especially, the uninvited were perfectly satisfied. Vodka and champagne flowed into mouths and gushed back out in honey-sweet speeches. By popular demand, the young couple kissed on the lips, and everything was going just as it should. But then, following the main course, Lida, feeling slightly squiffy, lowered her little head onto her husband's shoulder. No, that's not quite right . . . She lowered her little head, but the shoulder wasn't there. Lida looked and Zhora wasn't there either. 'Well,' she thought, 'he's slipped out somewhere.' But a quarter of an hour went by and her husband still hadn't come back. Lida started to get worried, hoisted up her crinolines and set off to look for him. She walked round the entire cafe and even glanced into the men's toilet, but Zhora was nowhere to be seen. Lida went out onto the porch, where several men were smoking. She glanced into all their faces, but didn't recognise any of them as her husband. 'Have you seen Zhora?' she asked. One of the men pointed round the corner and said: 'I think he went that way'. The bus made in Lvov was standing there, just round the corner. One of its doors was open and the driver was striding up and down beside the bus with a cigarette clenched in his teeth. 'Have you seen my husband?' Lida asked again. It was a ludicrous question to ask – how could the driver know who was whose husband? 'No, I haven't and I don't want to!' he replied angrily. 'My bus isn't some shagging-shed for you lot – I'm leaving, I've had enough!' At that very moment, Lida's ears were assaulted by moans of passion. I specifically mentioned earlier that the bus was made in Lvov, because those LAZ buses had a large, undivided seat at the back that was warmed by the motor and came in very handy for a quick spot of how's-your-father. (They don't export those buses to Russia any more.) When Lida glanced in through the door from which she had heard the moaning, she uttered a moan and fainted away. And then it all came out: Zhora was in the bus with his cousin Rosa (who had always wanted it), and she had come to Moscow especially in order to put one over on Lida and get a Moscow residence permit for herself. So the abortion was arranged after all – it still wasn't too late. However, these events transformed Lida's father into a radical anti-Semite; and the saddest thing of all was that Lida started putting on weight as a nervous reaction.

Lida's next official nuptials did not come soon – only

about fifteen years later. But don't get the idea that she spent all those years sleeping in a crystal coffin. No, she suffered a lot and thought a lot. She had various sexual partners. Despite her sumptuous figure, or perhaps even because of it, Lida was always in demand. But, of course, she dreamed of true feelings.

She was quite frank with her old school-friend Tamara.

'If I came across one like that,' she dreamed out loud over a glass of Cinzano, 'loving and genuine, I'd go running after him. No matter what.'

'No matter what?' Tamara asked doubtfully. 'What if he turned out to be a sloppy engineer with holes in his socks?'

'You don't understand,' Lida laughed. 'I told you – genuine.'

'Genuine as in well-to-do?' I suggested.

Lida gave me a sideways glance.

'Well, sort of . . . I've had enough of those types with holes in their socks.'

'Sure, sure,' said Tamara, nodding understandingly.

In life, however, the loving ones and the genuine ones fell into mutually exclusive categories. The loving types brought their love to Lida in rusty old Zhiguli automobiles, while the genuine types drove her to restaurants in good cars, but they were never more than up for it. Things went on like this, I repeat, for about fifteen years. But one day Lida showed up at our place completely transformed.

'Can I help you . . .' I muttered as I opened the door and only recognised her a second later. 'Come in, Lida.'

She had a new hairdo and bright evening-style makeup

and was even looking a bit slimmer, nothing like the Surkova who used to snivel about life in our kitchen.

'I'm with someone,' Lida said with a bashful smile. 'My husband.'

The husband, who was standing on the stairs, was immediately presented to us.

'Mikhail,' he said, introducing himself without a smile. 'Barbotkin.'

Tamara was glad for her friend. She hastily laid the table and we and the Barbotkins had a cosy supper in the twin couples format. When Mikhail went to the toilet to answer the lesser call of nature, Lida asked Tamara in a whisper:

'Well, what do you think of him?'

'Not bad,' Tamara whispered back. 'But why doesn't he say anything?'

'He's not a loudmouth like other men.'

'Sure, sure,' said Tamara, nodding understandingly. 'So what is he then – a genuine man?'

'Of course. He's very well-off! I can't even imagine why two wives have left him.'

Mikhail finished answering the call and came back. We had coffee and soon after that said goodnight.

But a little while later, Lida realised why two wives had left Barbotkin, despite his being so very well-off. Mikhail really was a man of few words, so when at the end of their honeymoon, without offering any explanations or even saying a word, he attempted to take her in a perverted position, Lida was shocked. She certainly couldn't complain of any lack of pre-marital sexual experience, but the extent of that experience was quantitative rather than qualitative. For Lida the art of love consisted of shaving her bikini zone and assuming poses appropriate to the circumstances and the scene of action. What Barbotkin tried to make her do was beyond her comprehension. Lida attempted to distract her husband with exquisite haute cuisine, in which she was highly proficient. By deceitful means, she bore Mikhail a delightful daughter, hoping that the joys of fatherhood would counter his perverse tendencies. It was all in vain and two or three years later, their marriage was annulled by mutual consent. The female judge shook her head as she divorced them, and we can only share her amazement at the petty trifles over which good families sometimes fall apart.

Be that as it may, the taciturn Barbotkin disappeared over the horizon and I am glad that I never made friends with him. Once again Surkova was left alone, but with an appendage in the form of a small daughter. Other appendages, rather depressing ones, attached themselves to Lida in the region of her waist and buttocks. That, basically, is the full story of her two failed marriages, as I know it, mostly from what Tamara told me.

Now let me tell you about the third, successful marriage. But first a brief digression. Moscow, as everybody knows, is a very big city. A vast number of men live in it and visit it. But if you're an unmarried woman of middle age, then you know how difficult it is to find a genuine man, especially one who's not already taken, in order to build a serious, long-term relationship. I suppose that Dmitry Pavlovich, who snatched away my ex-wife, was one of the last remaining specimens.

But unmarried women also know something else: large as Moscow may be, it is not the only inhabited world. While we nocturnal smokers gaze up into the murky Moscow skies, what do you think the unmarried ladies of Moscow are doing? They are sitting at their PCs, monitoring the inhabited universe, near and far, for all they're worth. The glow of the screen is reflected in their eyes; their right hands caress their mice. The ocean of dating sites is infinitely deep and broad . . . With how many men does the statistically average, unmarried Moscow lady spend the night? How many does she reject, how many does she mark as 'selected'? This is not for us to know . . .

Trying to catch men on the Internet is just like fishing, only backwards. Imagine a pond in which there's a huge glut of hungry, but mostly inedible fish. You spend all your time taking them off the hook and tossing them back into the water. The important thing is to remain vigilant, otherwise, when a worthwhile fish does turn up, you could automatically toss it back as well. I have also heard about another problem. Women anglers can sometimes get so caught up in the process of virtual man-hooking that when they finally land their prize, they no longer know what to do with him. Like my dog, Phil, who loves to go hunting for rats in the park, but loses all interest once he has polished them off.

However, regardless of certain overheads, catching a man on the Internet is far more convenient than granny's old method of natural acquaintance. It allows you to be economical with your own distinctly limited resources of charm and magnetism. You don't even have to put on makeup and buy new outfits. Just drop in the bait – a photo of yourself twenty years ago – then sit and wait. It's a shame that the Internet only became a universal presence so recently, and most of the women in my age group first sat down at the keyboard when they were already well-battered by pre-computer reality.

Now, why did I start talking about that? Ah, that's right! Our friend Surkova has also, at long last, become an IT fan. There'll be another gap in my story here, because this was the period when Tamara and I were separating, and I had no time to spare for Lida and her electronic HR. It was a rather edgy time for us, although in the end everything worked out okay. No one committed suicide, and Tamara began her new life with Dmitry Pavlovich with a clear conscience. I even became an infrequent but – as they assured me – welcome guest in their home. And then one day when I was at their place – I can't remember for what reason – I met Lida Surkova again. She arrived with someone, a sandy-haired, balding individual with an embarrassed smile.

'This is Tim,' said Lida, introducing us. 'He also answers to Timosha.'

We all smiled at Tim-Timosha and said we were very pleased to meet him. And then, without moving from the spot, Lida informed us that she had found him on the Internet, and although he looked a fright and was nothing at all like his photo, he had a beautiful soul. Tamara remarked that she shouldn't say that in front of the man himself, at which Lida laughed and said:

'It's all right in front of him. Timosha's from Canada and he doesn't speak a word of Russian.'

'Not speak a word,' Timosha confirmed with a smile.

That evening Timosha was our main topic of conversation. He really seemed like quite a decent guy to us, but he was rather timid.

'Just imagine,' Lida laughed, 'he's even afraid to go to the bakery. And why, do you think?'

'Why?'

'He's afraid of the KGB.'

Hearing that acronym, Timosha sprang up in alarm, but Dmitry Pavlovich (who had already drunk quite a lot) gave him a friendly hug and started explaining in broken English that we didn't have any KGB any more, we had the FSB, which wasn't interested in half-witted Canadian visitors.

After a while Tim, unaccustomed to the liberal scale of Russian hospitality, fell asleep on the sofa. But we carried on discussing him at the table.

'His surname's Aiken,' she said, 'which sounds almost like "I can". But actually he can't do anything.'

We learned that Tim didn't have any job and he had no financial resources, apart from his disability benefit. He found Lida very attractive as a woman, of course, but he never went to bed with her without Viagra, and even then it took her a long time to persuade him.

As we listened to her, Tamara and I were astounded: Timosha's image was so far out of keeping with Lida's descriptions of a genuine man. He might have a beautiful soul, he might even dote absolutely on Lida's daughter. But surely we had plenty like him here in Russia? Why did she have to import yet another lame duck from distant Canada?

'So tell me, what do you really see in him?' said Tamara, trying to worm an answer out of her. 'Confide in me as your friend.'

And that was the first time I ever saw Surkova blush.

'I don't know. . .' she answered, almost whispering. 'I suppose I fell in love with him. . .'

NASTENKA

Have I really missed her?

As she unpacks her suitcases, Tamara twitters incessantly about the charms of scuba diving – she has clearly spent more than enough time in underwater silence. Dmitry Pavlovich has barricaded himself off with phones and is booming something in a deep, authoritative voice – he's already completely engrossed in his business affairs. I stand there, looking out of the window at a distant plane glinting in the sky. I wonder if it's taking off or landing. Seen from their windows, Moscow is quite different from the way it looks from mine. At my place I can see an area for walking dogs, the roof of a grocery shop and the neighbouring panel-built high rises, some lying on their side, some standing upright; they are, of course, arranged according to a specific architectural concept, only from my balcony that concept doesn't make any sense. The view from here is quite different. From the height of the twenty-fourth floor, the city unfolds in a majestic panorama that is perfectly intelligible. I'm sure that the estate agents who sold this panorama to Dmitry Pavlovich charged him extra for it. Well, never mind, Phil and I have admired it for two weeks entirely free of charge, while the amorous couple have been taking their sea dips. Now I'm thinking about how long it will take Tamara to sweep all the dog hair and other traces of our presence out of the flat.

The riddle of the plane remains unresolved: it has simply crept behind a cloud. It's time for me and Phil to creep away too. We've met and kissed, and now it's goodbye: they need to rest after their journey. We can only hope that the hot water has come back on in our own building and feel a little regretful. Even the sentinel in the entrance had already begun to recognise us. Generally speaking, Phil and I are not much like the inhabitants of this place, so at first I had a feeling that the concierge was just dying to ask who I was and what business I had here. But he was a proud ex-military man and he didn't ask, so now he will never know that I'm a writer and I was moved in here temporarily, to water my ex-wife's plants. And also because in the low-class housing development where I live, and which is where I belong, they fix the leaky water mains in the summer.

For two weeks, while Tamara and Dmitry Pavlovich basked in the natural delights of the Adriatic, I have basked in the amenities of civilisation. How very pleasant life is in an elite neighbourhood! In the morning here there's no gurgling, sneezing and hacking from old Zhigulis out in the yard. They don't demand anybody's attention, because they aren't there, but even if they were, no one would hear them through the triple glazing. At dawn the silent, mysterious yard keepers have already done their job and dissolved into the bright rays of sunshine, like little elves. The fountain has woken up and started sparkling. And there are gentlemen in high-quality suits, striding from the entrances to the parking lot along freshly washed pavements, still glittering with moisture. They swing their high-quality leather briefcases in their hands and twirl the keys of their high-quality automobiles on their fingers. These gentlemen are Moscow's upper middle class, the hope and support of the new Russia. Meanwhile at this hour the new Russia that has been born here, in this monolithic brick tower, is snuffling in its cradles or already eating its pap. After the heads of families have driven off to their offices, the only people left in the building and the general neighbourhood are dependents, the individuals for whom the toiling gentlemen are a support in the literal sense: their little children, their beautiful wives and their mothers, who have been brought in from somewhere in the Lyubertsy district. And although this entire community left behind here creates no added value, they are the ones for whom the avenue with the babbling fountain has been laid out in the spacious courtyard, it is for them that the top-class playgrounds for children and dogs have been built, and the health club, with its 'OPEN' sign already on display first thing in the morning.

Phil and I have lived a very, very comfortable life in this elite neighbourhood. Of course, there are even classier places in Moscow and the surrounding areas, only they say that no one ever comes back from there. But wherever Phil and I might live, whether temporarily or permanently, in the morning we always rise in response to the call of nature. That is, only when Phil can't hold out any longer and he starts licking my nose to make me sneeze and wake up. This usually happens some time during the hour before noon, that is, at a time which in any urban courtyard, elite or not, could be called the hour of the dependents. The bemedalled gentleman in the hallway has watched us pass by with a bewildered, questioning glance. On several occasions I felt an urge to explain myself to him, but I couldn't, because Phil's natural needs would brook no delay. And anyway, a retired military man was hardly likely to understand the difference between a writer without a job and an idle loafer.

On our way to the dogs' area we could observe a scene of unmitigated demographic well-being within the bounds of a single courtyard. Children's buggies ploughing unhurriedly across its surface like yachts during a regatta, drifting along the pathways or swaying at their moorings beside the benches. The faces of infant passengers turned heavenward in their lacy icon-settings. Mums, nannies and grannies shepherding multicoloured herds of individuals of various ages as they master the dry land. Filled with the patter of little feet, snuffling and incessant twittering, the children's playgrounds are like flowerbeds that have come alive. How much life and energy there is in these small creatures! One of them pauses momentarily to search for something in his nose, but then his gaze falls on a doggy pulling a comical man along on a lead. The child breaks into happy laughter, and his nose purges itself.

A charming scene every morning, but we had no time to admire it. Phil's pressing needs drew him on towards the dogs' area, and he drew me along like a speedboat pulling a water-skier. The dogs' area here is a positive paean to cleanliness. You won't believe me, but it is possible to walk from one end of it to the other without stepping in fresh excrement even once. A box on a pole has even been placed in the corner, with special plastic bags that you can tear off, although I never saw anyone make use of them. Philip and the other male dogs used this pole as their post box. I hope to describe this dogs' area in more detail some day and do it full justice, but I won't show the description to Phil. He didn't share my rapturous delight; the area beside our own building was dearer to his heart, the one I can see from my window, and which is never empty. All it has to offer dogs is an old, rotten wooden beam and a well-gnawed lorry tyre, but there are plenty of other amusements. The benches around its edge – those of them that are still intact – are usually occupied by local beer-lovers. If you wag your tail for them and raise your eyebrows expressively, you can sometimes get a small piece of salted fish. In the evening, after the sun has gone down, teenagers kiss on these benches and carve messages to the world into them with penknives. They don't have anything edible, apart from chewing gum, but there's a friendly word for a doggy, and the girls will scratch you behind the ear.

Anyway, I'm waxing lyrical, and if push comes to shove, it's possible to relieve yourself anywhere at all. Phil's next half hour passed in honouring his debt to nature, and mine simply passed. Then we made our way back to Dmitry Pavlovich's flat. After breakfast, there was personal time for both of us. Before he went to sleep, Philip sprawled out and licked his stuffed belly, or tested Dmitry Pavlovich's furniture with his teeth and I ... what did I do? I won't even try to argue; at that hour I had been presented with all the necessary conditions for sitting down to work. My laptop glowed invitingly on the desk in Dmitry Pavlovich's study, there were no neighbours stomping about overhead or cars whistling under the windows (as I have already mentioned). Even the tap in the kitchen didn't drip. A sterile, distilled silence enfolded me. But believe me, while silence like that is good for the middle class to relax in and for dogs to lick their bellies, creative work in such a silence is absolutely impossible. Some people might say it's a question of habit. Maybe so, but I'm a sensitive, creative individual. Getting me tuned into operational condition is difficult, but knocking me out of it is a pushover.

So I didn't write after breakfast. I smoked a couple of cigarettes by the window, contemplating my bird's-eye view of the city, not to set my swarming ideas into order, but only to convince myself that I didn't have any. Perhaps I was wrong to blame Dmitry Pavlovich's flat for everything. To be quite honest, I had suffered similar bouts of empty-headedness previously, indeed I still get them under the most varied circumstances, and I had known for a long time what I should and should not do in such circumstances. Basically, there are two recommendations: don't try to work, because it won't happen anyway, and go for a walk.

I followed my own advice, based on my experience of life and writing. That is, after having a smoke by the window, I put on my coat and shoes again, left Phil in charge of the flat and set out for a stroll with a clear conscience. From the stratosphere of the elite flat I descended once again into the fragrant Eden of the elite yard. I walked into the avenue and stationed myself on a bench near the fountain. Here in the shade of the watery jets, I froze, transfixed, for a long time – still without any thoughts in my head, simply in a state of bliss. I resembled a statue in a park. Pigeons journeyed between my feet and hopped up fearlessly onto my shoes. Promenading mothers ceased to notice me, and I could clearly hear intimate confessions that would no doubt have amazed even their own husbands. For my part, I observed them surreptitiously. I don't feel ashamed of spying and eavesdropping on people because, even without a thought in my head, I always remain a writer.

The mums in this yard were quite attractive. Attractive in the same way – no other comparison occurs to me – as military officers' wives. I had seen those wives in the old Soviet days, when I was still a teenager, living in Vaskovo. At that time there was a military garrison not far from us (I don't know if it still exists now) and we used to slip through a hole in the fence, bypassing the checkpoint, in order to buy food. Well, apart from the commissary shop, that garrison had other things that were well worth a look. From the distant parts to which they travelled in the line of duty, the officers there brought back women so beautiful that they simply took your breath away. At least, they made a powerful impression on us provincial youths and we expressed it in our own, naturally crude style. 'Women with equipment' – that was what we used to call them, and whatever that expression might have meant, I recalled it as I gazed at the mums in the elite yard. Although I realised, of course, that the equipment here had not been nurtured by the bounty of nature in distant parts of the country but by the endeavours of cosmetic medicine. Where, nowadays, can you find natural female beauty without prosthetic devices, untouched by the scraper or the scalpel, unmutilated by exercise machines? The only hope left is for the revival of the army: then the military garrisons will be rebuilt and young officers will go flying off again to those distant parts.

But there are exceptions to every rule and I was fortunate enough to be granted proof of that right here, in the elite yard, by the fountain, while observing the local elite mums. The exception came drifting along the avenue entirely without haste, like all the other mums, pushing along a buggy that was also like all the others. But I picked her out immediately. Believe me, you women, no beautician in the world could ever give you such pretty dimples in your cheeks, or such an enchanting smile; that is nature's work. She was wearing a loose summer frock, but I know how to see into the depths of things. Beneath the thin material, I could divine the natural perfection of her body and the free oscillation of its parts. Here was a genuine example of natural, pure, organic female beauty. I wouldn't say that I have already reached an age at which such masterpieces are admired disinterestedly, but at that moment I observed her with the eyes of an artist . . .

Her name was Nastya Savelieva. I probably wouldn't have found out her name if it hadn't been such a warm, sunny day. Because of the fine weather, so many people were out strolling in the yard that there were no free benches left beside the fountain in the avenue.

'Do you mind?' I heard a gentle voice say and glanced up. Her frock was transparent against the light.

'Of course not!' I exclaimed, half-jumping to my feet.

In the buggy that she was pushing, I made out the tiny, dusky patch of an infant's face.

'What a delightful child!'

'Yes, that's what everyone tells me,' she said, smiling so that the dimples in her cheeks twinkled.

If not for that grateful smile of hers, perhaps I wouldn't have had the nerve to start talking to her at all. I would have sat there, examining her with surreptitious sideways glances and making up various stories in which she might have played the leading role. But the beautiful young woman smiled, I beamed brightly at her and we slipped into conversation as if we were old acquaintances. And so I didn't have to invent anything, because she told me everything about herself. For a single compliment to her little baby (to whom I offer my separate thanks) she made me a gift of her own story and, although I don't dare to hope for compliments, I feel obliged to share it with you.

So, once upon a time there was a girl called Nastya, or Nastenka, who lived, not in Moscow, or in some distant part of the country, as you might have thought, but more or less halfway between. The city of N-burg, where she grew up and blossomed, was large but provincial. And owing to this provinciality, many of the boons of civilisation, such as nightclubs with dance floors, for instance, had until recently remained something of a novelty to the N-burgers. Although many of Nastya's girlfriends had already visited establishments of this kind, she herself had never been to one. Not simply out of financial considerations, but mainly because they were places where so-called 'heavy types' hung about. In N-burg at that time the wild excesses of the period of transition had not yet completely retreated into the past. Big, beefy men with grim faces could be seen everywhere, especially in the night clubs, and they had such bad manners that any place where they appeared immediately deteriorated into a seedy joint. These heavies seemed very unpleasant and dangerous individuals to Nastenka. And that, essentially, was exactly what they were, although in a certain sense they were to be pitied, for their time was already coming to an end, even in the city of N-burg. They were like the remnants of a routed army, soldiers who had missed the end of the war and been left hanging about at a loose end, jangling their rusty weapons and pulling ferocious faces at everyone to conceal their bewilderment. But then, this is about Nastenka, not them.

I've already said that she didn't go to nightclubs, and that's true. She didn't go even once, until her roommate in the student hostel – I think it was Katya, she still writes to Nastenka even now – until this roommate persuaded her to break her vow. So one fine evening the two girlfriends linked arms and set off to a nightclub, one where Katya had already been twice, but Nastya had never been. The evening actually brought Nastenka nothing but grief. Firstly, the one long drink that she permitted herself cost half of her grant and, secondly, she was terribly disappointed by what one could call the male contingent. No, don't get the idea that Nastya went to the club with the intention of picking someone up. It was just that . . . well, as you might expect, all the students at the medical college were girls. The club was swarming with individuals of the male sex, but what kind of men were they? Apart from the heavies (Nastya was afraid even to meet their eyes), there were odd, sweat-soaked youths staggering around the hall in a state of unnatural excitement. As a professional medic, she deduced the cause of their excitement from their dilated pupils and did not find this excitement in any way infectious.

The music in the club was thunderously loud and her friend Katya had disappeared into the thickets of dancers long ago. But Nastya didn't dance, she sat on her high stool at the bar and sipped at her endless long drink. She couldn't go without finishing it – that would have been a betrayal of her squandered grant money. But everything comes to an end some time and the ill-starred cocktail was no exception. Nastya swung round on her stool and stretched out her shapely legs, intending to stand up on them and leave this idiotic establishment. And that is what she would have done if those legs had not – literally for just one brief moment – betrayed their owner. The drink had a bad effect on the legs and they buckled slightly. Nastya lost her balance, swayed on her slim heels and – who knows? – might even, to her undying shame, have ended up on the floor. But at that very moment a strong pair of hands grabbed the young lady and retained her in a seemly, vertical position.

'I beg your pardon, I must have jostled you,' a pleasant male voice said from somewhere over her head.

The girl looked up . . . and the words of gratitude froze on her lips. Her rescuer was a tall man, very broad in the shoulders. 'A heavy!' The thought flashed through her mind that it would have been better to fall.

'It's started . . .' she muttered in a trembling voice

'I beg your pardon, what's started? Allow me to assist you.'

But he has a lovely voice . . . Strange . . . And such a kind face . . . Nastya's thoughts, like her legs, had slipped slightly out of control. She lowered her head in embarrassment. If she hadn't lowered her head, but said straightaway: 'Yes, please help me out of here' – or, even better: 'I feel dizzy, please help me sit down' – if she hadn't lowered her head, but said that, then the evening – that same evening! – could have turned out to be wonderful. But when Nastenka lowered her head, she saw that her tights had laddered. How she could have snagged them on anything was a mystery; perhaps they had been defective to start with? But that wasn't the point, as you well understand, the point was that with laddered tights, any move towards closer acquaintance was out of the question. Having made this appalling discovery, Nastya sobered up in a trice.

'No,' she said coldly. 'Thank you, but I'll find my own way out.'

That concluded her outing to the nightclub. It cost her half her grant and one pair of tights, but we could say that she got off lightly. Her roommate Katya didn't show up until the early morning and confessed she had lost something that couldn't be bought for any money. But then, she had been behaving all evening as if that was what she was trying to achieve and, anyway, we're not concerned with Katya's problems here. After that incident, Nastya didn't go to a nightclub again. Not because she didn't have another pair of tights, but simply because she didn't have the time. Practical training began at the medical college and Nastya was assigned to do hers at CH – the N-burg Central Hospital. They didn't believe in pampering students there and Nastya, with her accommodating character, wasn't pampered at all. She often ended up on the night shift, and not in some quiet therapeutic ward but in A&E, which is the kind of place you wouldn't wish on anyone, either patient or medic. A brief visit to A&E is enough to put you off gallivanting round nightclubs, or even leaving the house, for a very long time. In a month of practical experience, Nastya saw things that would have robbed any girl without medical training of her sleep and her sanity for the rest of the life.

The injuries suffered at night in N-burg were mostly criminal in nature. Carelessly dressed individuals of mature age ended up in the department following domestic knife fights, and those who were younger and stronger generally came in with bullet wounds; these were the heavy types, who were still having gunfights with each other out of force of habit. The patients with knife wounds behaved modestly, while the heavies were insolent and aggressive, but Nastya wasn't afraid of them here at work, and she decided for herself who should go straight onto the surgeon's table and who should wait in reception for a while. Nastya worked shift after shift. One week followed another and very soon she would have completed her practical training and been enrolled in the Medical Institute. In time she would have married a decent man, become a district doctor – a paediatrician, for instance – and the children would have loved her. That's how everything would have turned out, if Nastya had completed her practical training. But then, that would have been a different story, and she and I wouldn't have been sitting by a fountain in a Moscow courtyard.

Events took a different turn. A turn for which Nastya should be eternally grateful to her superiors at the hospital, who condemned her to serve those shifts in A&E. One wonderful evening – definitely wonderful this time, probably the only wonderful evening in the entire history of that sad institution – an ambulance brought yet another poor wretch into the A&E department. Nastya took a brief glance: the patient was large in build and dressed in a tracksuit.

'A firearms case?' she asked professionally, addressing the paramedic in the ambulance.

The paramedic shrugged.

'Seems not. He says it's an ordinary dislocation.'

'Strange . . .' Nastya took a closer look at the patient and her heart started pattering: standing there in front of her, holding one arm with his other hand, was the polite stranger from the night club. 'Strange . . .' she repeated, as her cheeks turned pink.

It hardly needs to be said that from that moment on, he became Nastya's personal patient. She led him past the waiting casualties, all the stabbed and the shot, straight to the doctor, who put the shoulder back in in a jiffy, before Nastya could even leave the room. The young man merely yelped in his pleasant voice, and the job was done. The doctor winked at Nastya.

'We could do with more patients like that,' he said, pleased. This doctor was fond of dislocations and fractures, and he didn't like sewing.

The patient breathed in sharply, thanked the doctor and turned towards the nurse. And that was when he recognised her.

'Why, we've met before,' he said with a smile on his still pale face.

'I remember,' Nastya replied, and looked down. But this time her tights were all right.

'So this is where you work. And I thought you were one of those . . . evening girls.'

'And I thought you were one of those heavies.'

'Oh no,' he said, smiling again. 'I just dislocated my shoulder in the gym.'

'I'm glad.'

'Children, perhaps you could save the rejoicing for later?' the doctor interrupted. 'I've got a waiting room full of clients.'

Dr Popov was not an ill-natured individual at heart, but he had practised all his life in A&E and that had toughened him up a little. In any case, he was right: work is work. Nastenka expressed the hope that the young man would take better care of his arm in future, and went back to performing her duties. Nonetheless, during the remainder of the shift, her thoughts flew off repeatedly to somewhere very, very far away from the A&E department.

All of the above-described can, however, be regarded as merely the prelude to the real fairytale, which began in the morning, when Nastya finished her shift. Right outside the gates of the Central Hospital she was met by – who do you think? – yes, the owner of a pleasant voice, an ordinary dislocation and also, as it turned out, a very decent automobile.

'Good morning!' he said. 'Allow me to introduce myself at last: I'm Ivan Saveliev. How would you like to have a coffee with me?'

'I'm tired,' Nastenka replied. 'But I'll have a coffee with you. I'm Nastya.'

It had slipped her mind that coffee wasn't served in the catering establishments of N-burg at such an early hour. And even if it hadn't slipped her mind, she wouldn't have refused. But if any of you are thinking that she was hoping to become intimate with this almost total stranger, Ivan, you are mistaken. Firstly, Nastya was tired after her night shift and, secondly, she wasn't that kind of girl. Anyway, she got into the car. Ivan pressed a button somewhere, and the car was filled with beautiful music. The car drove away. On the way, Nastya felt slightly nervous, but eventually she dozed off. When she opened her eyes again, they had arrived.

As was only to be expected, Ivan had not brought Nastya to a cafe, but straight to his own block of flats, a simple building of five storeys. Reassured by a quite unaccountable trust in her companion, Nastenka walked up the stairs with him and into his flat. Ivan's residence was rather well furnished, especially in comparison with the medical college hostel. The girl's host seated her on a plump leather sofa, while he went off to the kitchen to brew coffee, not forgetting on the way to press a button on the music centre. The music poured out, filling the room, in the same way as it had recently filled the automobile. Lulled by the music and the sofa, Nastenka started feeling dozy again, and then even dozier . . . until she fell asleep completely.

And this time too, nothing happened that a girl might subsequently regret. Nastenka woke up on the same sofa, only now there was a cushion under her head and she was covered with a rug. She opened her eyes and saw Ivan sitting in the armchair opposite her. In fact, they both opened their eyes at the same moment because, after settling Nastya, Ivan had admired her for a while as she slept, until sleep overcame him too. Their glances met and Ivan said:

'How happy I feel, seeing you wake up under my roof.'

Nastenka smiled.

'You have a nice flat.'

He shook his head.

'The flat's not bad, but it's not mine, it belongs to the

firm. My flat's in Moscow, I'm here in N-burg to develop the business.'

'So that's it . . .' The smile faded from Nastya's face. 'So you're on a business trip. Now I understand.'

'You don't understand a thing,' said Ivan, upset. 'You think I'm just looking for a good time with you, but my intentions couldn't possibly be more serious. I promise that I won't make any advances until we're married. And once we're married, I'll take you away to Moscow. We'll live in a beautiful flat and there'll be a fountain in the courtyard.'

'I need to think about it,' Nastenka replied. 'And you were going to make coffee.'

She told me what came after that in brief, because it was time for her to go and feed her baby. They got married the same day, so Nastya didn't think about it for very long. She never went back to the A&E department or the college. When Dr Popov met her in the street by chance, he told her that she was stupid to throw away her career. Nastya laughed a lot at that. A month later, the Savelievs moved to Moscow. Ivan was promoted, and let us hope it will not be for the last time.

REAL ESTATE
DIVORCE

So here we are back home. I could recognise my own dear abode with my eyes shut. Have you ever noticed that once a place has been thoroughly lived in, it acquires its own distinctive aroma? Our Vaskovo house, for instance, had a smell of its own too, for as long as my parents were alive. But when they died, the smell evaporated.

To become aware of a place's aroma, you have to go away for a while. When I used to visit Vaskovo from Moscow, I could smell it, but my parents couldn't, because the furthest they ever went was to the vegetable patch or the grocery kiosk.

My bachelor flat has two primary smells – the ash-tray and dog hair. When Phil and I are away, these are securely preserved by the closed windows. I lock the small window panes shut whenever I go away for long, although I couldn't say why. A reflex response. But at least when I get back I can sniff the air and say: 'So here we are back home!'

Incidentally, there once used to be a more complex bouquet of aromas here, with notes of borscht and perfume woven into it, along with everything else that denotes the presence of a woman. But then Tamara went away and no locked windows could retain the female aroma in the flat. It lingered for a few months, gradually fading out of the upholstery of the sofa and the deepest corners of the wardrobe, and finally disappeared completely. This flat no longer has the smell of Tamara's borscht. While we were married, I never enquired about how it was made – all I can remember is that Toma always used to hum to herself in the kitchen. And now my foolish pride won't let me ask for the recipe.

In those days, it's true, there was no smell of dog hair. Phil was only born a relatively short time ago and he has no idea of the drama that unfolded within these walls. He knows Tamara, but for him she's Dmitry Pavlovich's woman. Well, let Phil think so, especially since it's true.

Phil is dozing on the sofa from which Tamara's smell evaporated long ago and he is not haunted by any memories. If something clatters in the kitchen, Phil won't wake up – he knows it's only a poorly balanced plate. And if a draught sets the front door jerking at its lock, that won't disturb his sleep either. But sounds like that still sometimes give me a jolt in the chest. For a second, or a split second, I forget reality and expect to hear Toma purring in the kitchen at any moment. Or I expect the door to open and slam shut, and then I'll hear the words: 'Yoo-hoo, darling!' Shoes kicked off weary feet will clatter onto the floor and tumble across it. And I will sigh in relief because it really is her, and because today I am 'darling'.

During the final years of our cohabitation, she didn't call me darling often. The blame for that was entirely and completely mine, for that was the time when I had taken up with prose, which was exactly the same as if I'd brought another woman into the house. I couldn't see anything wrong with it myself: let one console me and grant me rare moments of delight, and let the other feed me, wash my clothes and lecture me. Unfortunately, both my women proved to be too jealous. Tamara was angry because my writing had made me neglect my obligations as a husband – earning money and vacuum-cleaning the carpets – and as for prose, well, she simply couldn't tolerate Tamara's presence.

But the reason for Tamara's departure was not my graphomania. On the contrary, if not for the divorce, I'm sure she would have defeated her rival. It wouldn't have been the first time she had strangled my creative impulses. When I, being young and foolish, decided to take up artistic photography, Tamara only needed a year to convince me that I had no talent. And back then, of course, she still really loved me.

But let's not talk of love. In any case I'm certain that the dirty carpets were beside the point, and our marriage fell victim to the societal changes taking place in our country. I have this theory that there are two kinds of people: the thinking type, or people of thought, and the practical type, or people of action. When drastic changes occur in society, the thinking types slither down the social ladder and the practical types make careers. The catch is that not everyone knows in advance what type he belongs to. So when the tide of change crashed over us and I went plummeting downwards, I realised I was a man of thought. That was when I developed my enthusiasm for photography, Tamara, however, got a job with one firm and then another, and she has been moving on up the career ladder ever since.

But of course, it wasn't just a matter of our typological differences. A man and a woman are different in general, but as a general rule that doesn't prevent them from being married. It was a fatal confluence of circumstances: it just so happened that on one and the same day Tamara was promoted yet again and someone, who has remained nameless, puked in our lift.

I'll never forget the evening of that day. I was sitting at the computer, much as I am now, trying to create. But prose was being capricious. She didn't like the way I started and became distracted every time the door of the flat trembled. I was listening to the door, much as I am now, but on that occasion I really was expecting Tamara and I was a little concerned because she was late for supper. Anyway, the door was too slow in announcing her arrival, I had already recognised the clatter of Tamara's heels and heaved a sigh of relief long before the key turned in the lock. After that everything happened as I described four paragraphs earlier, only for real. The door slammed, the shoes went tumbling . . .

'Darling, it's me!'

I was surprised for a moment, because she hadn't called me 'darling' very often just recently. But I had to rise to the challenge, so I walked out into the hallway for a kiss, and there all was made clear. My darling was tipsy.

'How about that, I've been promoted again!' she informed me, looking herself over in the mirror.

'Congratulations,' I responded morosely. 'Are you going to have supper?'

'A substantial promotion,' said Tamara, making a significant face. 'And there's something important I want to talk to you about.'

'What's that?'

I was immediately on my guard, because I knew from experience that every time she was promoted and given a raise, it triggered an eruption of her consumerist ambition. Our sofa and our kitchen furniture and our home movie theatre were all milestones along the line of Toma's professional advance. So now I expected her to go back to the subject of the refurbishment that our little flat had needed so badly for so long, and which I tried so hard not even to think about. But it was even worse than that . . .

'It's this,' Tamara said with a frown. 'We can't go on living like this. Someone puked in our lift today.'

'But what's that got to do with me?' I asked with a shrug. 'Watch where you tread.'

Then it all came pouring out. Breathing fresh cognac fumes, Toma first inveighed against our puking neighbours, then declared that she found the entire building disgusting and all 'the rotten dregs' living in it, and our entire rotten, loutish neighbourhood too. The essential point of her impassioned monologue was this: with the status she now possessed, she absolutely refused to tolerate this squalid existence. Aware in my heart of hearts that I too was a part of Toma's squalid existence, I kept mum, in order not to put that idea into her head. I merely tried to hint that perhaps it was time for her to get changed and take off her makeup. But Tamara wasn't listening to me: she belonged to the practical type and people of action don't blather on simply in order to share what's been eating away at them recently. They round off every conversation with a constructive suggestion, as they are taught to do in their management schools. And Tamara didn't get changed that evening until she had given expression to her new idea, which was far more constructive even than refurbishing the flat.

'We need to change the place we live!' she declared.

You know, I've never been able to argue with women in suits. And apart from that, I was hoping a good night's sleep would restore Toma's sense of reality.

But next morning Tamara started talking about moving again, and from then on she came back to the subject regularly, over morning coffee and evening tea. The accursed lift had been cleaned out, I had expressed my willingness to refurbish our flat with my own hands, but it was all useless. The constructive idea had taken firm root in her head and alarm had invaded my heart. Don't imagine that I had suddenly developed a powerful sentimental attachment to my genuinely unenviable domicile. It really wasn't that I was afraid of all the hassle inevitably involved in a swap, either; I always left stuff like that to Tamara. The most likely explanation is that when I contemplated the bright future, the natural instincts of a man of thought suggested that such a future would hold no place for me.

Naturally, this didn't stop at words. Toma studied the question for a while and then, realising that this nut was too tough for her to crack on her own, she entered into relations with a certain real estate agency. When I first heard about this, I was delighted. The ladies and gentlemen of real estate, I thought, would soon bring Tamara to her senses, they would explain to her that fools had become extinct in Moscow a long time ago. I was certain that the best swap we could hope for was the trash-for-garbage kind. After all, the only asset we had was this poky two-room flat and our modest savings would all have gone on setting up the new home and the agents' fees. But no such luck: it turned out that the estate agency business is flourishing as it is precisely because there are still plenty of fools among us. And one of those fools is writing these lines.

The estate agents began by talking Tamara out of the idea of an exchange. They advised her to sell our flat, take a mortgage loan from a bank and buy a good flat in a future construction development. 'A beautiful flat,' they said. 'A business-class building, solid brick, look, here it is in our computer. And don't worry about your two-roomer, we'll have it sold before you even know it.' I disliked this new plan even more than the previous one. At that stage the beautiful flat only existed in the estate agents' computer, whereas the two-roomer had to be sold now, immediately. Even worse, the very word 'mortgage' frightened me. When I informed Tamara of my misgivings, the answer I received was that

I didn't understand anything about such things and I was a pedestrian kind of individual in general. What was my word against the estate agent's, if the agency had such a sumptuous office and the women who worked in it were all so nice, just like Tamara?

Nonetheless, the estate agents' remarkable plan ran into a problem at the very first stage. And, precisely as I had expected, because of the mortgage. But what I hadn't expected was that *I* would be the problem. The catch was that the bank couldn't loan the sum required as long as she had a dependent, i.e. me. I don't like that word: call me a non-working family member, a sponger, if you will, anything but a dependent. However the dull-witted counting house had insisted on defining me with precisely that term and for Tamara I had now been transformed into a problem that had to be solved. But how? If the first thing that comes to your mind is to make me get a job, then you are no novelist. Possibly a poet or a scribbler of flimsy fiction, but not a novelist. Because you don't know that, having once become a novelist, a man ceases to be anyone else. To go off and work somewhere in order to keep himself fed is as unthinkable to him as to change his sex – unless, of course, his nature prompts him to do so. But Toma's pay was quite adequate for my nature and I definitely did not wish to sacrifice my art in order to appease some mortgage bank. Tamara went off to consult with the estate agents again, leaving me adrift on a sea of dark premonitions.

My premonitions did not deceive. In the morning (it was a working day), I was invited into the kitchen for a talk.

When I walked in, Toma had already had breakfast and was wearing her makeup; there was a coffee-cup with a lipstick stain standing in front of her and a cigarette trembling in her hand.

'Darling,' she said, with a flutter of fresh mascara, 'don't you want to know what they told me at the agency yesterday?'

I gathered myself.

'Yes, very much.'

'They said . . . Don't get upset . . . but they said that to get a mortgage . . .'

'Be quick, dear, or you'll be late for work.'

'Yes . . . Basically, they said we have to get a divorce. A fictitious one, of course.'

The long pause that ensued could have been even longer, but Tamara was pressed for time.

'Why don't you say something? How do you like their creative approach?'

'What can I say . . .' I forced out. 'If we have to, we have to.'

'That's great then,' said Toma, sighing in relief as she stubbed out her cigarette. 'They were worried about how you might take it. In case you might suddenly turn round and demand that we divide up the flat and all the rest of it . . . But I told them what a civilised individual you are and they said, well, if he's as civilised as that, it won't be problem . . . Darling!' She was about to kiss me, but remembered her makeup and limited herself to an ordinary hug.

Pleased at having managed the conversation so well, Tamara darted out of the house and strode off, heels clacking cheerfully, to her job in her corporation, ready to achieve again and again. So what could I do? Closing the door behind my already almost ex-wife, I went to work too, that is, I shuffled out of the hallway into the room where my computer was waiting. However, prose did not visit me that day, and I achieved nothing at all.

The dissolution of our marriage took place soon afterwards, in a civilised manner. I demonstrated my civilised character on every point and didn't contest anything in court, which prompted Toma's friend Surkova, a specialist in such matters, to tell her that she was a woman to be envied. The divorce was supposedly fictitious, but even so a couple of months later Tamara was striding into the mortgage bank untrammelled and creditworthy, while I, having packed all my junk higgledy-piggledy into a taxi, was setting out to reside at Vaskovo. It was Toma's idea, to move me out to the *dacha* temporarily, in order not to prejudice forthcoming showings of the flat and, in general, so that I wouldn't get under anyone's feet. So in fact our notional divorce turned out to be very much like a real one. It was as if Toma and I had got into different trains: hers was setting off forwards, into the bright, comfortable future, and mine, the Vaskovo train, had gone off in the opposite direction.

Moreover, my own native parts failed to notice my return. For our Vaskovo neighbours, many of whom had known me since my childhood, I had long ago ceased to be either one of their own or a stranger; I was just another summer resident. Even I felt that my status was somewhat unreal. Who was I? A squatter in voluntary exile; a fictitious bachelor . . . The night after I arrived, I was woken by voices under my window. I thought at first that it was petty thieves on my land, but when I looked, I spied a young couple who had made themselves comfortable on my bench, as if it was in a city park. The girl was timid to begin with and kept looking round at the house, but her boyfriend reassured her by saying: 'Don't be afraid, no one lives here'. I didn't begrudge the young people the use of the bench, especially since they were fairly quiet on the whole, but the assertion that 'no one lives here' stung me. The next day I wound up my parents' wall clock with the pendulum, installed my computer and washed my *dacha* trousers: I hung them outside to dry, like a flag, as a warning to all wandering couples.

I started grafting myself onto village life with a change of image. In order to be less different from the local men, I started wearing my father's old jacket everywhere instead of fancy imported anoraks. I only shaved now when it was absolutely necessary, or when I couldn't sleep because of the prickling. I actually changed surprisingly quickly, as if some kind of genetic programme that had been switched off in the city had suddenly started to work. In the same way that a dog, abandoned by its masters, turns into a synanthropic wolf – unless, of course, it simply dies.

I wasn't really trying to make anyone like me, but my neighbours took a benevolent view of my reversion to a primordial state. They started recognising me and saying hello to me. One day Vyacheslav, who lived in the house opposite, stopped me in the street and started complaining at great length about his wife Lenka, who was 'whoring'– all the signs were that she was whoring, only he didn't know who with. Perhaps Vyacheslav was just sounding me out because he suspected his Lenka was whoring with me, but I took the very supposition as a compliment and surprised myself by responding with a torrent of such sympathetic, heartfelt obscenities that Vyacheslav suggested there and then that we have a drink together in a spirit of male solidarity. And as it happened, he already a bottle with him, tucked into the front of his trouser belt, like some American's pistol. So we drank it right there by the fence, without any snacks to go with it.

But in all fairness, there was something fictitious about my new life. No matter how bad his hangover was and regardless of his problems with Lenka, my neighbour Vyacheslav went to work every day. My other neighbour Mikha, an alcoholic, didn't go to work. But he turned up early every morning for a daily briefing at the beer kiosk. Vyacheslav earned his money by forging iron in a hardware factory. Mikha and his friends fetched and carried for the Azeris at the market. But I acquired my means of subsistence from the only cash machine in the whole of Vaskovo, and I felt slightly ashamed of that.

I worked too, of course, although I wouldn't have had the nerve to make such a claim to Vyacheslav or Mikha. Judge for yourself. Every morning, in complete and utter ignorance of all printed and televised news, sometimes without even putting on my underpants, I sat down at the computer with a cup of coffee. To write. The open window on the left of the monitor looked into the garden, where apples were ripening on the elderly trees and falling to the ground with a thud. And the words in my head ripened and fell like those apples. Their fall was also accompanied by thudding – the sound of the keyboard, which attracted the attention of a fat crow, who often flew onto my plot of land. It looked to him as if I was pecking at something tasty and he wasn't that far wrong. That crow was the only creature in Vaskovo who knew what I did, but even he could hardly have considered it work.

The only thing that could interrupt me was urgent physiological necessity or the trilling of the mobile phone. It was Tamara calling, of course. I pressed the green key with a sigh and an energetic rustling stirred in the handset.

'Hi! Didn't wake you, did I?'

'No.'

'Then why does your voice sound like that?'

'I was working.'

'Tell me another! All right then, listen . . .'

And I would receive the latest despatch from the flat-swap front. Certificates, agreements, negotiations . . . information that my ears simply didn't need to hear.

'Good, good,' I said, interrupting the assertive flow of Toma's report, 'why don't you tell me about how you're getting on?'

'Me?' she said, breaking off. 'About me? Listen, I haven't got time right now – I'll tell you when I come.'

Tamara had been promising for a long time to choose some day at the weekend to come out and see me in Vaskovo.

'I have to see how you've set up house, and apart from that . . .'

Her 'apart from that' meant she hadn't forgotten that for each other we were still husband and wife, regardless of any paper divorce. However, week after week went by; a month went by and then another, and my appointment with Toma kept being postponed, as the phrase goes, 'due to circumstances beyond our control'. And then the telephone link between us was broken off, but that was my fault.

The misfortune occurred during one of my walks. The thing is, when someone from the city has made the move to the bosom of nature, he is simply obliged to go walking in the forest and down by the river. He may write or be an idle drone, he may or may not drink vodka with the locals, but going out in the evening to feed the mosquitoes is a sacred responsibility. So every evening, if there was no rain, I set off to ramble through the countryside around Vaskovo. Sometimes I clearly recognised memorable places from my childhood, but more often I found them greatly changed. The familiar forest clearings were overgrown, the little river had shifted its banks in places, young trees had grown tall and many old ones had been struck by lightning. I didn't feel sad, though: nature is changeable and fluid, but manages to remain itself, even as it changes, unlike the city.

Well, anyway, it was during one of these walks of mine that disaster struck. I remember that I was already heading for home, walking along the riverbank. Having staggered a fair distance, I was feeling a bit tired and when I spotted a log protruding from the water's edge, I decided to sit down on it to take a rest and have a smoke. The log proved to be wet and muddy, so I didn't sit down. But I did light up. And just at that moment I seemed to hear an inner voice. Or rather, not a voice, I simply felt an impulse. 'Look,' said the impulse, 'what's that? There's something on the bottom.' That kind of thing happens to me quite often, I hear promptings inside myself: 'Look over that way' ... 'Do such-and-such' – and every time I obey unthinkingly. I did the same this time, leaning down over the water to get a good look at this ostensibly interesting something and, as I did so, the mobile phone slipped out of my breast pocket and plopped into the river. My impulse-cum-voice had deceived me, as also happens quite often; there hadn't been anything interesting on the bottom. But now there was, of course: my mobile phone. There was no point in fishing the phone out of the river, so I didn't even try.

From then on Tamara didn't call me. That is, she probably called, but she couldn't get through, because I'd drowned my mobile. But she didn't come either.

Autumn was approaching. The nights were getting cooler and so were the days. Showers arrived more frequently and lasted longer. When the sky loured, I battened shut the little window on the left of the monitor, the one that looked onto the garden. The rain drummed on the tinplate window-ledge; I drummed on the keyboard with my fingers; the words dripped into the text and flowed into the horizontal rivulets of lines. I still devoted the best hours of the day to my beloved prose. Nothing distracted me and my time was only measured out by the muffled chiming of the bells of Vaskovo's little church. But one day my efforts were interrupted by an unexpected knock at the door. I put on my trousers and went to answer it. My neighbour Vyacheslav was standing on the porch.

'Howdy!'

'Howdy!'

I thought I heard a challenging note in his greeting.

'Are you going to let me in, or what?'

'Come in . . . To what do I owe the pleasure?'

'Nothing special. Lenka didn't come home last night.'

'What's that got to do with me? She's not here.'

'I can see that . . .' Vyacheslav muttered sullenly. 'But what's your fly doing open?'

'Well, I wasn't actually expecting visitors.'

Perplexed not so much by the visit itself as by its early timing, I enquired why Vyacheslav wasn't at work. It turned to be a Saturday.

'Ah, neighbour, you've really hit rock bottom,' Vyacheslav remarked sternly. 'Even Mikha can tell Saturday from Friday. You need gingering up a bit.'

Naturally, Vyacheslav had a bottle under his belt and we sat down in my little kitchen to drink it. I got the impression that, once he had set his mind at rest about me, my neighbour forgot all about his Lenka, because initially our conversation ran along abstract lines. But after the third or fourth shot, Vyacheslav's thoughts came full circle – not to Lenka, but to myself.

'What I can't understand, neighbour, is how come you're on holiday all summer long. Leave in compensation for a dirty job, is it? Let on where to find work like that, will you? I forge iron and I only get two weeks off in the year.'

So I had to let on. I told Vyacheslav I was a literary man, a kind of writer. And even though I was out at the *dacha*, I was busy all the time. And so he wouldn't feel envious, I lied and said that forging words was no easier than forging iron. Naturally, Vyacheslav didn't believe me.

'All right, forget it,' he said. 'You get by without working, good for you. But how do you get by without a woman, that's the question. I haven't seen that little wife of yours around for a long time.'

I opened my mouth to say something, I don't remember now exactly what, but that's not important, because my reply was never uttered.

'Who's that you're talking about?' a familiar voice asked from the doorway.

It was Tamara.

'Speak of the devil . . .' Vyacheslav muttered. 'All right then, time I was going.'

He started pulling himself together and a minute later he had disappeared, taking the unfinished bottle with him. Dumbfounded by Toma's sudden appearance, I froze, uncertain whether I should approach her. I was expecting immediate castigation for drinking so early in the day, for the disorder in the kitchen and for goodness only knows what else . . . But strangely enough, Toma looked almost as embarrassed as Vyacheslav when he fled.

'You know what,' she said in a quiet voice. 'I'd like to have a drink with you too.'

I couldn't believe my ears.

'But he . . . Vyacheslav took the vodka with him.'

'That's no problem,' Toma said with a bashful smile. 'I've got something better than that.'

She took a bottle of cognac out of her bag.

Now I wasn't just dumbfounded, I was absolutely flabbergasted. As I tidied up the dining table, I tried to think what could possibly be the reason for Toma's unprecedented bonhomie. If she had come to celebrate the purchase of a new flat, where were all the fanfares? Why was she not flaunting her triumph? An alarming premonition was already constricting my chest, but I didn't jump in with any questions, deciding it would be best if things were clarified over a glass of cognac.

Finally everything was ready and we sat down at the table. Tamara opened the cognac herself and poured some for both of us.

'Off we go!' she said, obviously nervous as she raised her glass.

'Where are we going?' I enquired cautiously. 'What are we drinking to, dear?'

'You'll find out in a moment . . .'

She downed her glass in one and took a bite of an apple. I did the same.

'Well, let's hear it.'

Toma became embarrassed again, but made an effort to carry on.

'Here goes then . . . Basically, as they say, I've got good news and bad news. Bad for you, that is . . . or maybe it isn't, I don't know, I don't know anything. Let's have another drink.'

We had another drink, only it didn't seem to help Toma much. But she ploughed on notwithstanding.

'The first piece of news is: we're not selling our flat. Are you glad?'

Taken aback, I simply shrugged.

'And the second piece of news is: I don't live there any more.'

'Now that is interesting . . .' I muttered. 'May I have a few more details?'

Tamara had to take another drink. And so did I.

'Well you see,' she said, steadying her breathing, 'we met in this estate agency, he was buying a flat too. And so we thought, why do we need two?'

'We?' I asked, turning numb.

'We,' she whispered, and tears sprang to her eyes.

I got up. I was fearsome, appalling.

'I called you!' Tamara cried out. 'I called and called! Why weren't you available?'

I dropped the stool and walked out of the kitchen. A minute later I came back. Toma was sobbing and gnawing on an apple. Without saying a word, I grabbed the cigarettes off the table, jerked my umbrella off its nail and ran out of the house.

I marched on and on. Striding along without even seeing where I was going. It started raining, but I kept on marching. Suddenly I heard a thin, childish voice.

'Mister! Mister!'

But my ears heard without hearing and it was some time before I realised the voice was talking to me. When

I did realise, I automatically flung up the hand with my watch on it.

'Quarter past two, little girl.'

Only then did I realise there really was a wet little girl standing in front of me, clutching some kind of bundle in her arms.

'Mister, take the doggy,' she said, obviously not for the first time.

'All right,' I said without giving it a thought and took her bundle, in which something promptly started whimpering.

'Thank you,' the little girl said with a smile and ran off through the puddles.

I ought to have asked what the doggy was called, but I didn't think of it. And I didn't know the little girl's name either. When I got back home, I studied the contents of the bundle carefully. The creature proved to be a male, about six weeks old. I glanced into the calendar of saints and baptised him Philip.

MARINATED ORCHIDS

What is the absolutely primary public good? Of course, a shop that's only a step away from home, an EAS (Easily Accessible Shop). Price accessibility is taken as given, although this is a relative term. If we had EASs everywhere, there wouldn't be any need for the president's CC (Civic Chamber), because every shop like this is a citizen's forum *par excellence*. We assert our rights loudly on the sales floor, we conduct protracted debates on the steps, and in the alleys behind it we exercise personal freedoms that are not established in law. And all this without distracting the government from affairs of state.

As for my own neighbourhood, in this respect it could not possibly be better provided for: the nearest shop is located directly under my windows. So if I should get the urge, it's within spitting, as well as walking distance. When the shop was built a long time ago, it was called simply 'Bakery'. Nothing was ever actually baked there, but you could always buy bread and those rock-hard Soviet spice cakes. Later, when all the changes everyone knows about took place in the country, the shop was privatised and its name was changed to 'Rosa Bakery Shop'. Who this Rosa was – the first owner of the shop, the owner's wife or his beloved, nobody knows these days. During the next fifteen years this retail outlet changed owners several times; the shop sign was renovated and the words in it switched places, but the set always remained the same. I realise that 'Rosa' can't be taken off the sign, because that's the brand now. But I am surprised by the stubbornness with which our little shop continues to call itself a bakery, when they still don't bake anything there. On the other hand, it now has low-quality versions of everything. The undemanding consumer who lives only a step away, including myself, always does his or her shopping at the 'Rosa'.

However, if I absolutely must have freshly-baked bread buns or some other product that isn't out of date, I have to take a step further. Located about two hundred metres from my building is a large, modern grocery store. It's considered to be economy class, but that doesn't mean the customer can make any huge savings there. In wintertime the old ladies tumble like ninepins on its icy steps, and the air on the sales floor is stale and stuffy in both winter and summer, not to mention the chronic shortage of shopping baskets and little keys for the lockers where you leave your own shopping bag. The economy-class grocery store represents our second level of consumer prosperity.

The third level, and the highest in our district, is exemplified by the 'Throne' shop, which is distinguished from the first two by its automatic doors and certain strict internal security measures. And also, of course, by its prices. This third level is only three steps away from me, but it is well beyond the reach of my wallet and, indeed, of most wallets around here. We usually walk past the 'Throne': the miraculous doors gape invitingly wide, but all they catch is air. The checkout lady here is not overburdened with work: she spends the whole day leafing through a glossy magazine with her manicured fingers or flirting with the security guard.

The third level of consumption is not my level; my level lies somewhere between the 'Rosa' and economy class, and that's only when my financial affairs are in relatively good order. My finances are subject to disruption when I have to make any large purchases – shoes, for instance, or trousers. In such cases I sometimes borrow from my brother-in-law, as I call Dmitry Pavlovich, my ex-wife Tamara's husband. I don't find it pleasant to do this, but I really have no choice. I'm a writer and, therefore, a public figure and, therefore, there's no way I can manage without a decent pair of shoes. That's the way I see it, and Tamara agrees with me, although nothing here really follows from anything else. My relative celebrity as a writer of prose simply allows me to get past face control at certain literary clubs in Moscow without any problem. Every now and then I attend other people's presentations at one place or another, provided, of course that the functions are accompanied by a buffet meal. I don't go for the pleasure of it, only to demonstrate to Tamara and Dmitry Pavlovich that I am an item of some cultural significance. Otherwise, I suspect he wouldn't loan me the money for shoes, and I wouldn't be able to go.

When my indebtedness exceeds my creditworthiness, Dmitry Pavlovich doesn't write it off, he restructures it. I don't find the moral aspects of this process very pleasant either. 'Forget about the money,' says Dmitry Pavlovich, 'pay it back when you can.' The first part of this phrase doesn't tally with the second, because if I forget about the money, then I'll never give it back. But that's okay. What's worse is that he moves on to speculate about fixing me up with some kind of work, not so that I can pay him back, of course, but so that I can buy my own shoes. Our conversations on this subject are ritual in nature and never lead to any practical conclusion. Never, that is, with one single exception, which I am going to tell you about now.

One day Dmitry Pavlovich called and informed me that I was invited to dinner. Dinner sounded good; I rarely decline invitations of that kind. But it was strange that he called in the middle of a working day. If I try to contact him at that time, Dmitry Pavlovich doesn't immediately recall who I am and addresses me in an intimidating, bossy tone of voice. This time too, in fact, the tone was peremptory, brooking no objections.

'Be ready at half past seven. Tamara and I will pick you up.'

I tried to ascertain the occasion for the prospective dinner, and why my presence was required, but Dmitry Pavlovich didn't go into the details.

'I've got no time to talk to you now,' he snapped. 'It's a business dinner, you'll find out what's what there.'

Not entirely satisfied with his answer, I phoned Tamara. Managers of her level don't give themselves such airs and anyway, to judge from the occasional slurping sound in the handset, my call caught her at coffee in the corporate canteen.

'What is it you don't understand?' Toma asked with a slurp of surprise. 'Dima's found you a job and wants to introduce you to the people you need to know.'

'So that's it,' I muttered, 'I see. But I'd like to be in the loop too.'

'In what loop?'

'Well . . . where we're having dinner and who with.'

'Didn't Dima tell you?' Toma slurped. 'We're dining at Gridlevsky's place, Griddle.'

'But who with?'

'Gridlevsky, of course.'

I paused for a moment, gathering my thoughts. The surname surfaced slowly out of the depths of my memory, trailing vague gastronomic associations . . . and then sank again.

'And who is he, this Gridlevsky?' I asked cautiously.

Tamara gasped in amazement:'

'What do you mean, who is he? And you a writer! He's a celebrity, all your lot eat at his place.'

'My lot?'

'Yes, your lot – the cultural fraternity. He's read you and he liked you. He wants to commission you to write a book.'

'A recipe book?'

'Why a recipe book . . . well, maybe it is a recipe book. What do you care, as long as they pay for it?'

The situation had been more or less clarified. The idea of a recipe book didn't exactly inspire me, but I thought I probably ought to get to know Gridlevsky and his establishment. After all, it's rather frustrating to be known as a Moscow writer and not know where the cultural fraternity dines – the part of it, that is, that has the wherewithal to eat out at restaurants.

At eight o'clock or, to be precise, eight-forty, the Geländewagen rolled up to the entrance of my building with Dmitry Pavlovich, Tamara and the driver Little Dima in it. I got in, kissed my ex-wife and we set off.

We drove through Moscow: traffic jam – spurt, traffic jam – spurt . . . There were lots of restaurants on both sides of the road, with gilded turnstiles and guards who looked like Little Dima at the entrances. The red-carpet tongues of these establishments licked up patrons as they arrived, but these patrons didn't look like the cultural fraternity. Then the Geländewagen turned off the main avenue and started threading its way through side streets. There were no more opulent signs here, but there were many tightly-parked expensive cars. Half of them were compeers of our Geländewagen – steep-sided jeeps – and the other half were meteoric sports models as flat as squashed insects. All this gave the impression that the local population consisted entirely of safari-lovers and demon drivers, but I knew this was not the case. The cars stood along the wall like lacquered shoes in a hallway and I felt inclined to pity them.

'How inconvenient to live in the centre,' Tamara remarked. 'There's not even anywhere to park.'

'Uh-huh,' responded Dmitry Pavlovich.

It seemed to me, however, that they weren't being entirely sincere with each other.

Meanwhile Little Dima whispered something unprintable as he spun the wheel hard and cast rapid glances into both mirrors, straining to hold the Geländewagen in check. Eventually we squeezed backwards into a small space at the pavement.

'Out you get, we're here!' announced Dmitry Pavlovich.

Naturally, this order was intended for Tamara and me. Little Dima slumped back in his seat and stuck a cigarette in his mouth. I clambered out of the Geländewagen and looked round, but failed to observe any entrances with carpet runners nearby, or any entrances of any kind.

'We've got to go into the courtyard,' Dmitry Pavlovich announced.

Tamara took hold of his arm and we proceeded on foot, polishing the glossy flanks of the endless automobiles, and soon our leader turned into an arched passageway that smelled of cats. Alarmed, Tamara pressed up closer against Dmitry Pavlovich while I, on the contrary, felt that we were on the right track, although there was no sign of the cultural fraternity just yet. I was not mistaken: once in the courtyard, we discovered a handwritten inscription on the wall of the building: it said 'Griddle this way'. A crooked arrow pointed to a flight of steps leading down to the basement. At the end of the steps was an iron door with a similar handwritten inscription: 'Entrance'. The door yielded without a creak.

Everything inside the basement establishment was just as I expected: walls of whitewashed brick, pipes, valves and pressure gauges. True, the reading on the gauges was zero. Underground ambience, but not entirely so: the pipes had been neatly painted, and the tables standing in the open space all looked spick and span. There was a thick scattering of clients, not flamboyantly dressed, but hanging loose, drinking and eating something off plates that were small, not like the ones at free literary buffets. On looking closer, I discovered several familiar faces in the restaurant. Someone even waved a hand to me. Tamara had not lied: this was a place of culture.

Having ascertained from the manager that Gridlevsky hadn't dropped by yet, we sat down at the reserved table and picked up the menus.

'Let's see how our intelligentsia feeds itself,' Dmitry Pavlovich joked.

I opened my menu card. The fare on offer proved to be extremely varied: apart from every possible variety of griddle cakes, there were dishes from all round the world, from Ukrainian borscht to Argentinian carbonado. Russia was represented by genuine fifty-per-cent-alcohol moonshine, which was called 'the house tipple' for reasons of security. But anyway, before we could actually order anything, the owner of the establishment showed up.

'Ah, there's Gridlevsky,' Dmitry Pavlovich announced, but he needn't have bothered, because I had already spotted him myself. The stocky man with a curly beard was walking round table after table, exchanging a few words with his guests. He gave some of them a friendly slap on the shoulder and clasped the select few in a tight embrace. When he eventually reached us, he immediately started pawing Dmitry Pavlovich

'Hello, my dear friend ... hello ...' Dmitry Pavlovich muttered between the kisses. 'Allow me to introduce ...'

Gridlevsky turned towards me.

'A-a-ah! I've read you, I've read you ...'

Before I could even take fright, he fell on me too. It's a good thing I don't wear any facial hair, or Gridlevsky's beard and mine would have entwined and we would have remained like that, pressed cheek to cheek, forevermore. Nevertheless, I felt flattered and happy to feel the envious gaze of the cultural fraternity on me.

After our mauling, we resumed our seats and Gridlevsky assumed command of the table. He ordered from hither and yon and all points in between, rapidly transforming our dinner into a culinary degustation. What an array of dishes we sampled at his insistence – I can't recall them all now! Only the moonshine, with which we washed down one item after another, lent any semblance of structure to the gastronomic chaos. I've also forgotten the conversation that accompanied the meal; I think we talked about football. But whatever that discussion was, we never finished it. I don't think it would have been possible to finish any discussion with Gridlevsky, because cultural celebrities kept coming up to him to be embraced. There was only one short-cropped lady who greeted Gridlevsky simply, without any kissing. In fact, she took a free chair and sat down beside him.

'Allow me to introduce you,' he said with a sideways glance at the lady. 'Irka. My executive director, who also doubles as my wife.'

Irka smiled at us with just her lips. She laid a device halfway in size between a mobile phone and a laptop on the table and enquired in a business-like tone,

'So, how are our negotiations going?'

'Negotiations?' We exchanged puzzled glances.

'We're still eating,' Gridlevsky explained in an affectionate tone of voice.

'So I see,' said Irka. 'But it's time to get down to business.'

'Then down to business it is!' said Gridlevsky, wiping his lips with a napkin.

His face started glowing and his eyes sparkled.

'My dear fellow!' he said, turning to me. 'Take a look at the diners . . . Who do you see here?'

I looked around.

'Well, over there there's a political analyst sitting with someone else. I saw him on the telly yesterday.'

'And over there,' he said, pointing with his fork, 'is a film director. And at that table – do you see them, embracing? – two writers, both poets. And so on – no room to spit for all these people of culture sitting here, dining in cultured fashion . . . And why is that, do you think?'

'Why is what?'

'Why are they sitting here at Griddle and not somewhere else?'

I shrugged.

'Maybe you give them a special deal? A discount or whatever you call it.'

Gridlevsky nodded.

'The discount, that goes without saying. And the basement, and the pipes – of course, that all has an influence. But what's the most important thing? The most important thing is that we believe the cultural process and the digestive process are inseparable. That's our angle!'

'Maybe the angle is in the precise balance . . .' I tried to suggest cautiously.

'The angle is their inseparability!' Gridlevsky retorted. 'You can't imagine how many creative careers have been shaped in this basement . . . Director drinks with director, poets drink with each other . . . people of art come here and find each other. And you . . . I want you to find inspiration as a writer at Griddle.'

'I'd be glad to,' I murmured, 'only I don't quite understand . . .'

'Ah, what a slow Joe Blow you are,' Dmitry Pavlovich put in unexpectedly. 'Write something beautiful about all this . . . about the way destinies are defined. The establishment gets a boost for its image and you, you fool, get paid a fee. There's the balance for you.'

'Yes, write about it,' said Irka, 'you could do a good job.'

Four pairs of eyes gazed at me expectantly. It would have been simply indecent on my part to refuse now.

'I'll put my best foot forward,' I promised. 'Let's drink to inspiration.'

Irka entered my phone number into her device and we drank to the success of the undertaking. Gridlevsky announced that to celebrate he would treat us to a special dish, then summoned a waiter with a snap of his fingers and whispered something in his ear. We waited for about fifteen minutes until the dish came floating over to us in the hands of the chef de cuisine himself. It was thin slices of dusky meat, set in a surround of delicate blue flowers.

'What is it?' we exclaimed in chorus.

Gridlevsky paused, savouring the effect.

'Smoked antelope with orchids.'

'Antelope – that's really something,' Dmitry Pavlovich said approvingly.

'It looks so lovely!' Tamara exclaimed in delight.

'Help yourselves, ladies and gents!'

Gridlevsky stuck his fork into an orchid and despatched it into his mouth. Spotting the horror on my face, he laughed.

'Don't worry, writer, they're marinated!'

I couldn't bring myself to sample the orchids, but that didn't save me from an upset stomach. After that dinner at Griddle, I spent a restless, sleepless night. The process of digestion was tempestuous, and the process of thought quite inseparable from it. Every new jolt in my belly set my thoughts scampering off in a new direction: I swung wildly between castigating myself for being a literary prostitute and calculating how I would use the fee from Gridlevsky to go to Europe.

By morning my intestines had settled down and the tempest in my head had abated. I fell into a state resembling sleep but not, as it turned out, for long. I was roused from my bed by the trilling of the phone.

'Not calling too early, am I?'

It was someone called Irina Kirillovna from Griddle Inc. In my drowsy state I didn't realise it was Irka from the day before.

'We have to draw up a contract. We'll expect you between eleven and twelve. Okay?'

'Okay,' I responded dully. 'Where shall I come to?'

Thus began the first morning of a new life for me.

Well, there was no going back now. I consulted with my stomach one last time, had a wash and a shave, drenched myself in eau de cologne and set off to Griddle Inc. at the address provided. To draw up a contract.

How often has that word caressed my ear? Well ... a few times. You take the metro to get to the publishing house and the wheels keep drumming it out: 'a contract, a contract'. If you've never written books, you can't understand what an invitation to draw up a contract means to an author. It means that his creation will not be despatched directly to the noosphere, but will first tarry for a while with the public. It has been accepted by mankind as fit for consumption, approved for publication and, perhaps, someone might even read it. The typesetters at least will read it, showing it to each other and tittering into their fists.

But on that morning when I received the invitation from Griddle Inc., I didn't have a completed piece of creative work. It might seem that nothing could be better: you haven't done a stroke yet and already there's a piece of paper waiting for you somewhere with the amount due to you clearly stated in figures and words. But somehow in the metro, on my way to the coveted meeting at that office, I wasn't exactly feeling overjoyed. The carriages rattled and rasped deafeningly as they raced along, and from time to time the driver broadcast hoots of alarm into the darkness. What the driver imagined he could see there, I don't know; but I tried to convince myself that I had nothing to worry about. Especially since I had brought the indigestion tablets with me – just to be on the safe side.

At the office I was met by Irka – now Irina Kirillovna. She greeted me with a meagre smile and led me straight through to the conference room. We had barely even stationed ourselves at the long table before a young woman arrived and set a bowl of sweets down between us.

'Would you prefer tea or coffee?' she asked me.

I preferred coffee.

'The usual for me,' Irina Kirillovna instructed. 'And get in everyone we need.'

The young woman was back in a flash. Tea, coffee and everyone we needed appeared almost simultaneously. While the sugar was still dissolving in my cup, I managed to make the acquaintance of a lady designer and a lady marketologist (both shorn to match their boss's cropped style), a young culturologist, an old gastrologist and a representative of a PR agency on friendly terms with Griddle (a middle-aged man with manicured nails). Noticing that they had all come to the meeting with folders, I felt guilty because I hadn't brought anything apart from my indigestion tablets.

'Let's talk about our book,' suggested Irina Kirillovna. 'Does anyone have any ideas?'

The colleagues briskly opened their folders, but I merely drummed my fingers on the table. Ideas were not slow in coming: the lady designer had four versions of the cover ready, the young culturologist advanced the familiar thesis that culture and nutrition are inseparable; the lady marketologist demanded that the work reflect the positive trend in seat-occupancy rate. The man from the PR agency advised me to give artistic expression to the fact that nowadays going to visit people and drinking at each other's homes was irrelevant, old hat, just like making your own moonshine, because now moonshine was sold at Griddle.

The only ones who didn't have any ideas were the old gastrologist and me. He was obviously too old, and I, to be honest, was too frightened. It was only natural that I should be frightened when I realised I would have to work as part of a team. This was unusual for me: the last time I'd been a part of a team was when I went stealing apples with the other kids in Vaskovo. As she summed up the brainstorming session, Irina Kirillovna turned to me and said that Griddle Inc. was not expecting any self-expression from me and they didn't want 'a novel for the shelf', what they wanted was a contemporary perspective on the culture of nourishment and the nourishment of culture. The production meeting concluded on that note. The colleagues gathered up their folders and left, each collecting a sweet on the way out. I just sat there, totally exhausted.

The young woman who had served the coffee earlier brought a stack of paper.

'Familiarise yourself with the agreement,' Irka told me.

The lines started jumping about in front of my eyes. My head wasn't working too well, but even so I was surprised when I got into it.

'What's this – you call me "the Contractor". But I'm not a builder.'

She shrugged.

'If there's a client, there's a contractor. We have a standard contract, and in your place I wouldn't nitpick over words.'

She was right, there was no point in nitpicking. I felt firmly put in my place, but the 'Remuneration' section appeared to compensate for all the linguistic inelegancies.

In short, I emerged from Griddle Inc. no longer a free artist, but a normal employed citizen. Out on the street, I gazed around with new eyes, washed as clean as office windowpanes. Office buildings, rank upon rank of them – working Moscow encompassed me on all sides. A stream of men wearing ties with broad knots engulfed me and for the first time in my life I felt the urge to look into their hearts and ask: 'What's *your* salary like, for example? What's *your* remuneration?' I felt the urge to bond with them, to hint that now I was no stranger, I was one of them. I could have suggested going somewhere (perhaps even to Griddle!) for a drink of something à la mode to ease the stress. Yes – I could afford that now! I could, because the envelope with my advance was lying in my inside pocket, pressed against my heart. I stood there bewildered, not recognising either the city or myself.

How had it happened that I – I? – had been hired on a stand-ard contract, like any of these individuals in ties? I wanted to go down into the metro, deafen my ears and anaesthetise my soul with all that comforting clatter. I wanted to make a quick getaway with this money that I hadn't earned, lie low, disappear completely. 'You can go whistle for your book!' I muttered vindictively.

Such were the distraught feelings with which I emerged from Griddle Inc. that day. Two or three days later, however, the tumult within had subsided. Naturally, I failed to come up with a saga on the gastric mechanisms of cultural trans-mission; I didn't even make much of an effort. I spent the advance, as I had planned, on a trip to the Czech Republic (a wonderful country!) But I didn't have to lie low after making my getaway. Griddle Inc. carried on for a while trying to get hold of me through Dmitry Pavlovich, then they gave up and wrote me off, like spoiled antelope meat.

A BLOWN GASKET

In the old days, as you know, there used to be so-called 'writers' houses' in Moscow. In fact, there were entire neighbourhoods of writers' houses. I don't intend to discuss this phenomenon here from the politico-historical perspective or from the standpoint of undiluted envy. I merely wish to mention that those buildings are still standing today and quite a large number of literary people still live in them. Of course, I'm not talking about the original residents, those Soviet writers who once had honours and favours heaped on them by the Party and the government, but who now repose in a state of eternal peace or profound senility. I mean their living descendants, who have inherited a love of literature. As a rule, these descendants write neither verse nor prose, but that's a good thing, because their second hereditary disease is dyslexia. This, of course, does not prevent them from participating actively in a vigorous literary process. They serve Russian literature honourably as critics and reviewers in journals, as editors and literary secretaries of all kinds, members of juries for literary prizes ... and in God only knows what other capacities. They are the small screws, levers and pinions of our large, complicated literary machine, a locomotive that is kept in steam even while standing in a siding. And they live in the former writers' houses.

However, I don't mean to backbite or talk shop. I simply don't understand how they have managed for so long, all those literary people together. How they have survived without putting their philological suburbs to the torch or flooding them, or blowing them sky-high with the domestic gas supply. I know that blowing a gasket or two is the intelligentsia's favourite pastime. I even have a literary anecdote involving gaskets and the intelligentsia.

It didn't happen in some writers' ghetto, but here in our working-class district, where the literary men can be counted on one finger and one thumb. These two digits are myself and Sasha Prut, who lives in flat number 27A, three blocks away from me. Sasha (in formal terms he is Samuil Solomonovich) works for a newspaper as an essayist and literary columnist. He is the son of another, better-known Prut, who founded something or other in Soviet literary studies. So Sasha is the genuine article, a literary scion cast up in a working-class housing district by the whim of fate. Why the Soviet authorities neglected to provide his father with a worthy apartment, I don't know, and I don't ask. But I suspect that this circumstance is a source of secret suffering for Sasha.

It would definitely be stretching a point to call us

'brothers in the pen', but Prut and I are friends, despite the difference in our origins. Simply because in the entire district we are the only men of letters, and there is no one else to gossip with on subjects that interest us. Sasha is married, with children, and so, until Tamara left me, our two families socialised on symmetrical terms. Then Prut's side acquired numerical superiority and also developed, I would say, a preponderance of interest. They – especially Sasha's wife, Sonya – imagined that I had suffered a tragedy and was devastated by my loneliness. Indeed, after the divorce I did become a more frequent visitor to the Pruts. Not, however, for the sake of their compassionate solicitude, but because as a bachelor I was lured by the home-made rissoles. A couple of times a month Prut and I used to drink, snack on Sonya's rissoles, gossip about literary subjects and drink again, this time without snacks of any kind, to the cosy accompaniment of the kitchen tap dripping. My heart was warmed by the awareness that it was not I who would have to wash the dishes.

But month by month the dripping in the Pruts' kitchen gradually accelerated, until it developed into a continuous gurgling that became an irritating factor. It even seemed to me that this trickle had begun to erode the Pruts' domestic idyll. Sonya would occasionally resort to rhetoric: 'Can it be possible?' she would exclaim, 'can it be possible that things like this happen in other homes?' Sasha and I tried to take refuge from the subject of the water supply in conversation, but even without Sonya the tap reminded us of its presence ever more insistently.

The malefic trickle babbled away in the Prut's kitchen

by day and by night, carrying off an amount of water beyond all measuring. But among the innumerable drops of which it consisted there was one – although by no means the last – which caused the cup of Sasha's patience to overflow. Indistinguishable among the vast shoal of its fellows, it slipped down and away through the rust-rimmed plug hole of the kitchen sink. This happened at night, when everybody in the flat was asleep. Neither Sonya nor the children sensed the fatal drop – only Sasha did. Waking with a shudder, he started listening to the familiar gurgling coming from the kitchen. Gazing into the darkness, he was suddenly filled with an inexplicable hatred for the incontinent old tap although, properly speaking, its condition was the objective result of its age. 'I have to put an end to this!' Sasha muttered, grinding his teeth. 'Tomorrow or never!'

And then tomorrow came. Prut woke again, this time in the usual manner. In the morning the babbling of the trickle in the kitchen was not so intrusive; it merged into the other sounds of newly woken life. But strangely enough, sleep had not obliterated Sasha's memory of the nocturnal incident. Marvelling at the strength of his own resolve, he clambered into the closet where, out of sheer sentimentality, they stored items that had outlived their time. There was an old Olympia typewriter, a Neva photographic enlarger, a Yauza four-track tape-recorder and all sorts of other things in there. From in among the other stuff Sasha retrieved a yellow pigskin case containing hand tools that he had inherited from his father the literary scholar, who had inherited it from Sasha's grand-dad, a cobbler from Kiev. Tipping the contents of the case out onto the floor, the scourge of the cantankerous tap selected the weapon best suited to his purpose – that is, naturally, the largest and most fearsome pipe wrench. With a tool like that even a puny man of letters is capable of wreaking havoc.

The fateful moment arrived. Having excluded all extraneous personnel from the kitchen, Prut summoned up his martial spirit and moved in to attack. He clamped his mighty weapon on the tap and heaved. The madman didn't even take the trouble to close the shut-off valve, which – as emerged later – didn't work in any case. That poor old tap! In its thick, furry coat of salt deposits, it looked like an impregnably secure stalagmite, but it proved as brittle as a rotten branch. Sasha heaved and – crunch! – the tap was left clutched in the jaws of the wrench and a hot geyser at a pressure of four atmospheres shot out of the wound in the mixer. Only then did it become clear what a destructive force the old brass fossil had been straining to hold in check. Enveloped in a cloud of steam, Prut dashed from the kitchen into the toilet to close the shut-off valve – but to no avail! The shut-off valve was the same age as the kitchen tap, it had turned downright crusty long ago and the only function it now served was as a decoration on the pipe, except that Sonya occasionally hung the floor cloth on it to dry. All Sasha could do with the shut-off valve was bend it badly and scratch it. And that was all he did. I won't paint a detailed picture of the subsequent events and what the real plumbers said to Sasha. I could never, in any case, do that more vividly than Sonya. The most significant outcome of Sasha's efforts with the pipe wrench was that he became much better acquainted with the inhabitants of the sixteen floors below his own. They had previously greeted him more or less politely when they met in the lift, but after this tragic event Prut came to know another side of his neighbours. However, I won't go into the details of that either.

Although the case of the flood that Sasha had loosed was eventually settled on the basis of compensation for costs, the incident itself spawned an entire chain of consequences. The first, and least significant, was that Samuil Prut wrote a novel, which related the bitter fate of a sensitive and educated man obliged to live in aggressive and soulless surroundings. Written in a fury in only three months, the novel failed to win the approval of his contemporaries, which was hardly surprising, since Prut had set his hand to a trade that was not his, but it was strange that he was so upset by this. He wasn't the first and he won't be the last; who can tell how many failed novelists there are in Moscow? The catch, however, is that although there are many novelists, not all of them write literary columns. Prut decided to wreak vengeance for the fiasco suffered by his novel in his journalistic capacity. His reviews became violently critical; the hot bile dripped from his pen, gathering into a trickle that soon became a toxic torrent, poisoning the sluggish flow of our literary waters. Everyone got it in the neck from Prut! They said that his criticism even gave one elderly writer a stroke that paralysed his right side, and now, supposedly, the old man is obliged to learn to write with his left hand.

Sasha did not spare my modest creative efforts either. True, I didn't suffer a stroke, but when Prut discovered unjustified social optimism, a compromise with reality and something else of a similar kind in my work, I stopped going round to his place for rissoles.

We hadn't seen each other for some time and only met by chance at a buffet meal after some literary event. He was drinking alone, in a Byronically sombre mood. I didn't pretend, as many others did, that I hadn't noticed him, but made an effort and walked over with my glass.

'Hello, Sasha!' I said. 'Why so gloomy?'

'What's there to be happy about?' he replied. 'I stand here and observe the insignificant nonentities. I'm an outsider at this Vanity Fair.'

'You've become very strict with the human race,' I protested. 'These are your fellow professionals. Not great talents, perhaps, but good-hearted people. Or is it true what they say, and you've got a bleeding ulcer?'

Sasha laughed darkly.

'It's nothing to do with an ulcer. You try flooding these people's flats, then you'll discover just how good-hearted they really are.'

'Maybe you're right,' I observed, 'but you behave as if you were the one who was flooded.'

I don't remember how he answered. Our conversation didn't lead anywhere in any case, like all conversations at buffet meals. And then the buffet meals stopped, because summer arrived and literary life came to a standstill. Summer is a time of hibernation for those who write – this is what differentiates us from the rest of the animal world. Creative hibernation, that is, of course. Men of letters spend these three months trying to heal their haemorrhoids and their nerves and rid themselves of the fatty deposits that have accumulated in their buttocks as a result of their sedentary work. Then in the autumn, refreshed, they gather at the familiar places and recognise each other again, like school classmates after the holidays – with the difference that writers don't grow over the summer.

Only one sub-species of writers has a hard time in summer – literary columnists. The paper must come out, complete with the review. Columnists conjure up subjects out of thin air and write nonsense that they feel ashamed of for the next year. And no one invites them anywhere to give a talk and have a drink. Literary reviewers wander through the summer like lost souls, they shamble about like insomniac bears. During this period their psychoses are exacerbated.

In saying this I am hinting at Sasha Prut, who seemed to be finally broken by the summer. In late August I met his wife Sonya in the economy-class shop and found her in a state of emotional distress. When I asked how she and Sasha were getting on, she replied that things were bad and she thought Sasha had gone to pieces.

'Has he started drinking?' I asked, puzzled.

'No, I didn't express myself correctly,' said Sonya, shaking her head. 'Sasha's flipped his lid. He's gone round the bend,' – tears glinted in her eyes. 'I'm afraid – he's not all there!'

There are numerous popular expressions for what had happened to Prut – the people know how to diagnose such problems. But Sonya was not a woman of the people, and so she got her terms confused. Prut was there all right, all of him, including his misery, and that was what was driving her and the children round the bend. He had got into the habit of lying down the whole day through, with his face turned to the wall, and then in the evening he would suddenly become agitated, leap up and walk out of the flat without even combing his hair, sometimes in his slippers. He rambled round the neighbourhood, scaring solitary passers-by and courting couples, and even the packs of freaky teenagers made way for him . . .

As I listened to Sonya, I asked myself a question: What really was the cause of Sasha's mental breakdown? And I couldn't find an answer. My extensive wisdom could come up with no more than a single phrase:

'These things happen . . .'

She would have carried on pouring out her sorrows to me, but it was too awkward in that place. As I have said, Sonya was not a woman of the people, so she felt embarrassed tattling in the middle of a supermarket.

'I'm sorry for not inviting you round,' she told me as we said goodbye. 'We don't make rissoles anymore, you know, because there's no one to work the mincer.'

And Sonya set off with her burden of groceries and untold woes. Naturally, she forgot about me instantly.

We hadn't seen each again other or had any kind of contact until yesterday, when Sonya phoned me in a terrible state. From her disjointed monologue, I gathered that Sasha had been missing for more than two days. She had already run round our neighbourhood and all the others nearby, rung all the morgues and loony-bins and alerted the militia. And now she was calling me, without really knowing why. Concerning the militia, I thought she was deluding herself about their alertness, but as I listened to her, I blushed bright red in shame.

'Forgive me, Sonya,' I muttered. 'I didn't think he had left without saying anything. You reassure the militia and I'll get him back to you soon without fail.'

Sasha, who was sitting opposite me, glared wildly . . .

'So he's there with you!' Sonya shrieked, bursting into floods of tears.

It took me a long time to persuade her not to come running to collect her husband there and then, and when I did manage to persuade her and hung up, I gave Sasha a severe look.

'You're a real bastard, Prut,' I said. 'How could you set me up like this?'

I might as well have asked Phil why he had eaten my glove. Without even waiting for an answer, I sighed and said:

'All right. We'll go there one last time – and then it's back home at the double for you.'

'There' meant the River Moscow. On the two days for which Sasha had been living with me, we had taken Phil and gone to watch a dock crane at work. We sat on the riverbank and drank beer while the crane pecked pinches of sand out of a barge and dropped them onto a pile. The pile was huge, with a little bulldozer creeping perilously across it and a tiny, intrepid man sitting in the bulldozer. But sometimes the crane suddenly dropped its scoop bucket into the barge and froze, as if lost in thought, and at that very instant the bulldozer on the sand hill fell silent. The drivers climbed out of their cabins and got together for a bite to eat and a drink. They dined among the sands, like Bedouins, except that Bedouins don't drink vodka, but the drivers did, and they spoke in Russian, only not about literature.

THE HAMMER DRILL

I was once invited to a writers' congress in a certain developed country. I don't think I need to explain what a writers' congress is. The only functions that have ever been more boring were the old Soviet trade union conferences. But I went – I went as a matter of principle, to get one up on certain colleagues of mine, because I had been invited and they hadn't. The organisers put us up in a Hilton – a certain kind of five-star hotel. On the first day the congress delegates wolfed down their five-star breakfast and went about their writers' business. Those who had a good grasp of English took up their folders and set off to give readings and listen to them, while those whose grasp was poor (mostly writers from the undeveloped nations) set out to do some shopping. And only I, being no great master of the English language or the art of shopping, went back to my room after breakfast. I battened down the window, so that I wouldn't be disturbed by the sirens that sounded more frequently on the city street here than at home, and climbed back into bed, intending to snooze for an hour or two. Snoozing is one art of which I am a true master. But no such luck! No sooner did I start nodding off than I heard a repulsive rasping sound. It was clearly coming from somewhere inside the building, not from the street. But regardless of where its origin lay, its focus was at the very centre of my brain. This scraping that merged into a regular staccato hammering and then soared up into a whine was produced by a hammer drill – mankind's most heinous invention since the torture wheel. Supposedly this device is intended for various kinds of repair jobs, including in hotels.

Greatly displeased, I subjected the word Hilton to five-star linguistic torment as I prepared to get out of bed in order to catch up on my sleep at some conference session, when suddenly someone knocked at my door. It turned out to be the maid, who had come to tidy my room. She came in with a bright, beaming Hilton smile but her surprise on finding me in bed was so great that the smile instantly faded from her face. According to her foreign ideas, it was inexcusable to be in bed at such a late hour.

This incident demonstrates how poorly our world is adapted for sleeping during the day. It's exactly the same here in Moscow: any repairs and renovations anywhere, except in the metro, are carried out in broad daylight. The only ones who doze peacefully to the murmur of the city at midday are the metro workers, Phil and me. The difference is that the toilers of the underground, having toted all those heavy sleepers, sleep so soundly themselves that you couldn't wake them with a canon, but my writer's sleep is delicate.

... My sleep may be delicate, but the customary noises don't disturb it. The squawk of an ambulance driving into the yard or the screech of faulty plumbing somewhere in the building, or a fly buzzing past – these are all nothing to me. It's only the stran ... what's that?

'... Brrrrrrrrrrrrrrrrrr!' I hear. 'Vzhzhzhzhzhzh!'

I dream that I'm back in the Hilton, skiving off the writers' congress in bed. And once again I use bad Russian words to curse these foreign habits ...

I wake up with those words on my lips. My watch says ten thirty, absolutely genuine Moscow time. Someone in our building has started renovation work. Some single, separate individual in some single, separate flat. Many years ago, when the building was young and the residents were youthful, improvements used to be carried out everywhere at once. Hammers pounded simultaneously on all floors; people walked in through the entrances with bundles of wallpaper that they had managed to pick up somewhere. The wallpaper was rubbishy, but the people's faces shone with joy. There weren't any hammer drills then, but happiness was possible. Every roll of pre-pasted paper bought on the side, every can of Finnish paint obtained by dubious means seemed to us like manna from heaven. Tamara and I also renovated our flat here – for the first and only time. How long ago that was.

The hammer drill falls silent just long enough to give me hope of deliverance ... and then starts howling again. From the pattern of its behaviour, I know it is being directed by the uncertain hand of an amateur: it either whines at maximum velocity or whirrs like a dying housefly. I hear the unknown handyman miss some unknown target and wish with all my heart that he would hit his finger.

Phil wanders round the rooms with his tail drooping. Instead of working, I set up a game of patience on the computer screen. Do my other neighbours really not give a damn about this outrage? They do not. In the flat to the right of mine the only people left in during the day are a young mother and her baby. Right now he's taking her breast and she's watching a soap on TV, and the earth's crust can split open as far as they're concerned. The man living on the left is an army veteran, as deaf as a post – he's probably polishing his medals without turning a hair.

The most annoying thing is that at this hour of the day there's no legal redress against the damned hammer drill. I'm no lawyer, but I know that. After all, if that sort of thing is allowed in the Hilton . . .

. . . brrrrrrrrrrrrrrrrrrrrrrrrrrrrrrrrrrrrrrrrrrrrrrrrrrr!

But if there's no legal means of redress, maybe I can find some extra-legal means? The concierge Nasir told me about an incident in which one resident on our stairwell punched another one in the face. The other one had supposedly annoyed him in some way too – by making noise or simply by the way he looked. The one who threw the punch was actually put in prison later, but for a completely different reason. Why shouldn't I give it a try? Go and tell this eager beaver: 'If you don't stop clattering away with that machine of yours, I'll . . .' Basically, threaten to stick his damned hammer drill up his you know where. Of course, he'll wax indignant, reply insultingly, and I'll promptly smack him with a right – one!

– and a left – two! Great. Even if I can't give him a drubbing, I'll certainly spoil his mood for him. Of course, if I don't give him a drubbing, then he'll give me one and rearrange my face for me. And that's too high a price to pay. Isn't there any way I can spoil his mood without a fight? With just words, for instance? After all, the word is also a mighty weapon, isn't it? On reflection, I find the verbal alternative more to my liking – it's the only course worthy of a civilised individual.

. . . BRRRRRRRRRRRRRRRRRRRRRRRR!

My patience snaps; and I put on my trousers. Before I leave the flat I straighten up, square my shoulders and look at myself in the mirror. I look so menacing, I even give myself goose bumps.

I sally forth to the enemy camp or, rather, in search of it. The hammer drill's roar fills the stairwell from top to bottom, an organ note from a monstrous music of the spheres . . .

Proceeding at random, I walk up one floor and I'm in luck: a trail of chalky tracks runs from the rubbish chute right across the landing. Chalk means whitewash, and where there's whitewash, there's refurbishment, and that's where I should seek my foe. I estimate the enemy's shoe size. No larger than mine. I follow the trail.

There's a door facing me. The hammer drill thundering away behind the door makes it hard for me to concentrate. I repeat to myself the verbal diplomatic note that I have prepared, pluck up my courage and press the doorbell. The hammer drill falls silent. My heart counts off the beats in the silence that has fallen. Time drags on, second after second, as I wait . . . But then the hammer drill starts wailing again.

No one has opened the door. I ring again, and the howling of the hammer drill breaks off again. But once again no one comes to the door. This is beginning to resemble some stupid game, but I'm sorry, I'm not in the mood for games today. I force the bell push in with the firm intention of holding it there until the victory is won.

Well, at last! The latch clatters and the door opens, pushing me aside.

'Oh, I'm sorry! I was wondering if someone rang my bell or I was hearing things . . .'

Standing there before me is a long-haired, bespectacled young man in briefs and a t-shirt. The t-shirt bears the logo and phone number of some firm – like the ones they give out at company parties – but the briefs are ordinary ones, from a shop. The young man's spectacles are covered with cement dust and his bare knees are smeared with the same substance.

'Pardon my appearance,' he says with a smile. 'As you can see, I'm doing a bit of work on the flat.'

'I can see that, young man, and I can hear it very clearly too.'

I tried to make my voice sound stern and authoritative, but it came out cranky and peevish. Immediately I was deluged by expressions of regret, as if they were tumbling out of a sack – oh, he didn't know, he didn't realise, he took the day off especially to do it during the day, so he wouldn't disturb anyone . . . The final part of this rapturous apology was addressed to my back.

It takes only a minute, no longer, to complete the return

march, close the door of my own flat behind me and catch my breath. The army is back from its campaign. Phil looks at me enquiringly – is the army victorious? That's something I don't know myself.

An hour goes by after my return; the building is silent. But this silence has cost me dear. As a well-known poem puts it: 'both steed and dragon's body side by side on the sand'. The hammer drill has been vanquished; now I should be able to create unhindered. Board the glorious ship *Prose*, weigh anchor, hoist aloft the taut sails of invention and forward, into the fictive sea that is my element. Sail on, leaving astern the fading furrows of the lines. But alas! After the battle my head is filled with nothing but a windless calm and the sails of invention droop limp and impotent. The characters that make up my tight-knit crew have all hidden away from me in the hold and are keeping schtum.

I've closed the game of patience on the screen so it won't tempt me, but now there's a face in spectacles gazing back at me instead. What's that there behind those dusty lenses? Could it be reproach? Big deal – so he took the day off specially! But writers don't have any days off, only back-to-back periods of idle down-time for various stupid reasons.

I wonder what that barefoot weirdo's doing up there now? Probably sitting there sighing over his wasted day too ... I open the game of patience that I saved ... and then close it again. The situation has a whiff of the absurd about it.

Phil watches, perplexed, as I climb into my trousers. Yes, my friend, I'm going back up there again ...

This time the young man opens the door immediately, as if he was sitting right behind it. His eyes glitter defiantly, but in their depths I see fright.

'If you heard anything, it wasn't me,' he reports. 'I haven't even switched on the drill.'

'Quite right too,' I reply unsmilingly. 'You don't have a clue about how to use it.'

By the way, I have every right to tell him that. I happen to be very adroit when it comes to handling tools – nature herself designed my hands for it. Sometimes I take up a drill or a hammer just to prove to myself and the people around me that I am, after all, an individual endowed with certain abilities. As for my bespectacled neighbour, of course I have no intention of trying to prove anything to him. It's just that where he's concerned I feel . . . well, basically, I feel rather guilty.

The young man doesn't immediately understand that I am offering to help him and when he does understand, he tries to decline the offer gratefully. In the brief battle of magnanimity and counter-magnanimity that ensues, I emerge victorious, politely battering down Four-Eyes' defences and insinuating myself into his flat. A short while later he and I are crawling round on the floor together, drilling holes for skirting boards and installing them. Or rather, I am drilling and installing them and Vasya (that's his name) is crawling around with me out of a sense of solidarity and getting in my way. He thinks he's picking up the knack from me. A naive young fellow without any natural ability, the most he'll do is skin his knees unnecessarily. But then, that's what a master class is for in any case: to boost the maestro's self-esteem.

And then, working with a hammer drill is so satisfying! How easily it eats through the concrete, with such cheerful greed. I could go on drilling and drilling for ever. It must be admitted that a hammer drill arouses entirely different feelings on different sides of the same wall.

While we're crawling about like this (and it goes on for several hours), Vasya and I talk and learn a few things about each other. For instance, Vasya is an interior designer by profession, and he has set about renovating his flat because he's planning to get married. Only somehow he can't decide on the final design for this interior. The renovation is going slowly, because Vasya is tormented by doubts.

'About what?' I ask ironically. 'The design or the wedding?'

He shrugs.

Well, whichever it is, I can understand him. I'm often tormented by doubts too, which is why my prose advances so slowly.

'But you fairly dash along with the repairs,' Vasya says encouragingly.

'Then maybe we should swap places?'

I'm joking, of course. Vasya laughs.

'No, honestly, thanks very much for the help, it's a pity I haven't read your books.'

He admits that when he reads fiction he falls asleep on the second page. The only material he reads without slumbering is professional, otherwise it's all computer, computer . . .

'What a coincidence,' I say. 'I fall asleep on the second page too, but only when I'm writing.'

Combined with our fruitful labour, these conversations help the time pass imperceptibly. Evening arrives, it's getting dark outside. My lower back aches from crawling about on all fours for so long. I'm tired, but it's a benign tiredness that refutes the conclusions of reason by demonstrating that the day has not been lived in vain. I think that today we have brought Vasya's wedding day significantly closer. But enough is enough, even of a good thing.

'Isn't it time we called it a day? You never know, the neighbours might come round and raise hell.'

'Oh, you're right!' Vasya exclaims, suddenly realising. 'Let's wind things up.'

'Yes, let's.'

We wind things up in due order, by drinking to our heroic exploits in Vasya's kitchen. Of course, we drink tequila, the preferred tipple of designers. Vasya shows me his designs for the future interior and photos of his fiancée. The designs are different and the fiancée is the same everywhere. But it's all the same to me what I drink and what I feast my eyes on. I'll sleep well tonight, even though I haven't written a single line. Although in fact, for me these two things are not connected – I just hope no one starts whirring away with a hammer drill.

IN BED WITH
AN ESTATE AGENT

Ludmila gets home from work at seven thirty. She could get back at seven fifteen, but on the way home she always calls into the supermarket. At that time Konstantin is only just making the change from the circle line to our radial line on the metro. He's never home earlier than eight. They are not acquainted.

But their children know each other very well, since they grew up playing in the same yard. Ludmila's daughter Masha and Konstantin's son Seryozha are sixteen. They hang out together, like the same kind of beer and have identical mobile phones. Normal young people. Masha and Seryozha are in a sexual relationship, but they won't set up a family, of course, because soon they'll swap their mobiles for different ones and their ways will part.

Ludmila and Konstantin have no chance at all – not

even of meeting each other. And even if they did meet, where would that get them? If they ran into each other in the lift in the morning, for instance? Konstantin uses Issey Miyake cologne, and Ludmila uses Trussardi perfume: fine fragrances, taken separately, but just try mingling them together in a cramped lift! He and she would turn their noses in opposite directions and ride on like that, dreaming of reaching the ground floor as soon as possible.

Theoretically speaking, however, Ludmila and Konstantin are perfectly suited to each other. Not merely because he's a man and she's a woman, but in purely human terms – at the level of their preferences. Only Ludmila already has a lover who comes to her place. A decent man, married, but a confirmed masochist. When they're alone, he puts on a harness and makes Ludmila ride round the flat on him. She rides around, thinking: 'If only Masha could see me now'.

Konstantin's contacts are not really to his taste, either, although he has far more of them. He works as a senior editor for a magazine publisher and draws his partners from among his young female colleagues. The publishing house is what is called modern and sophisticated: all the girls in the offices, without exception, are devotees of slang and piercings. Every time he encounters either or both of these things in an intimate context, Konstantin shudders. These girls can only be caressed with great caution and they constantly stain the sheets with self-tanning lotion.

All this is sad. Of course, within the bounds of the present novel I, as the author, am empowered to arrange the fates of my characters as I see fit. It's not hard for me to fix things so that Ludmila and Konstantin meet somewhere at a Housing Management Association meeting, introduce them to each other and make them fall in love. Masha and Seryozha don't even have to be introduced; all that's required is to instil in them a more serious attitude to life. And how well it would all turn out: the parents would move into one flat, and the other would be left at the disposal of their children.

Yes, I can do that. I can marry anybody I like – or you like, dear reader – to anyone. But I won't do it, and don't expect it to happen at the end of the story. Because in my art I am a devotee of the realist school, that is, I take my lead from another Author, who writes all of us. My present characters live in Moscow and as you know, while having granted Muscovites many comforts in this life, He has been rather stingy in endowing them with family happiness.

Sometimes I think: Why does it work out like that? Millions of men and women living alongside each other, all on the same patch of land, so to speak, and they can't sort themselves out into couples. And if couples do form then it's purely by chance. To walk through life hand in hand is given only to very few. I suspect that heaven is to blame here, the same heaven that is responsible for making marriages. Moscow's department of heaven is like a nursery school teacher who has despaired of ever creating a balanced group. Or a sports trainer whose bench of players is too long, so he constantly experiments with the team. But perhaps heaven is not quite as clueless as it seems. It could be that from heaven's perspective we are relatively insignificant and the welfare of the megalopolis is of greater importance. After all, what would happen to Moscow if we all suddenly found our other halves, got married and immersed ourselves completely in our private lives? The city would become lethargic and drowsy and lose its metropolitan status. Do you want that? No.

What does it matter that our urban life does not facilitate the creation of enduring ties, when on the other hand we have so many momentary, fleeting contacts that we don't even notice! In the metro, in the shops, in the streets, everywhere where there are many of us – and there are many of us everywhere – we are woven, minute by minute, into a web of countless lines of communication. Contacts spark constantly and we feel no shortage of adrenalin without love or hate or any of that old provincial drama. The sparking of contacts of this kind doesn't produce children, but it does generate a great sense of community. These contacts are the soldered joints that hold together the universe of Moscow, and each of us is a tiny bright lamp in the sky of that universe.

We each move in our own orbit, sometimes colliding, less often forming twin star systems. This, however, does not happen simply according to someone's whim, but according to the objective laws of urban mechanics. And we must also bear in mind that not only our bodies move in set orbits, but our thoughts as well. Ludmila is not destined for Konstantin not only because their work timetables don't match, but also because it is very unlikely that he would ever set his sights on her. His dating profile – as life has moulded it – is sophisticated girls with slang, tattoos and piercings. Even in the metro, when he gazes around because he has nothing to read, he only notices girls like that. And when he looks through the end windows into the next carriage, he finds the same thing there. He wouldn't notice Ludmila, he wouldn't appreciate her attractive, natural appearance, her well-rounded, womanly forms. Everything that is truly feminine – soft breasts, cabbage soup on Saturday and conversation without slang, with long pauses between thoughts – none of this has existed for Konstantin for a long time. It fled from his life about twelve years ago and ran off to Europe, where, of all things Russian, naturally rounded femininity enjoys the highest demand.

But then Ludmila would hardly be likely to pay any attention to Konstantin in the metro either, even if they were put in the same carriage, facing each other. She has got used to switching off in the metro and focusing on her own thoughts. On the way to work all her thoughts are about Masha and household concerns, and on the way back her head is full of work matters. Ludmila tries not to think about her lover any more than necessary: she's fed up of his whims and of having to hide his idiotic masochistic paraphernalia from Masha. And in general she thinks it's time she finished with him, and if he turns up next time without champagne and flowers, that's what Ludmila will do.

Of course, I feel a little bit sorry for both of them. Ludmila and Konstantin have been two separate pages since they were born, but I have become quite fond of them. However, to be quite honest, I don't very much want to help them in their affairs of the heart. Are they themselves even ready for an encounter with what people call 'a great love'? I'm afraid not. Konstantin wants a girl with more curves and no piercings, and the limit of Ludmila's dreams is a lover with flowers and no insane streak. They can find that kind of happiness without me.

They don't want a great love; and nobody wants one, as a matter of fact. I'm not talking here about Masha and Seryozha, they have their own interests, the concerns of youth, I mean those of us who have long ago developed mature personalities. We assume, of course, that we *are* these mature personalities; we cherish them and try to maintain their integrity. But love is always 'hi-here-we-go-again'. We know from our own experience, or from books, what profound psychological and even hormonal consequences love brings in its wake, and we hide from it. This is like the instinct of self-preservation: it is pointless even trying to make us see how paltry our mature personalities are.

And then, why should I sort out the lives of some characters when I can't even sort out my own? Only last summer I was involved in an episode that was almost a love affair – and what came of it? As was only to be expected, nothing came of it or, rather, it came to nothing. Not even my family know about this story, if Tamara and Dmitry Pavlovich can be considered my family. Even I sometimes think that it's a story I wrote. The first thing I find hard to explain is why I was in the flat in the city on that day; after all, it was summer outside, and my place was in Vaskovo, at the *dacha*. The second thing, of course, is that I opened the door. I think I've already told you how our main entrance is arranged – basically the same as all the 17B series high-rises. There's a TV camera outside it, somewhere under the canopy of the porch, and the concierge Nasir sits inside and watches two television sets. The first set has nothing to do with the camera, it's needed to prevent Nasir falling asleep on duty, but the second one is a monitor, on which Nasir can see who wants to come into the hallway of the stairwell. And let me tell you, getting in is no simple matter, because there's a strong iron door with an entry phone and an electronic lock. If a resident is sober and he has one hand free, that's okay, because he takes the key with the round tab on it out of his pocket with his free hand, presses it against the right spot and the door squeals, inviting him to come in. If the resident's hands are occupied or his key has got lost somewhere then Nasir swings into action. He has a button of his own under his desk. He presses it, the door squeals, the resident comes in and thanks Nasir. But that's if it *is* a resident. Not for anything will Nasir let in a stranger – that's why he's been put there. It's simply unthinkable for an outsider to infiltrate our entrance, so it's a total mystery to me where these strangers in the stairwell come from. But every single day there they are walking about, people delivering promotional trash or selling potatoes, sociologists with questionnaires and God only knows who else. They trudge from floor to floor and ring all the doorbells, one after another, looking for some fool who'll open up for them. Only there aren't that many fools among us. As a rule, in such situations we lie low and pretend we're not at home. I personally open up – that is, not open up but go and look through the peephole – only if the person ringing the doorbell demonstrates exceptional stubbornness. So I absolutely cannot understand why on that occasion I started and hurried straight to the door.

I walked up, looked through the peephole and saw a young woman. Have you ever looked at a young woman through a peephole in a door? What can you see there except the nose? But, believe it or not, my heart immediately skipped a beat; it was a very long time since anything like that had happened to me. The young woman outside the door could have been a promotional agent for a perfume company, or a thief's 'finger'; she could have been absolutely anyone apart, perhaps, from a potato-seller. And yet I opened the door for her, Instead of quietly lowering the cover of the peephole and tiptoeing back into the room, I opened the door for her without giving a thought to the consequences. And I realised that my heart had not skipped that beat in vain.

The young woman was charming, so charming that she couldn't possibly be a 'finger' – for some reason I decided that straight away. We can attribute that decision to my unregenerate romanticism, but she was genuinely good-looking: red-haired, slim, wearing a flowery summer frock. And she had such touching pink slippers on her little feet, like a child's gym shoes.

'Hello!' the young woman said to me happily. 'I'm so glad I found you in!'

'Me?' I asked in surprise.

'Yes, of course. For some reason there's no answer from your phones.'

'You know my phone numbers?' I asked in even greater surprise.

'Well, naturally,' the young woman said with a slight shrug. 'But perhaps you'll let me in?' I invited the young woman into the hallway, where Phil was already whimpering in his desire to meet her.

'Ah, what a lovely dog!' she exclaimed. 'Are you a boy or a girl?'

I gave them time to decide that question and express their mutual liking. However, there was something I wanted to find out too.

'Pardon me,' I enquired eventually, 'but who are you, miss?'

'Ah yes,' she said, slightly embarrassed, and held out her hand. 'My name's Marina.'

'Pleased to meet you,' I replied, quite sincerely, and introduced myself too.

'Me too . . .' Marina replied. 'But . . . it's strange, I've got another name written down here.'

It was only then I noticed she had an office file with her – pink, like her slippers. Marina opened the file and took out a sheet of paper.

'Here, read for yourself: Vladimir Anatolievich Kozlov.'

A minute later we were both laughing merrily. As you have already realised, a perfectly ordinary misunderstanding had occurred. Marina wasn't any kind of salesperson, but a representative of an estate agency. She had come to take a look round the flat of a certain Kozlov with a view to selling it, but got the address wrong and ended up with me. She apologised, again offering me her little hand, this time in farewell . . . but I kept hold of it in mine.

'Since this has happened,' I suggested boldly, 'perhaps you could take a look at my kitchen too – with a view to a cup of coffee.'

To be quite honest, I wasn't really hoping that she would agree. But she did – perhaps Phil helped there. Marina scratched him behind the ear and smiled.

'Well now, I won't say no. Only I'll just go and wash my hands.'

At that moment I realised that fate had presented me with a challenge. There was only one thing that I wanted in all the world: to persuade this charming estate agent to stay with me, by any means at all. To win her away from Vladimir Anatolievich Kozlov by seducing her immediately, right now, while we drank coffee. Time was tight, but a desperate plan matured instantaneously in my mind. In effect, I had to play Marina at blitz chess, so I did – and I won.

'So, Marinochka, why don't you really take a look round my flat?'

She shrugged one slim shoulder.

'What for? You're not selling, are you?'

'Ah, that's where you're wrong. I very definitely am selling. Only I still haven't decided which agency to use.'

'Really?' Marina laughed.

'On my word of honour!'

She looked hard at me, thought for a moment and sighed.

'All right, show it to me. Nobody's answering at Kozlov's place anyway.'

Oh, well done, that man! I even turned away to conceal

my triumphant expression. And they say you can never hood-wink an estate agent! However, the door of the cage had not yet slammed shut behind the little bird . . .

Marina and I finished our coffee and went to look round my accommodation. I had a two-room flat with the standard lay-out, designed for a standard building. But Marina studied everything carefully, even the balcony, making notes all the time on a sheet of paper. I informed her that I was single, in the sense that I was the only owner of the flat – she recorded that fact too. When the inspection was finally completed, Marina put the sheet of paper covered with writing away in her pink file.

'Well then,' she said, lowering her eyelashes. 'I suppose I'll be going now . . .'

Going! In my place only a total blockhead would have let her go. Her nearness was so thrilling.

'Oh no, Marinochka,' I protested tenderly. 'I won't let you go just like that.'

Her eyelashes shot up.

'What do you mean to say by that?'

'Why, that you still haven't seen everything. You've seen the building and the flat, but what about the surround-ing area? We have a wonderful large park not far away – it seems to me that having something like that close by should add to the property's . . . what do you call it . . .'

'Capitalisation.'

'Precisely.'

Marina looked at Phil as if she was expecting advice from him.

'Close by, you say? That's interesting.'

Five minutes later the three of us were already downstairs. I pushed open the mighty door and let my companions out of the entrance into the air, into the sunshine. Outside Nasir was striding to and fro, smoking and screwing up his eyes against spots of sunlight reflected from the glossy flanks of a small yellow car that had almost driven up onto the steps.

'Yours?' I asked Marina.

'Yes. How did you guess?'

'It looks so pretty. Only why isn't it pink?'

Marina lowered her eyes.

'There weren't any pink ones in the showroom.'

The little car was so yellow and shiny, I felt like licking it, but Phil limited himself to delicately sprinkling one little wheel.

The weather that day was just what I would have ordered, warm and sunny. For our part, Phil and I tried to make Marina's walk as pleasant as possible. In the park he ran ahead of us on patrol and I fanned my female companion with a small branch so that no gnat or mosquito would dare to land on her delicate, gently freckled little shoulders. On a couple of occasions I was even fortunate enough to carry her over small pools of water.

And then we watched the River Moscow and the city of Moscow from the high riverbank. The greenish river looped through the endless plantations of real estate, only every now and then shuddering slightly, as if it was feeling chilly. Having tickled the river, the light breezes flew on to us and caressed the exposed areas of Marina's body. We stood on the steep bank and gazed at the distant prospects of Moscow. With an estate agent's practiced eye she identified the recent residential developments and unerringly distinguished reinforced concrete from solid brick facing. I listened to Marina and feasted my eyes on her. So slim, so luminously orange against the light, during those minutes she seemed like a little sister to the sun that was already preparing to set.

The day was coming to an end. Moscow, with its new developments, chimneys and historical districts was gradually dissolving into an off-white haze. Evening blurred the beautiful features of the city's face, covering them with a smog as subtle as gossamer stockings. Marina's ginger-haired brother, the sun, bade us an affectionate farewell as he gradually sank down onto the roofs of the city, soon to seep through them, steal into the buildings through the chimneys and fragment into the light of a thousand windows.

It was time for Marina and me to be going. We'd had a very successful walk; she hadn't even got her slippers wet. All the way back the girl held my hand and I could practically feel my personal capitalisation growing. Phil plodded along as good as gold beside us, without barking at anyone or jerking on the lead even once. We didn't even notice that we had reached my building, didn't realise that we had been standing there under the canopy of the entrance for a long time already. Marina was the first to wake from the trance.

'I suppose I'll be going, then . . .' she whispered, glancing round at her little car.

It was dozing serenely, its little face nuzzled up against the steps.

'But what about your file?' I protested. 'It's still up in my place.'

'Then . . . then let's go up.'

'For the file?'

Marina sighed.

'For the file.'

I'm certain the scene of our non-parting was observed by Nasir, because the entrance door squealed invitingly before I could press my tab-key against it. We went up to my flat and found the pink file. Marina took 'my' sheet of paper out of it and immediately noted down the information gathered during the walk.

'Before I forget,' she said with a bashful smile.

What happened after that? After that Marina sighed and agreed to have supper with me. The supper was romantic, with a bottle of Chilean wine. I drank and she drank too so, sighing apart, Marina couldn't drive in any case. After dinner she went to the bathroom and I went to the bedroom, to set the stage for the bedroom scenes.

The majority of readers are familiar with the nature of bedroom scenes, so I shall omit all stage directions and merely reproduce our dialogues.

Scene one

Marina (blissfully): What a glorious client I've found.

I: Better call me a partner.

M: Of course, we're partners. Your flat will sell – don't even worry about it.

I: Darling, let's talk about personal matters . . .

M: I am talking about personal matters. I feel so at ease with you . . . You can't even imagine what a hysterical lot our clients are: all nervous and suspicious, never knowing what they want . . .

I: But I know what I want!

Scene two

I: (blissfully): What a glorious agent I've found!

M: Say it again . . .

I: What a glorious . . .

M: What sweet words . . . you should hear the things people say about us estate agents.

I: They don't know your best side.

M: Can you imagine, they even confuse us with property developers! They think we're scroungers, getting fat on rising real estate prices.

I: You haven't got a single spare centimetre.

M: Thank you . . . They think they can do everything themselves, without our help.

I: But I only want to do everything with you. Come here . . .

Scene three

M: (blissfully): Tired?

I: A little. How about you?

M: This isn't tiredness. Sometimes I get home squeezed out like a lemon, and I think: What do I want with all of this . . . It's the chains that really do me in.

I: What chains, darling?

M: Deals that involve lots of swaps. This flat for that flat, that flat for another one . . . Loads of subtle nuances that you have to tie together. If one link comes unstuck, the whole chain falls to pieces.

I: What strong nerves you need to have!

M: We're not supposed to have any nerves at all. Just you try drawing up a statement of agreement from the agencies of child guardianship and custody if you have any normal human nerves! Can you imagine, sometimes the same procedures are governed by quite different rules in districts next door to each other!

I: I suppose you have to give bribes?

M: What do you think? We live in the real world.

I: I lose my sense of reality with you.

M: And I do with you.

Scene four

M: (joking drowsily): That's it, don't call me again . . .

I: I'll give you a buzz later.

At that the curtain fell, and no more scenes were played out that night.

There was also the scene of parting – the next morning, immediately after breakfast. Phil and I went down to see our guest to her car. As we said goodbye, Marina scratched my dog behind his ear and looked into my eyes for a long time with her hand set on my shoulder. Then her glance accidentally fell on her watch, she came to her senses, ducked into her car and slammed the little door shut. The little yellow automobile came to life and its motor started murmuring. It gave out a smell, but not of petrol, more like perfume or confectionery. I even felt sad at the thought that I would never see that likeable inanimate creature again.

Two hours later Phil and I were already decamping from the flat to the *dacha*, I stayed out there at Vaskovo until October with my mobile phone switched off. In time, of course, Marina realised that she had been mistaken about me, but evidently I had found my way into some kind of estate agents' database, because even now I still get calls from women with pleasant voices, enquiring if I would like to sell my flat.

THE TRAFFIC CONTROLLER'S BOX

We often liken a city to a living organism. And that's right, because it has arteries, organs and nerves. The arrangement of a city, like that of all living things, is inconceivably complex. It breathes, feeds, produces waste – and therefore it really is a creature of nature. But if that is so, then a city cannot, as some assert, be a creation of human genius, even cumulatively. Firstly, man is not capable of creating anything natural and, secondly, there is no such thing as cumulative genius. There are only various different institutions and organisations, which themselves do not always know how they function.

True, they do say that a certain genius, although not of the cumulative kind, once used to live in Moscow. He was a unique specialist on sewerage networks, a sorcerer and magician of his trade. In some incredible manner he could sense waste pipes under the ground, even the ones that weren't shown on any plans or diagrams. No one ever started digging a foundation pit in Moscow without consulting with him first. But then the specialist got old and retired, and there wasn't another one like him. Let us note, however, that even this unique individual only understood the sewerage system and, after all, there are many other systems and services in the city, under and on and above the ground, even all the frequencies of the airwaves are occupied.

If we acknowledge that a city is a living organism, we must acknowledge its place in creation. And in so doing, we shall be obliged to cede our priority and accept that it is not we human beings who are the crown of creation, but the city. Because although we are also organisms, we are only small particles of the city, and a part cannot transcend the whole. It is not we who are godlike, but our city. It is the arbiter of our destinies and the master of our wills. Without it we will perish or, at best, revert to the wild. Without it we would not be who we are. Yury Mikhailovich Luzhkov would not have become mayor, Vasily Stepanovich would not have become a trolleybus driver, I would not have become a writer. And you, dear readers, would not have become readers, since without the city the metro would not exist.

It was also the city that was responsible for Vasily Stepanovich's wife, Raisa, going to work as a railway traffic controller. As a child Raisa had dreamed of managing the roundabouts in Gorky Park, and then of being someone else, but certainly not a traffic controller. However, as is the way of things, the city had its own plans for her, and in order to realise these designs, it chose to house Raya and her mum and dad close to the railway goods station. Her parents themselves were not railway workers (they both worked in some kind of factory) and they died early. But shortly before her demise, mum gave her daughter some useful advice.

'Raya,' she said, 'you go and work at the station. It's so convenient. Five minutes and you're home.'

If her dad had not already died by then, he would not have been likely to advise her any differently. But even without mum and dad's advice, everything had already been decided, as I said, by the city. Regardless of her aspirations and dreams, Raya, was a ready-made railway employee, without even being aware of it. She was well-acquainted with the smells of creosote and coal smoke from the tea urns in long-distance carriages. The clanging of the buffers, the swishing of the points and the whistling of the shunting engines did not disturb her at night, just as a villager is not disturbed by dogs yapping, or a fisherman by the murmuring of the sea. Raya could follow the meaning of the traffic controllers' echoing, rumbling speech. She just didn't know that she was destined to inherit that rumbling.

And then the moment came for what had been ordained to be accomplished. In order to prevent any possible mishaps, the city bolstered mum's advice and the aforementioned predisposing territorial circumstance with additional causative factors. It introduced Raya to Vasya, a young trolleybus driver with the temporary right of residence in Moscow, and in the dense growth of one of its parks it provided the conditions for the expeditious conception of their future child.

Most importantly of all, it arranged for there to be no free places for the child in any of the municipal nursery schools nearby. There were places in the railway department's nursery schools, but for a child to be accepted there, one of the parents had to be employed by the department and Raya, who had only just turned eighteen, was not employed anywhere yet. Faced with this situation, what do you think the young woman did?

You guessed. Raya went to the railway division, or whatever it is they call it, to ask for a job. She was a strong-looking girl and, of course, she prudently said nothing about being pregnant. I don't know how she fooled the medical examining board, but she was taken on as an assistant coupler. This is a rather interesting profession in its own right, lively and responsible work, involving physical exertion and the danger of catching cold. Couplers are the people who connect up brake hoses and ride on the step boards of wagons; they used to have whistles, but now they have walkie-talkies.

Raya, however, was not a coupler for long – only three days. On the fourth day she fainted, and almost fell under the wheels of a diesel-electric locomotive. The girl was promptly taken to the medical unit, where her secret was revealed. When they learned that personnel had let in a pregnant girl, the bosses swore profanely, but there was nothing to be done: the Labour Code didn't allow Raya to be sacked. She was transferred to the position of assistant traffic controller, and thus she came to the job appointed for her by destiny – or the job came to the Raya appointed for it.

Many years have passed since then, but Raisa

Grigorievna is still at her post. From her high box she confidently controls the traffic within the limits of the goods station and the movements of workers pottering about on the lines in those orange waistcoats that make them look like fans of some football team. She communicates by radio most of the time now, of course, and only rarely makes use of the PA system, but if a loud clarion call should suddenly rumble and echo across the station and its surroundings, know that this is the voice of Raisa Grigorievna. 'Attention, locomotive shunting on line six!' – that's her.

Raisa Grigorievna is a reliable, experienced railway employee. For her services to the sector she has been awarded diplomas and a badge that was presented to her by the head of the division himself, a man holding the rank of General of Traction. Raisa Grigorievna knows her professional duties off to a T – there can be no doubt about that. And yet there are many things about a railway that she doesn't know and never will. Because there's not a single person in the world who *could* know everything about a railway. Raisa Grigorievna doesn't know about the structure of a locomotive, and an engine driver, for instance, doesn't have much idea about the work of a traffic controller. A General of Traction supposedly possesses information about both these things, but only in the most general terms. And I, for instance, am a total ignoramus in all of these matters, even though I am a passenger of long standing and wide experience. Through the window of my suburban train I see only an incomprehensible tangle of rails and cables, carriages crowded together on sidings and the stroboscopic flickering of trains going in the opposite direction. If my train suddenly gets stuck, like now for instance, at an inappropriate spot like this goods station, all I will do is gaze obtusely at the traffic controller's box that has popped up unexpectedly nearby and puzzle over unprofessional questions like: Why are we standing here and what could it mean?

One other thing Raisa Grigorievna has learned is the way home from the traffic controller's box. The concrete slab fence enclosing the station's territory has a break in it at one point. By using this break, she can shorten her journey so that it is exactly as long as her mum said: five minutes. At home or, more often, on the bench beside the entrance, Raisa Grigorievna is met by Vasily Stepanovich, who is retired on a disability pension. He drove his trolleybus honestly for thirty years and repaid his temporary resident's debt to the city in full. But five years ago there was an unfortunate accident: Vasily Stepanovich's own trolleybus gave him a severe electric shock. It didn't kill him, but medical science confirmed partial paralysis of the right side of the body. The incident was discussed at the trolleybus depot and it was decided to write them both off, the trolleybus to the scrap heap and Vasily Stepanovich to a pension. Vasily Stepanovich is of no benefit to the city now. However, since he still possesses control of the left side of his body, he participates to the best of his ability in family affairs, in particular by minding his grandson.

Raisa Grigorievna's and Vasily Stepanovich's grandson was produced for them by their son Kirill, the same child who was first placed with the railway nursery school, and then with the railway kindergarten. The grandson Alyosha is still, so far, an obedient little boy, but Raisa Grigorievna has problems with his father. The trouble is that Kirill, in his own opinion, has still not really found his place in the world. Well, his life just hasn't worked out. Despite the fact that, like his mother, he grew up close to the station and also received a departmental pre-school education, Kirill flatly rejected the path of the railway, without explaining his reasons. Nor did he wish to fill the driver's seat in a trolleybus, but that was understandable: after all, he was a native Muscovite. But apart from that he wasn't offered work anywhere except, perhaps, with the militia. As a native resident, Kirill took offence when no interesting vacancies could be found for him in the whole of Moscow, and entered into an ongoing dispute with the city. In simple terms, he became a drop-out, getting involved in all sorts of dubious business and even – oh, horror! – at one time almost becoming a drug dealer. That's all in the past now, though; Kirill is married and he works in some theatre or other, lugging the stage flats about. But he still nurses a grievance against the city, although the city, as you understand, couldn't really give a damn.

Raisa Grigorievna believes that to stop Kirill growing up as a waster, he should have been given more discipline as a child. But she herself never raised her voice at home because a traffic controller has to take good care of her vocal cords, and Vasily Stepanovich simply didn't know how to be strict. He was a soft, weak-willed man: he never really settled into Moscow, he yearned for the Volga and the city of Kostroma that he had left behind. In his yearning he used to drink in secret with the attendants of the post and luggage carriages, and then feel guilty afterwards.

But I don't agree with Raisa Grigorievna, in my opinion it's not a matter of discipline, but simply the fact that the city needs people like her Kiriusha too. Not everybody can be attached to a job; there must be someone there just for fun, someone whose destiny can be toyed with – the city enjoys that sort of thing.

In my young days I had a sidekick who was a marginal drop-out. His name was Felix, his mother had a job at a printing works and at first he studied in college with me. To be precise, he stuck it out for a year and a half, and then gave up. He was right, too: he would never have made any kind of engineer. I realised the same thing about myself, only much later.

When he gave up college, Felix decided he was going to earn big money – he had the potential for it. In those days people who could work for the direct benefit of their own pocket, while sharing with the state, earned a lot: jewellers, for example, or cobblers. And Felix had been gifted by nature with clever Jewish hands, in the best meaning of the word. The trouble was that those hands were the only smart thing about him. He got himself taken on as an apprentice in various workshops and made a successful beginning everywhere, but as soon as he was allowed anywhere near hard cash, he immediately spent it on drink before he got around to sharing with the state. So he was given the boot. Not that Felix was an alcoholic, that is, he became one later on, but at that time he simply didn't know how to wait. The moment money appeared, no matter whether it was his or the government's, he used to call me at the student hostel: 'Greetings, student! I've got dough in my pocket, let's hit a tavern!' Taverns, as he called them, were his passion. In those years Moscow was not as generously endowed with places of amusement as it is now, and an outing to a restaurant was almost the only way you could offload your ready cash. In one year Felix and I made the rounds of a host of Moscow restaurants, and in the breaks between restaurants we drank at his place, in order to keep our hand in. We drank industrial alcohol, with oily streaks in it, which Felix's mum brought from the printing works.

Fortunately, in the third year at college I met Tamara, and that drew me away from boozing with Felix. But he still carried on in the same old way: every now and then he got hold of some money, spent it, got himself sacked and sank into a state of penury. The city toyed with Felix, tossing him up and dropping him down, and Felix didn't like it: he felt resentful, like the aforementioned Kirill. The periods of penury gradually became longer and then merged together into a life of unrelieved gloom. Nobody would give Felix a job anymore. Without money, taverns were out of reach, and he switched to his mum's industrial alcohol. But even this final source dried up when his mum passed on (I suspect that she died of grief). In a short time Felix sold everything in his flat that was of any value, and then the flat itself. And when, having sold the flat, for the first time in his life he found himself with a decent sum of money on his hands, he started thinking seriously – also, perhaps, for the first time in his life.

Felix was facing a choice: either to wander from one dubious acquaintance to another – and they, of course, would rob him blind – or to leave the capital, move to somewhere in the country and try to start a new life. Since he was so unused to serious thinking, Felix stupidly chose the second alternative. As was only to be expected, his subsequent career proved short. He temporarily gave up drinking, bought some kind of hovel in an outlying area of the Moscow region and got a job in a logging enterprise. But, say what you will, a non-drinking Jew in a team of Russian lumberjacks can only be a double misfit. Felix's new comrades couldn't do anything about his racial origins, but they could at least force him to 'loosen up'. Felix got drunk once, then a second time, and the third time he got drunk in a hard frost and fell asleep under a fir tree in the forest. He fell asleep forever.

The moral of this story is simple: never argue with the city. If Felix had chosen the first alternative and become a normal Moscow street bum, he just might have still been alive today.

And by the way, on the subject of the departed. I think I've realised why our suburban train has got stuck here at the goods station. Two people in white coats are carrying a stretcher with a body, covered by a blanket, out of the traffic controller's box that I've been contemplating all this time. I assume it's Raisa Grigorievna's body. She has passed away suddenly at her place of work, so there's a temporary hitch in traffic on the railway. But I'm sure the city will find a replacement for her in a minute or two and we'll be on our way.

CLASSMATES

Today we have an unexpected visitor: Tamara. Almost before she says hello, she has inspected the flat and taken a firm grasp of the floor cloth.

Phil and I huddle into a corner, gazing at Toma's implacably advancing backside and saying nothing, partly out of surprise, partly out of cunning. And really, after all, let her wash the floor for us if she wants to.

'Feet!' the command rings out, and Phil and I make a dash for the divan.

I look at Toma's feet and the legs above them: firm, well-groomed, tanned in the tropics.

'And stop ogling me,' she growls without turning round.

I laugh.

'What makes you think we're ogling you?'

'I know you two.'

Tamara straightens up. Her face is slightly flushed; she has a stray wisp of hair on her forehead.

Okay, so she knows us. But then why is she provoking us? I should ask her straight out . . . but something tells me I won't get an honest answer. Well, a person can feel drawn to the old places, can't she? To wash the floor, and whatever . . .

'When was the last time you bothered to look in here? What a nightmare!'

Still on her knees, Toma presses her body against the floor and reaches an arm under the wardrobe. A supple arm . . . No, I have to put an end to this cleanup.

'That's enough,' I say, 'stop mocking me, will you. Let's go and have some tea instead.'

It's good to entertain a lady guest when that lady will tidy up the kitchen herself. It's good when you know in advance what she takes with her tea. In general it's good to entertain a lady who is your ex-wife. The only bad thing about it is not having a clue what her plans are. But anyway, for the time being I can chat about this and that. Ask how our Dmitry Pavlovich is getting on. Ah, so he's gone off to Yekaterinburg! A smart man, constantly expanding the business. And how is she doing (Tamara that is)? As far as work's concerned, there haven't been any changes for a long time; perhaps she has reached her ceiling. Clear enough . . . But what has she come round to my place for . . . No, better leave that for a while. In fact the situation clarifies itself. Since Dmitry Pavlovich is in Yekaterinburg, Tamara has come to stay the night. The only question is what we're going to do: will we watch TV together, as in the old days, or abandon ourselves to passion, as in the even older days? Or will we weep on each other's shoulders and complain that there is no happiness in life? Possibly, recalling the temporarily absent Dmitry Pavlovich, Tamara would prefer the third option, while I am inclined towards the second. But the important thing is not what we are going to do tonight. The important thing is that today Toma is with me. Dmitry Pavlovich is in Yekaterinburg, and she is with me. Now we'll take Phil and go to buy something for supper. And then, *que sera sera*; I'm even prepared to watch TV.

Any street is beautiful, if you walk along it arm-in-arm with a woman. Birdies coo as they peck at the asphalt and children prattle: they launch their little ball into the air and it comes straight to our feet. Right, now we'll pass it back . . . Thwack! Hey, where's it gone flying off to . . . 'Clueless, mister!' cries a voice as tender as a flute. Too right, kid, right now this mister really is clueless.

At moments like this I recall those characters of ours, the ones to whom I once denied simple human happiness. Come to me at such moments, all who have been abandoned and aggrieved by me without due cause, and I will do what I can to help you. But hurry, because such moments are brief.

Konstantin and Ludmila. When they were here recently I refused, but now I've changed my mind. After studying their case file more closely I realise that all is not lost for them. Believe it or not, it turns out that they once studied at the same college, at the same time, in the same department. This fact was established, of course, with the help of the Internet – a new site was set up recently, called 'classmates' (or 'college friends' – I don't remember). Although this site is relatively new, it has already become immensely popular. Not because all the old classmates or college friends have suddenly started missing each other badly, but because they all want to see how much each of them has aged. Naturally, even here the public employs a certain degree of cunning, especially the ladies. Not to the same desperate extent as on the dating sites, but even so . . . On her page, for instance, Ludmila has posted an old portrait which only the most benevolent of observers could possibly recognise as her present self. Konstantin has acted more honestly – he has at least posted a recent photo in 'classmates', although the expression on his face is the moody, Byronic one that he only uses for seducing girls.

That's why Ludmila hasn't identified his photo. I have decided to compromise my principles slightly after all and arranged for them to take a ride in the lift together (it's not important how; let's say I made Ludmila stay on late at work). And from that a simply incredibly cascade of coincidences has followed. A couple of hours later the man with whom Ludmila had travelled in the lift was gazing out at her from a computer screen. Gazing at her with a moodily Byronic expression and informing her on his page that he studied at the Publishing Trade College – that is, in the same place and at the same time as she did. Ludmila's memories came flooding back. She remembered, or seemed to remember, that yes, she had been in love with him at one point in her course, and he had shown certain signs of interest himself. But, as she recalled, he wasn't from Moscow, and neither was she, she was from Mariupol. And then someone else had turned up, a registered Moscow resident, who had ruined Ludmila's life, but resolved her accommodation difficulties. Ah, if only she hadn't been so practical when she was young, if only she had followed the promptings of her heart, then ... but what would have happened then? Ludmila started pondering: she wondered how life would have worked out if she had married this one then, instead of that one. Where would they, both non-Muscovites, have gone to after college? To her home in Mariupol? And now they'd be living on Ukrainian *hryvnias* ... No thank you very much. Or would they have gone to his home, somewhere out in Ivanovo? But that wasn't much better. Here in the capital, she had at least made a career; she'd had to walk over dead bodies to do it, but she had done it. Now Ludmila was the deputy personnel manager – and soon, perhaps, would be the manager – in a rather large holding company ... But then, from the look of things, this Byron was no slouch either, otherwise what would he be doing here in Moscow, in Ludmila's lift? And then it jumped out at here: What was he doing? He was going home! Of course, he was her neighbour, since he rode in the same lift as her. Ludmila re-read Konstantin's entire page avidly. Star sign ... studied ... ta-tee-ta-tee-ta ... aha! Divorced; divorced – that was great. And as for the address, which Konstantin didn't provide, Ludmila almost knew it already, the building and the entrance, that is. She went to bed very late that night.

Konstantin, on the contrary, fell asleep as usual. He hadn't recognised Ludmila since, as I already said, she had posted an old portrait photo in 'classmates'. And apart from that, he never switched the computer on in the evening, because he'd had enough of it at work. If someone in his dream had called him 'no slouch', Konstantin's inner face would probably have assumed the same expression as in his photo. But he actually found that expression hard to maintain. He had managed to hold it just long enough to seduce a certain professor's rather appetising, although stupid, young daughter, but not long enough to keep her. In his heart of hearts Konstantin was a straightforward, normal individual, even if he did work as a senior editor. But no one, apart from his son Seryozha, valued these qualities in him.

And so, they both fell asleep – he a bit earlier, she a bit later – separated by no more than a few concrete floor slabs. But that was not the end of the 'classmates' story. The next day Ludmila deliberately stayed on at work for a while, without any help from me. She took her time walking from the metro to the high rise, casting stealthy glances at the men overtaking her and for some reason stopping altogether at her own entrance as if she was pondering something, but then the concierge saw her on the CCTV, decided that she was looking for her key and opened the door. Ludmila started, walked in, thanked Nasir for being so thoughtful, and walked over to the post boxes. She stood by the post boxes for a few more minutes, during which time no one came into the entrance apart from one man with a dog (that was me and Phil). Then Ludmila sighed, got into the lift and rode up to her own floor.

I think she was not entirely aware of what she was doing on that occasion. She could hardly have hoped for a repetition of the previous day's chance encounter. Trying to catch someone in the lift is a futile endeavour. On the contrary, the people you come across in the lift are usually the ones you don't want to meet for some reason, or characters who have breakfasted on garlic, or dogs who rub their moulting sides against your legs. Be that as it may, on that evening Ludmila was behaving strangely; even Phil and I could see that, from the way she was hanging about by the post boxes.

When she got home, Ludmila deviated from her normal schedule there as well. Firstly, she didn't eat supper. It wasn't that she had no appetite because her nerves were in a state, it was just that today, for some strange reason, she had decided to lose weight. Secondly, instead of sitting down as she usually did to relax in front of the television with a cup of tea, Ludmila took that cup of tea straight to the computer.

As was only to be expected, during the twenty-four hours or so that had passed, no changes had taken place in Konstantin's page; nobody had written anything new to Ludmila either. Clicking from Konstantin to herself and back again, she drank two cups of tea and pensively smoked two of her slim cigarettes. But, to be quite honest, I have no idea what she had found to ruminate on. What could possibly have been simpler than to go ahead and type 'Hello,' and then something like: 'Kostya, it turns out that you and I are neighbours; here's the number of my flat, call round and we'll reminisce about our young days'. Yes, that's what I would have done in her place; but women are mysterious creatures, even when they're only characters. In some places they're prepared to walk over dead bodies, but in others they suddenly display extreme infirmity of purpose. In affairs of the heart modern-day women are not much different from those who wore corsets, the same timidity and delicacy of feeling. Anyway, the outcome of Ludmila's ruminations was not a bold decision to write to Konstantin directly; instead, she limited herself to posting her full address on her own page, just in case.

Meanwhile, that is, while Ludmila was sitting at her computer, her daughter Masha came home. Engrossed in her own dubious thoughts, Ludmila didn't even hear that her daughter had not come home alone, but with Konstantin's son, Seryozha, who went to the same school and was, as they say, her friend. The young people went through into Masha's room, locked themselves in and spent some time in there quietly. After about an hour they got hungry and came back out. Masha glanced in through Ludmila's door.

'Hi, ma!' she said in greeting. 'Tell me, what can we eat?'

'We, who's we?' Ludmila asked in surprise.

'We – that's us . . .'

'Hiya!' she heard Seryozha say, and his head appeared in the doorway.

'Ah . . . Hello, Seryozha,' Ludmila said with a reserved smile.

'Hey!' the youth suddenly exclaimed. 'That's my old man.'

'Where?' Ludmila asked with a start.

'There, on "classmates",' he said, pointing at the computer with Konstantin's photo glowing handsomely on the screen. 'So you play around with that too, do you?'

Masha didn't like the way he grinned.

'So what,' she said, coming to her mother's defence, 'all the old people do.'

'Like I said,' Seryozha agreed with a shrug.

While they bickered, a strange transformation took place in Ludmila. To Masha and Seryozha's immense surprise, she suddenly announced that she would make them supper. She led the children through to the kitchen and really did feed them, pouring their tea herself. She was especially affectionate with Seryozha, which might have embarrassed him, if only he had been capable in principle of being embarrassed.

And then, just as their tea-drinking was already drawing to a close, the doorbell suddenly rang in the hallway. Later Ludmila would claim that on her way to answer it, she already knew who was there outside the door; her heart, she would say, told her immediately. But I think that would be a case of rewriting after the event, although perhaps a forgivable one. Anyway, you've already guessed: it was Konstantin.

'Hello. Are you Ludmila?'

He smiled, not Byronically but pleasantly, a slightly self-conscious smile.

'It's an incredible coincidence, but I just logged on to 'classmates', and what do you think . . .'

He never finished what he was saying or, rather, I never finished inventing it, because I've been distracted by Tamara. An urgent question: what are we going to buy for supper: pork chops or rib steak? I'm not sure which is more appropriate to the occasion, basically it's all the same to me, but it's nice that she asks my advice. And tomorrow, when I'm finishing off that meat on my own, it will be nice to recall how the two of us went to the shop together. And in general, how Tamara and I got together on the sly. Not an entirely sad story, you must agree.

THE
NORTH-EASTERLY

A couple of kilometres away from me — that is, from my housing development — lie the so-called sprinkling beds. Those to whom this term seems overly poetic call them sedimentation tanks or sewage works. Basically, the whole place is one mega-cesspit, into which the faecal matter of the megalopolis flows. Not all of it, of course, but a substantial part, including my own. These beds are located to the north-east and I recall their existence when the wind blows from that direction. In former times, thanks be to God, the north-easterly was an infrequent visitor to our parts, but just recently I have noticed that the pattern of Moscow's winds has become less favourable to me, evidently owing to the general changes in the climate of our planet. For the last forty-eight hours I have been regaled continuously by the wind from the beds, which brings neither warmth nor rain, nothing but a ubiquitously intrusive aroma, from which even tightly closed windows offer no salvation.

My only consolation is the historical awareness that this smell has accompanied humankind down through the ages. Our forebears used to fight it by burning newspapers in the privy, and then they invented air fresheners. Of course, in this particular case the privy is too large: all the air fresheners in the world, together with the combined print runs of all Moscow's tabloid newspapers, would not be enough to freshen it. It's a well-known fact that at times of national disaster, during various upheavals and disturbances, this smell has matured and intensified to a fetid stench. Today, however, it is not so very terrible, making itself felt more as an ineluctable ambient olfactory presence. Who can put a number on the ineluctable presences that impinge on our other senses? Television advertisements, for instance – they swamp you completely, but you put up with it.

Anyway, I don't foresee any national disasters today; I'll just have to be patient and wait for the wind to change. And, for lack of anything else to do, analyse the associations that the north-easterly arouses in my memory. For me personally, it brings reminiscences of my childhood. You are already aware that my childhood was spent outside Moscow, in the small town of Vaskovo, where my parents had a little house of their own. These days we would have been called individual owner-developers, but at that time, together with the inhabitants of hundreds of similar houses in Vaskovo, we were officially termed 'citizens living in the private sector'. I don't even know which sounds better. Everything we had was private, i.e., individual, including our own sprinkling beds, although we didn't use that term. On every plot of land, in its most shady, overgrown corner, there was a special catchment pit and above it a structure of wooden planks with the requisite supply of old newspapers.

See how long I've been alive, if I can remember ancient times like that. But long before my birth, before the formation of any of these misfortunate 'sectors', even before the appearance of newspapers, Vaskovo already existed, and Vaskovites lived there. And very definitely, since they lived, to the extent of their natural capacity they produced waste and bestowed it on the earth. Calculate the amount of this waste produced by the many generations of Vaskovites, and it will be clear that the little town should have drowned in it long ago. Why, then, has this not happened? Why, in the hundreds of years of its existence, has Vaskovo not become mired in its own, to put it crudely, faecal matter? The person we have to thank for this, of course, is none other than the man with the bucket, a member of one of the most ancient professions. The sludge man is one name by which he is known, although earlier he was called something different. It is of him that I shall speak.

The Mongol Tatars were obliged to roam from place to place and constantly fight for territory because they repeatedly defiled their own camps. They were good warriors, but poor sludge men, and consequently failed to establish a stable state. The Vaskovites won the historical competition because they chose to follow a different path. They found a peasant who had no land and gave him a horse, a cart with a barrel and, most importantly, a bucket on a stick. Having equipped him in this fashion, the Vaskovites charged him with riding round the farms and scooping out the accumulated contents of the cesspits. That is why to this very day these pits are referred to in Russian as 'scoop pits'. And the man was called a 'scooper' (amended behind his back to 'shit-scooper').

I encountered this scooper with a bucket on a stick in my early childhood. Later they gave him a truck instead of a horse and cart, and the bucket was only retained as a measure of last resort, since the truck basically sucked everything out itself. For those who might not recognise the truck from the smell, they wrote 'sewage truck' on it. The scooper was similarly renamed a 'sewage operative', although they still called him the same as ever behind his back.

I realise, of course, that the scooper I saw in my childhood was a distant descendant of the first one who was drafted in to spite the Mongolian Tatars. But I simply can't understand how the Vaskovo scoopers could have had any descendants – as far as I know, they were all unmarried. For obvious reasons, young girls and not-so-young women shunned them, and men avoided shaking their hands in greeting. Such is the reverse side of this most essential, but thankless job.

The wind from the sprinkling beds . . . I remember how the jealous protectors of private property in Vaskovo used to drive us rascally little apple-scrumpers away. Many of us caught shot-gun blasts of salt on our nether regions for raiding other people's plots. But we used to take a cruel revenge: we would get hold of a packet of yeast from somewhere and secretly tip it . . . where? Why, of course, into our assailant's sewage pit! If you have somebody you truly hate, and he has a sewage pit, do the same thing to him. I assure you, the effect will exceed all your expectations: the product will gush out of the privy like torrents of lava and there won't be enough sewage teams in the entire district to deal with it.

Now that I've told you that, I have an uneasy feeling. Am I not being imprudent, inadvertently providing a lead to some potential terrorist? And what if someone gets it into his head to empty a dump-truck of yeast into Moscow's sprinkling beds? From a distance they look less like beds of any kind than paddy fields or large square ponds. The surface area of these ponds is quite vast. I don't know what their depth is, but I think it is also more than ample. I'd like to believe that children don't play anywhere near them – it's dangerous, after all. I remember something that happened to me once, when the other lads and I were playing 'Cossacks and Bandits'. I holed up on someone else's plot of land and jumped into this pit. Yes, you've guessed: it turned out to be a cesspit. I guessed too, when it was already too late. The owners had moved the privy somewhere else and left the old pit uncovered, perhaps even with malice aforethought. It was a deep pit and I couldn't get out of it on my own. My howls attracted quite a lot of people, but no one was in a hurry to pull me out. Someone even suggested sending for the scooper. Of course, it ended with my mother running up, squeezing her nose shut and dragging me, her treasure, out, as she had dragged me out of various other greater and lesser scrapes. She drove me home with a switch, like a goat . . .

Not the most cheerful of memories, although when I come to think about it . . .

Anyway, falling into a village cesspit is not the end of the world. If you fall into a municipal one, they'll never find you, even with frogmen. And what frogman would even go in there?

Or perhaps they do actually exist: special frogmen for diving in the product. I think they live in that housing estate built beside the sprinkling beds. The estate is also visible from my bank of the River Moscow. It's called the 'sewage operatives' settlement' and only scoopers and their wives live there. And, perhaps, those special shit-divers. I can make out some kind of infrastructure in the settlement – schools and kindergartens – so, unlike the Vaskovo scoopers, the modern-day scoopers of the capital are family people and they raise children. There you have the advantage of the big city: here everyone can find a mate from within their own profession in order to continue the family line. But the sewerage operatives and their women almost never leave their settlement, because people are reluctant to allow them into the metro or a trolleybus. And, to be quite honest, there's no point in them going anywhere: after all, there's no need any more to go driving round the courtyards of the city with a bucket. Things are arranged in Moscow so that the product flows to the same place from everywhere – all you have to do is filter it and mix it.

I wouldn't like to think that the sewerage operatives live in a ghetto, but tell me honestly: have you, for instance, ever been to their settlement? How familiar are you with their needs and their aspirations? About as familiar as I am. We only ever mention these people – and then with an unkind word – when there's a north-easterly blowing. That's the way you and I are constituted: we remember about the plumber when our toilet gets blocked, about the militiaman when someone nicks our purse, about the doctor . . . Ah, what am I saying – we only even remember ourselves when something starts to hurt. We have no time for it . . . From morning until evening we're busy with what is known nowadays as self-realisation, and meanwhile our organs are working away inside us, protecting, cleaning, carrying on with their modest work, which may not always be fragrant, but is very necessary.

Our memory and our feelings are also, as a rule, entombed under the bushel of urgent daily cares. Something special has to happen for them to be aroused. The northeasterly might start to blow, your ex-wife might call . . . But if both of these things happen simultaneously, accept that this is the end – no more self-realisation for you today.

'Hello, darling, how are you getting on?'

'There's a north-easterly, darling.'

'My God! I remember . . .'

And do you remember how happy we were in the balmy southerly? How we listened to the rain in the westerly, warming each other with our bodies? Do you remember how once, in defiance of all the winds that blow, we set sail together on the billowing waves of life? You and me, our little crew of two . . . It was amusing: our first quarrels, those stupid quarrels over trifles and those tempestuous, tearful reconciliations. Then the elements subsided and we were becalmed. You and I drifted for many long years, until you gathered up your goods and chattels and disembarked. On a foreign shore . . .

But then, maybe it's for the best. I won't drift very far, I'll wait for you, lying here at anchor. If you should decide you want to take a short cruise, bobbing about on the waves again – I'm at your service.

'You want to come over darling? Then come . . .'

Come, if the north-easterly doesn't bother you.

A MIGRATORY BIRD

Lev Naumovich Lebed lived to see the triumph of justice after all. Not universal justice, but historical justice of a kind, although, of course, only with respect to his own self. But even that is good, and he hadn't really been counting on anything more . . . My apologies for being so impulsive and running ahead of myself with this announcement so soon after the conclusion of the previous narrative. It's just that I'd like those of you for whom personal justice remains an unrealised dream to read this little story without sadness. Let my main character be your representative, as it were.

Now from the beginning.

Lev Naumovich Lebed is a senior researcher at the Pochechuev memorial estate museum, a literary scholar, a Jew and a Russian intellectual – delete as appropriate, as it says in the questionnaires. His views are generally liberal, but after taking a drink or two he proclaims himself a Kropotkinite anarchist. Sometimes he even hints that he is something of a Slavophile, but I think that is basically bravado on his part.

The above thumbnail sketch of Lev Naumovich is correct as of the present historical moment and was similarly correct on all points a quarter of a century ago. If you did not know how circumstances have changed in Russia during those years and all the extraordinary events that have taken place involving Lebed, talking to him for a while might give you the impression that no such events had ever happened. However, the events did occur, and he has returned to his former views and pursuits only quite recently, thanks to the triumph of justice to which I have already alluded above.

Lebed is twenty-two years older than me, so I can only judge how his journey in life began from what he himself told me. He told the story well. For instance, I learned from Lev Naumovich that in the past he had performed actions of great moral courage. When he ran foul of ideological coercion, either in his scholarly work or simply in the course of everyday life, Lebed fearlessly confronted the Party system of those times, taking great risks in the process.

When I made his acquaintance, which was around the time of the Moscow Olympics, the Party system and ideological coercion were still the same as ever, but Lev Naumovich was taking considerably fewer risks. The only way in which I observed him oppose the regime was by not attending the May Day and November celebrations. Afterwards he fobbed off the local Party committee with explanatory notes, in which he cited a cold and other non-political reasons. I personally cannot testify to any other conflicts that Lebed had

with the system. Of course, like all Soviet citizens, he suffered from the shortage of gourmet delicacies and the lack
of reliable information about what was happening in the
world. But the gourmet problem was not very high on Lev
Naumovich's list of priorities, owing to his miserly museum
salary, and he solved the information problem himself by listening to foreign voices on the radio.

Lebed had two genuine misfortunes: he had no formal
place of residence and his wife suffered from epilepsy. However, while the Soviet regime could certainly be blamed for
the first woe, it was definitely not responsible for the second.
And it wasn't exactly that he didn't have any formal place of
residence at all, but he was registered in the town of A. This
is an old, interesting town, but unfortunately it is located
beyond the limits of the Moscow region, while Lebed wanted
very much to be registered within that region, preferably
in Moscow itself. The fact was that Lev Naumovich felt a
strange, irresistible attraction to the capital; and apart from
that Moscow was where all the major libraries required for
literary research were located.

As for his wife's illness, Lebed's greatest tribulations did
not derive from the convulsive fits that his wife had once or
twice a year, or even her periods of temporary mental aber-
ration, which occurred far more frequently. Lev Naumovich's wife suffered or, rather, he suffered from fits of sudden
aggression on her part. Galina, as she was called, was also a
highly educated philologist, but in fits of irrational passion
she beat Lebed like some simple peasant woman. These fits of
hers could not, however, be attributed entirely to her epilepsy.

We met, as I have already said, shortly before the Moscow Olympics. Being a student at the time, I had decided to earn a bit of money during the holidays and taken a job as a guide at the aforementioned memorial museum of the writer Pochechuev. This museum is located close to my Vaskovo and is, by the way, quite well known. When my fellow-townsfolk have to explain to someone what sort of place Vaskovo is and where it is, they say: 'Well, it's near the Pochechuev Museum'. Literate members of the public immediately understand – after all, Russia is a country with a special regard for writers.

There I was, reciting the text of my guided tour for a man who bore a distinct physical similarity to the poet Pushkin – that was Lev Naumovich – when a short woman walked up, glanced briefly at me and remarked:

'Well, look at that, they've taken on another young blockhead.'

Then she turned to 'Pushkin' and added:

'Lev, the director wants to see you.'

That year there were endless pre-Olympic meetings taking place in the Pochechuev museum.

The short woman was Galina, Lev Naumovich's wife, who held the responsible post of senior curator at the museum, although she was not officially registered to reside in the Moscow region – like her husband, as you recall. In those days this was an explicit breach of the regulations, but in Soviet times regulations were honoured mostly in the breach, so it was impossible to tell which violators the authorities hadn't got around to dealing with yet and which they were deliberately turning a blind eye to.

Despite the difference in our ages, the illegally resident museum couple and I became friends quite quickly. We found common ground in our rejection of socialist reality, and I also proved useful to them on the domestic front. The board of the museum, valuing the Lebeds' erudition, had allocated them a poky little hut to live in, a hut located in the memorial park zone under its own jurisdiction – which was yet another violation of every possible rule and regulation. God only knows who used to live in that hut before the Lebeds and where that someone had got to, but it was in need of capital refurbishment. On my first visit to the philologists I fixed their gate for them, and then something else, and in this way I became a welcome guest in their home. That was when I learned a few things about Lev Naumovich's past, his relationship with Prince Kropotkin and the fact that Galina beat him.

The first time it happened right in front of me, I must admit that I was shocked.

One day for some reason, I don't remember what, possibly simply because a batch of fortified wine had been delivered to the Pochechuevo village shop, Lev Naumovich and I sat down together in his little kitchen to have a drink, two men together. Where Galina was at that moment is not important; what is important is that she appeared before we could even cut the metal cap off the bottle of Agdam. Slamming the gate, which I had mended only recently, and then the front door, Galina set the hut shaking with her heavy footsteps as she strode through into the kitchen.

'Come outside, I want a word,' she ordered Lev Naumovich.

I almost panicked, thinking that Galina was furious about our imbibing at that hour of the day, but it turned out that the Azerbaijani wine was not to blame. I realised that, because I could observe what happened next through the small window. This window was open, and it looked out into the yard, which was where Galina had taken Lev Naumovich although, owing to this same window, she needn't really have bothered. And this was what she had led him out there for: the moment he stepped down off the porch she clouted him – a resounding and, presumably, painful slap to the side of his head.

'Feel that, did you?' Galina asked sternly. 'That's for your whoring!'

That was what she said: 'whoring'. I froze at the window.

Lev Naumovich came back into the kitchen, massaging the left side of his face

'Sorry,' he muttered, hiding his eyes. 'Galya's not herself today. Well, what can you do, she's not a well woman . . .'

I think that on that occasion I beat a hasty retreat, but later I became accustomed to the strong expressions that Galina occasionally uttered and the slaps that she sometimes bestowed on Lev Naumovich. Well, you can't really blame someone who's slightly off her trolley. Especially since, apart from her illness, there were other, more objective reasons for those clouts.

In general, though, scenes like the one described above didn't occur very regularly, otherwise, of course, I wouldn't have enjoyed going to visit them. On the contrary, in fact, we spent most of the time in pleasant conversation accompanied by generally modest libations. The leading role in these conversations was taken, of course, by Lev Naumovich, a genuinely interesting raconteur. He spoke about his young days at university, jazz and literature, which, as a philologist, he understood very well. And also, of course, about the ideas of Kropotkinism. Naturally, in this ideological context he frequently lamented that our country was too large and too centralised. Lebed also had personal reasons to complain about Russia's great distances: he had measured them out in person in his quest to improve his formal residential status. The distance from Siberia (where Lev Naumovich began his career in the job assigned to him after graduating from university) to Moscow couldn't possibly be covered in a single leap, so Lebed had advanced in a series of tactical rushes. From province to province, from city to city, sacrificing good jobs, friends, square metres of floor space ... the best years of Lev Naumovich's life had been spent in reaching the town of A., which didn't even belong to the Moscow region. 'I'm a migratory bird, like a swan,' he used to say, not without a certain irony, and it was true.

But our discussions were not restricted to abstract subjects. Our minds were also exercised by the current political situation. In particular, in those days, everyone was talking about the forthcoming Olympics. I don't know about other Soviet citizens, but we Muscovites and residents of the Moscow region were all expecting something, only our expectations were confused and uncertain. In simple terms, we were simultaneously hopeful of receiving an appetising addition to our diet and fearful of repression. To some extent our uncertain expectations materialised: Finnish salami appeared in Moscow and mass deportations began: Individuals of No Fixed Abode (INFAs), gypsies and other elements not engaged in gainful employment or involved in sport. The importation of salami into the Moscow region was apparently not envisaged, but the plan for the 'purges' was handed down to us as well.

Lev Naumovich's response to the deportation campaign was nervous but dignified. 'They won't exile me any further than A.,' he declared courageously: the undesirable elements were being moved out past the so-called '101st kilometre', and the town of A. lay immediately beyond that fateful line.

However, the Vaskovo authorities failed to spot Lev Naumovich. They reported to higher authorities that there were no INFAs or gypsies in Vaskovo and dispatched to the 101st kilometre only a few individuals with suspended jail sentences or who had failed to pay the municipal charges on their flats. These malicious defaulters happened to include among their number the museum's stoker, an alcoholic called Matveev. When he found out about his sentence, Matveev was very upset. He staggered around the museum, drunk the whole day long, sharing his grief with the employees. 'Have you heard?' he asked, accosting every person he met. 'Have you heard about my troubles, brother? Now then . . .'

Eventually he got to Lebed.

'Have you heard, Naumich? I've got terrible problems . . . They're evicting me, moving me out beyond the 101st kilometre, they're moving me to bloody A.!'

'You don't say? To bloody A.?' said Lebed, interested.

'Why the blackguards ... Only I can't see that it's any great calamity for you personally, Matveev. What difference does it make to you where you do your boozing?'

'Of course it makes a difference!' said the stoker, offended. 'What kind of place are they going to move me into? Some kind of rotten communal flat, so I can feed the bedbugs?'

'No, you don't want to go into a communal flat! You know, I've just had a good idea about all this ... Why don't we take a stroll to the shop?'

Lebed's idea, naturally, was not to get drunk with the stoker. The treat was necessary to persuade him to accept a mutually advantageous exchange. As you know, the Lebeds were registered in the town of A., to which Matveev had just been exiled, and where the Lebeds had a small flat. Nothing special, a little dump of a place in a barracks-style building, with no gas or hot water supply, but without any bedbugs, because bedbugs have no interest in places where there are no people. The way Lev Naumovich figured things was this: Why shouldn't he and Matveev simply swap their living spaces? Of course, in the process the stoker would lose his Moscow region registration, but then Lebed would acquire it. And as he had already quite justly remarked, what difference did it make where Matveev did his boozing?

The plan seemed foolproof, but the stoker didn't accept it immediately. He changed his mind several times, became difficult and started demanding money. Sometimes he suddenly broke into swearing, in the way that alcoholics do, and made gratuitous references to Lev Naumovich's racial origins. Lebed incurred substantial expenditure by making several trips a day to the shop with him and even started to resemble his opposite number in negotiations. The siege continued for almost a week. Eventually Matveev surrendered, signed the necessary papers, gathered up his foul-reeking bits and pieces and departed tearfully for his place of exile.

And so, without even being aware of it, in their pre-Olympic frenzy the Soviet authorities helped Lev Naumovich to move one step closer to Moscow – the library and cultural centre of our excessively centralised country. However, Lebed still had one other problem in his life – his wife's mental illness. In speaking earlier of Galina's condition and the sudden fits of rage that it engendered, I mentioned another possible reason for these fits. Without in any way attempting to excuse Lev Naumovich, let me say that in this connection I find the expression *whoring* too strong. In Lev Naumovich's case the French term *adultère* would be more appropriate, although it doesn't translate as anything good either. In any case, people don't get slapped across the face for *adultère* or, if they do, then not as hard as Galina did it.

Let us admit it: Lev Naumovich was delinquent in *les affaires d'amour*. But what else could he have done? He was an interesting man who looked like Pushkin, with an extensive education, so he attracted the attention of the museum's female employees, among whom, believe me, it is always possible to find one or two decent lookers. Moreover, the events described here took place in the summer, and even if there are three sets of Olympic Games going on, summer in a memorial estate museum is the season of *affaires d'amour* and *adultère*. In summer all the even slightly interesting male employees and non-hideous female employees who are not involved in guided tours, stroll through the wooded memorial park together, read poetry to each other and hearken to the call of the flesh. Then comes autumn and the *adultère* either fades away of its own accord or advances to the stage of a substantial affair. But if Galina was concerned that her Lebed was ripe for an extra-marital affair, her fears were absolutely groundless: he had never been known to make life complicated for himself.

However, the male friendship between Lev Naumovich and myself was of a different nature. It did not fade away when autumn came but was renewed each time I visited Vaskovo and called round to see him. According to the season I visited him with my bottle of Agdam or Alabashly either in the flat, which smelled ineradicably of the stoker Matveev, or in the old hut, which now served Lebed as a *dacha*. Lev Naumovich and I discussed literature and the humanities and Galina, when she was not cursing and swearing, fed us rather tastily: she could cook well using simple ingredients. Later on, when I married Toma and became a Muscovite, Lebed started paying me visits. It was convenient for him to spend the night at our place after a day spent in the library or chasing round editors' offices.

By the way, all his beavering away in libraries and chasing round editors' offices was not entirely futile. Of course, the decade that elapsed between the Olympics and the collapse of the USSR was one of profound stagnation for society, but in his career as a scholar it was the most fruitful, resulting in the publication of four scholarly literary articles and one monograph devoted to Pochechuev. Nowadays nobody ever mentions that decade, those rotten eighties, except to abuse them, but I cannot subscribe to the general attitude, if only because Tamara and I spent those years in loving harmony. At bottom, however, everybody was dissatisfied with the existing state of things at that time. For instance, Toma and I wanted to have a child, but we couldn't, while Lev Naumovich still couldn't get himself officially registered in Moscow. He was also depressed by the lack of any changes 'concerning Galina's health'.

Well, Tamara and I did not see our hopes fulfilled, but Lebed successfully invoked changes of his own. They came crashing down on him immediately after the breakup of the empire, which Lev Naumovich, as a genuine Kropotkinite, initially welcomed fervently. As a theoretician, however, he should have foreseen that a great collapse would bring lesser collapses in its wake and the ructions would inevitably reach the Pochechuev museum, which they did. The former Party *nomenklatura* director was replaced and, naturally, the new one inflicted on the employees proved to be an embezzling villain. The first thing he did was to sack Galina Lebed as senior curator so that she would not hinder his plundering of the museum's holdings and assets. This dismissal, plus the reform of the currency, brought about serious changes concerning her health. Galina passed away in late 1992, after suffering a severe epileptic fit.

I wouldn't say that Lev Naumovich started moping after Galina's death, he simply fell apart. He wasn't able to feed himself tastily and cheaply, let alone clout himself round the ear for his most recent moral lapse. Moral delinquency and inadequate nutrition gradually became the norm with him; his life and his very personality were on the verge of total disintegration. Even his liberal views were shaken.

'Russia,' he told me one day, 'needs a new Pinochet.' Then he paused and added: 'But screw Russia anyway'.

This casual addition evidently expressed profound disenchantment on his part. I guessed that Lebed was directing his cumulative resentment for the failure of his own life against the country as a whole: his resentment for all those long years of wandering from to place, for the poverty, for the manuscripts rejected by publishers, for the years spent with a deranged wife: basically for his entire life, with its unrealised potential in human, philological and, perhaps, even sexual terms. And I also twigged that Lebed was ready to change his official place of residence again.

I was not mistaken. The next time he came, Lev Naumovich brought with him a three-volume edition of the poet Kirsanov and a lady's gold watch.

'I cleaned out my library,' he said, taking out the three volumes. 'Anyway, this is a present for you.'

'And the watch?' I asked.

'The watch is Galina's,' he replied. 'A memento, you might say. I'll let you have it cheap. I haven't got time to faff around with it now, and you'll be able to sell it for a good price or trade it for food.'

'What food?' I asked in surprise. 'And why do you say you haven't got time?'

'For food . . .' he explained, '. . . I mean when there'll be nothing left here to eat. And I don't have time because I'm getting out of here.'

That made everything clear. I didn't buy the watch, of course, but Lebed wasn't really upset about that. I think he sold it later to the same Azerbaijanis who bought his, that is, Matveev's flat from him.

Just before he left, Lev Naumovich came to see me with a bottle – for the last time. He wanted to talk, to explain himself, to sum up, I suppose, his more than fifty years of life in Russia.

'The most important thing,' he told me after the third or fourth shot of vodka, 'the most important thing I've learned in my life is that in this country nobody needs me. I wasn't needed in Soviet times and I'm needed even less now – even the girls have stopped valuing culture in a man.'

When he grew agitated, Lev Naumovich looked especially like Pushkin, but an old Pushkin with a Jewish nose. I listened to him, secretly bemoaning the fact that every shot only added to his vehemence.

'But after all,' he exclaimed, 'there are other states in the world, there are! States that take respect for every single human individual as the cornerstone of their values . . . no! – for them it's more than that, it's the very centre of the universe!'

I tried to protest, muttering that all this was obscurantist nonsense and even from the scientific point of view the universe couldn't revolve round a single human individual.

But I was inebriated, and therefore unconvincing.

A few days later Lebed departed, travelling light.

He abandoned our perverse country with the sincere desire to start a new life. However, his desire was not to be granted in full; life abroad was different, all right, but in certain respects it was still like the old life. The most annoying problem that Lebed encountered there was the same old one of an official place of residence. Those countries that took the individual human being as the cornerstone of their values were not yearning desperately to offer Lev Naumovich a place by that stone in the corner. Before he could settle into it, he had to live for a while in a certain small southern state where the cornerstone of values was not so much the individual as the absence of a foreskin on the individual's penis. And although Lebed met this requirement of the state, the state failed to meet his requirements. How and why he explained later in rather vague terms. Supposedly Lev Naumovich couldn't get along with the rabbinate in the small town where he was given accommodation. I think the real reason was actually that the small town didn't feel any great need for Russian-speaking philologists and the local girls didn't feel any great need for men of culture . . .

I start a new line here, although I don't know why, since the whole of Lev Naumovich's life in emigration could be fitted into a single paragraph. The only job that a Russian-speaking philologist could find in a small town in a small southern state was as a floor polisher in the local supermarket. He spent seven and a half years in this capacity, without the slightest chance of saving up enough money to make the move to a country where there was no rabbinate and his individual personality would find itself at the centre of the universe. But then, we must assume that he would not have made any better career for himself there. Lev Naumovich would have remained in that small town, a floor-polisher to this very day, gradually forgetting the Russian language, birch trees and all his subtle philological wisdom, but ... if you recall, I have already announced a happy ending to his story.

Good tidings, though tinged with sadness, reached him from his homeland. During the years that Lebed had spent far away from Russia, none of the terrible things he had prophesied had come to pass there, that is, here. The food supply had improved and the new ruler of the state was almost a new Pinochet. The birth rate in the country had increased, especially in the capital, although, unfortunately, without any assistance from Tamara and me. The death rate had declined but not yet, alas, been reduced to zero: old people still contrived to die one way or another, freeing up accommodation and bringing their younger relatives joy through tears. One day in the city of Moscow an old lady passed away in the course of this natural process. I did not know this old lady and, of course, no one informed me of her demise. But Lev Naumovich Lebed was informed, because the old lady's first name and patronymic were Faina Naumovna, her maiden name was Lebed and she was, in fact, Lebed's sister. Lev Naumovich had told me almost nothing about her; all I do know is that they were at loggerheads over some disagreement for years. I suspect that he simply resented her right to reside in Moscow, which she had acquired, like me, via a felicitous marriage. Be that as it may, when she departed for the next world, Faina Naumovna settled accounts with her younger brother by leaving him her Moscow flat.

After receiving this happy and sad news, Lebed repatriated himself so rapidly that he almost arrived in time for his sister's funeral. Somehow the idea of selling his newly acquired flat and finally departing to take up permanent residence in those countries where the individual human being is truly valued never even entered his head. Now he's back again working as a senior researcher at the Pochechuev memorial estate museum, although he only attends two days a week, because it's a long haul from Moscow to Vaskovo. Lev Naumovich drinks a little vodka, inveighs against Russian centralism and now and then expounds the teachings of Kropotkin. He doesn't reminisce about his life in foreign parts, but occasionally he subjects the work of the museum floor polisher to severe criticism.

As for his 'whoring' – that, of course, is a thing of the past: too many years have gone by.

A SLUM HONEYMOON

Everybody has places that hold special memories for them. Places where they spent their childhood or where they met their love or where they simply used to live and were happy, without even realising it. It's good to visit these places sometimes: to go there, stand there for a while and think; to sigh a bit, as if contemplating the grave of someone dear to you. Only sometimes it seems as if there is nowhere for us to go to, because these places no longer exist anywhere except in our memory. There are no ruins or ashes left behind; everything has been wiped off the face of the earth or, even worse, built over and transformed into something quite different by that indefatigable property developer, time. Of course, it's possible to journey back into the past simply in the mind, after all, no one has taken away our memory, it still belongs to us. Although who can say . . .

Blank spots . . . More and more often these days I find them not only on the outer surface of my cranium, but inside it too. I occasionally feel I would like to sigh sweetly and recall something special, something good from my life – but I just can't. It has been blanked out and built over with later texts, many of them composed by me. Perhaps the reader may sigh over them, but I can't manage it any more.

For instance, here is one text, already quite dilapidated at this stage, constructed by me on the site where a memory should live. It starts ... no, I don't remember where it starts. Somewhere in Moscow, in the vicinity of my college. I can't say precisely, because in those young years I had what my comrades used to call 'the wine weakness'. Not in the sense that I was especially devoted to wine, we were all devoted to it, but in the sense that I got drunk quickly. I got drunk very quickly at our student binges and afterwards I had only the haziest memory of the route we had staggered along, the young men we had fought, the girls we had kissed and all the other heroic feats we had performed. The next morning, when I woke up in the student hostel, I found out about everything from the stories that my comrades told – those were my first experiences of blanks in my memory.

I didn't always wake up in the hostel though. A post-binge awakening could find me in the entrance of some unfamiliar building or on a park bench or at a bus stop or in the monkey cage at a militia station – anywhere at all, basically. The only thing that all such awakenings had in common was the first thought that arose before I even opened my eyes: 'Better not wake up'. This is a fundamentally pessimistic, even downright depressive thought, but it is precisely this thought or, rather, the phrase that represents it, with which I am obliged to open my text.

So: 'Better not wake up ...' I thought before I even opened my eyes. At that moment I couldn't remember my own name or where I was, but I knew for certain that I was drunk again. It wasn't the first time this had happened to me: in some mysterious fashion this realisation arose in my consciousness at the very moment of awakening. But on this occasion I had the feeling that the fateful news had reached me from the outside.

'He's drunk, Tomka, why are you wasting time on him?' I heard an angry voice say somewhere above me.

Another, more compassionate voice, protested:

'Wait ... We can't just leave him like this.'

It was as if my two angels, the dark and the bright, were deciding my destiny.

The dark angel said:

'Well, please yourself. I'll be off then.'

But the bright angel stayed with me.

I felt a wet cloth on my face, probably a handkerchief. The angel was either washing me or trying to bring me round – in either case it felt good. Without parting my eyelids, I reached out with a grateful hand and found a bare knee.

'Hey-hey, no funny business!' said the angel.

And then I realised it wasn't the first time I had heard that voice. Awareness was gradually returning. By the time I made the decisive effort to open my eyes, I already had a pretty good idea of whose face I would see. But when it happened, when I finally unglued my eyelids, I recognised that face and didn't recognise it at the same time. Yes, I remembered those little cheeks, little lips ... Somewhere, it must have been at Felix's party, I had already tried to press my lips to those little lips (and heard that 'hey-hey'). Little lips, cheeks and nose: I remembered all of those, but I didn't recognise the eyes. Because now they were the eyes of an angel and they glowed with the light of compassion.

'Ah, you've come round at last! I've wasted my entire bottle of water on you.'

'Give me a drink,' I croaked in reply.

I propped myself up on my elbows and looked around to get my bearings.

'Where are we?'

She giggled.

'In Moscow.'

Suddenly I was swamped by the noise of the city, as if someone had jacked it up to full volume. Leading the acoustic assault with its screeching and howling was a trolleybus, followed by a tumultuous herd of invisible cars, roaring and snarling in every possible register. Birds' wings started clapping, music started playing, invisible crowds of people started babbling and scraping their feet. We were in Moscow.

When I pushed myself up off the grass it left dirty stains of rubber soot on my hands: the earth under it was warm and trembling. I didn't get up, it was the city that raised me to my feet and embraced me, supporting me with an arm round my shoulders. The city and I breathed into each other's faces: stale vodka fumes for stale engine fumes.

Toma – I'd already remembered what my angel was

called – allowed me to finish her mineral water. Then she dusted off my clothes and restored the parting on my head with her own little comb. We could probably have said good-bye then, but I wanted to clarify one final question: Where had she come from? She hadn't been sent down from heaven to help me, surely. Or if she had, then let her say so . . .

'Have you forgotten? We were all taking a walk together!'

So that was it! We were all taking a walk together. And then Felix had said: 'Let's put him down here – he can sleep it off, he might get picked up by the cops in the metro'. Then everybody left, but she had stayed.

But that still wasn't the answer to my question.

'Do you want to know why I stayed?' Toma asked. 'I don't know how to put it . . . Why don't we walk for a bit? If you're in a fit state, of course.'

I didn't know if I was in a fit state to walk for a bit, but no one knows that until he takes the first step. She took hold of my arm and I took a step. Then another one, and another; from one boulevard to the next; my legs became steadier, my speech became more rational . . . we walked round Moscow, round the inner boulevard ring, and a miracle of healing took place within me as we did so. It's good to be young! Only in youth are the body and the soul capable of such rapid metamorphoses. Was it really me who had been sprawled out on the grass, bleating pitifully, only an hour ago? And now here I was, washed with mineral water, my hair combed and parted, strolling arm in arm with a girl, and she found me interesting company.

I would not stay sober for long though. As we continued our walk, I pursued the obligatory exchange of highly significant nonsense with my companion, thrilling to every accidental touch between us, and felt myself succumbing to a different kind of intoxication, one with which, I confess, I was not very familiar. In those years I didn't suffer from 'the girl weakness'. Not that I was immune to girls, but casual kisses and other contacts with the opposite sex didn't trigger any kind of addiction. All the more surprising, therefore, that before we parted that evening I was already absolutely convinced that I was in love. In love with this Toma.

In and of itself, my discovery might appear insignificant. Lots of young men fall in love with girls after strolling through Moscow with them in the evening. The next morning or, at most, a week later, all that remains of these strolls is the narrative. That's the usual scenario, but my stroll didn't conclude so smoothly. I fell for Toma suddenly, almost without any reason, head over heels as they say. Some specialists explain this phenomenon by the action of a certain mysterious chemistry. I am inclined to agree, because you certainly can't call it psychology. Without reflecting any further on the matter, I confronted Toma with the full force of the primaeval feeling that had erupted within me; I gave her no chance to gather her wits and didn't even allow her to spend any time as 'my girl'. It all happened in the space of a few short weeks, from washing me with a handkerchief to signing on the dotted line at the register office.

Only the other day she had been Tomka from group three in our year and now she was my wife. Those little lips and little cheeks were all mine now; and I belonged entirely to her, complete with all my male virtues and accoutrements. Nature had endowed us with the necessary physical and mental prerequisites to begin a life together and as for all the rest, we were counting on getting that from our parents. By 'all the rest' I mean, of course, accommodation and the means of subsistence.

It was precisely when it came to the parents that Toma and I encountered our first difficulties.

Imagine the scene: I've brought my young wife to Vaskovo, to introduce her to my old folks.

'Oh, good Lord!' my mum exclaims, throwing her hands up in the air. 'She's so thin!'

'But then I don't eat much,' Toma tries to joke, blushing.

'Never mind,' my mum says reassuringly, 'we'll feed you up with milk. Look what a lovely little goat we have.'

The goat comes out. Toma shrieks:

'OhHey, it's chewing my dress!'

My father huffs through the cardboard tube of his *papyrosa* and darts a glance at her from under his eyebrows. Eventually he asks: 'Are you going to live with us?'

'Mmmm . . .' I reply.

'I see,' he mutters.

'What do you see?' my mum asks anxiously.

My father tries to strike matches – one, two . . .

'I see everything' he repeats angrily. 'Now his studies are down the drain and . . . I see the whole thing.'

'There you go, droning on already . . .' says my mum, glancing round to see if the neighbours can hear.

We leave the next day, after promising to 'visit more often'. We have been given a hundred-rouble note and a jar of goat's milk to be getting on with. Our mood is uncertain, tending towards bad, especially since Toma has broken a high heel at the station.

Now the action moves back to Moscow, to a flat in a building from the pre-Khrushchev era, with an extravagant superfluity of moulding on the high ceilings. These eighty square metres of useful floor space are occupied by Toma's parents, her younger brother Vityok, a deaf white cat and Toma and her young husband. I am the husband and son-in-law, an unexpected and extravagantly superfluous family member.

In the sitting room the date has been circled with a red felt-tip pen on the calendar with the half-naked half-Japanese girl – that's how Nikolai Stepanovich, Toma's dad, indicates the public holidays. After the official events are over, he invariably celebrates these holidays at the table with his nearest and dearest. Today his nearest and dearest include his wife, Irina Borisovna, his deputy manager for purchasing and supply, a colleague of his from the ministry with his wife, and his two children – Vityok and Toma. The cat has already eaten and is sprawling on the carpet. My plate has been perched right on the farthest corner of the table to make sure that I'll never get married again. The assembled company is drinking, eating and lending an ear to Nikolai Stepanovich's speechifying (everyone apart from the fortunately deaf cat).

Nikolai Stepanovich's orations, packaged in the form of

toasts, deal with a standard set of subjects arranged in order of decreasing importance. These subjects are:

a)   the international situation;
b)   the successes achieved by the reinforced concrete goods factory that Nikolai Stepanovich manages;
c)   the successes (if any) achieved by Vityok and Toma in their studies;
d)   praise for the hostess and this magnificent spread, with a kiss on the lips for the individual concerned.

At this point Irina Borisovna exercises her right of reply and remarks quite correctly that the credit for the grand spread belongs entirely to Nikolai Stepanovich. The thought that she leaves unspoken is that all the fine fare on the festive table has not come from the grocery shop, but through *nomenklatura* supply channels. The ministerial comrade and his wife nod understandingly. This compulsory programme usually winds up as the main course is being served. When Nikolai Stepanovich is eating, he is not capable of intelligible speech.

After the main course our host requires a break. He spends a few minutes searching for something in his mouth with a fork and seeming rather abstracted. Soon, however, his gaze clears and we come to the next item on the agenda – 'miscellaneous'. At this point nobody, including Nikolai Stepanovich himself, knows for certain what he will start talking about. He might speak about football or launch into some *nomenklatura*-type reminiscences. Or perhaps he might glance round the assembled company without saying a word and break into his favourite folk song. True, just recently Nikolai Stepanovich hasn't really been in the mood for singing. On its smooth passage round the table, his gaze inevitably stumbles over me and his lyrical mood evaporates.

Never mind, it's time for the next item on the programme. A carnivorous smile is already playing on Nikolai Stepanovich's face.

'And now,' he declares, 'I want to drink to my dear son-in-law!'

'Here we go . . .' I mutter spitefully.

'Daddy, don't . . .' Toma cheeps imploringly

But no, daddy really wants to do this! He simply has to take his revenge on me for his unsung song. Irina Borisovna suddenly needs something from the kitchen urgently. That snake Vityok is already chortling into his glass in anticipation of a scandalous scene. Nikolai Stepanovich tells the heartfelt story of how in my person their family has acquired a useful new member and how greatly its common budget has been augmented by my student grant. The couple from the ministry shake their heads; I know that their own darling son tried to pull Toma at one time, but without success, even though he is studying to become a diplomat. Daddy's deputy manager for purchasing and supply smirks openly: in this devious rogue's opinion I could hardly be a less valuable acquisition.

My patience is finally exhausted.

'You can take your budget and stuff it!' I shout. 'I married Toma, not you!'

Then I jump up, clattering my chair, and run out, giving the entirely innocent cat a kick on the way.

Let me add that in my new family scenes like the above did not happen only on public holidays. Nikolai Stepanovich sank his hooks into me on ordinary days too if he was feeling out of sorts – and he felt out of sorts every time he ran into me as he came out of the toilet or anywhere else. No, this was not the match he had wanted for his daughter. Although Toma was too thin for Nikolai Stepanovich's own taste, he knew well enough that in society she was regarded almost as a beauty. His comrades who had marriageable sons – and there was no shortage of those – had hinted repeatedly that they would not be averse to establishing family ties. And what comrades they were! Captains of industry, Party functionaries . . . The idea that his genealogical capital had been inherited by a miserable, rootless little student poisoned Nikolai Stepanovich's life. The least the miserable little student could do was be grateful!

I must admit that my father-in-law was right. I did behave insolently with him. And not only with him. I annoyed Irina Borisovna, for instance, by reading at the table. She regarded reading as a dubious pastime in general, but at the table it was simply indecent . . . However, Irina Borisovna rarely expressed her displeasure to my face, preferring to act through Toma.

Then there were the two secondary characters – Vityok and the cat – neither of whom was averse to playing me a dirty trick now and then. But I could always get my own back on them by employing physical force in secret.

I didn't want to waste time waiting for this charming *nomenklatura* family to get used to me. I admit quite frankly that I thought more than once of slamming the door behind me and clearing off back to the student hostel. But how could I possibly leave Toma? In the first place, I loved her and, in the second place, she loved me. However, as we all know, there is a way out of any situation, even if it seems that nothing could possibly be more stupid. After yet another battle with Nikolai Stepanovich, Toma and I resolved our situation by running away together.

Our stupidity consisted in the fact that basically we had nowhere to run to. They didn't accept married couples at the student hostel, especially if they were Muscovites. Vaskovo was too far away and, in any case, that was where the terrible goat lived. Without a single *kopeck* the only place where we could take up residence in the city was a railway station or my friend Felix's flat. We chose the second option, although Toma would probably have felt more at ease at the station.

Felix lived in a small flat with just his mother, that is, in a single-parent family, which was encouraging, as far as it went. To this day the only thing I know about his mother is that she worked as a storekeeper in some printing house. An indefatigable and inconspicuous working woman, who was equally inconspicuous in her private life, she was the most suitable mother possible for the numbskull of a son that my friend undoubtedly was. I don't remember her expressing any opinion concerning our sudden appearance. Felix himself took a sympathetic view of our predicament and agreed to take us in, although he warned us that his hospitality had its limits.

'With you here,' he said, 'I won't have any personal life at all.'

If by 'personal life' Felix meant the boozing sessions that he regularly held at home, his concerns were groundless. We lived with Felix for three days and throughout those three days I drank with him continuously, to Toma's absolutely horror. However, our drinking turned out not to be a total waste of time. On the third day of our session my friend had a flash of inspiration.

'Got it!' he exclaimed, swaying on his chair. 'I've got an idea!'

'What's up?' I asked, half-opening one eye.

'A most excellent idea concerning accommodation for you and Toma. A good place, and no need to pay any money. You'll thank me for this.'

It sounded improbable, to put it mildly, but it was my third day of drinking and I wasn't thinking too well.

'Why didn't you say anything sooner, dickhead?'

'God only knows why I didn't,' Felix replied with a shrug

To prove that he wasn't lying, Felix suggested we go there immediately – to find out if the 'good place' had been taken and come to an arrangement if there was a chance. I was happy enough to go and agreed without a second thought, but only because, I repeat, I was drunk. Anyway, I had nothing at all to lose. Felix and I supported each other as we raised ourselves, with some difficulty, to the walking position, put on our coats and set off, ignoring Toma's protests.

Once out in the frost, however, I sobered up a bit and asked where we were going and what sort of strange place it was where you didn't have to pay for accommodation.

'Who said you don't have to pay?' Felix asked in surprise. 'You did?'

'Did I? You must have misunderstood. Let's sit down and have a smoke.'

We plonked ourselves down on the nearest ice-bound bench and lit up, and Felix finally informed me that he was taking me to see Dmitrich.

'Who's that?' I asked, baffled.

'Dmitrich? Oh, he's a big wheel!' said Felix, pulling an appropriate face. 'Dmitrich is our head yard keeper. Not even a yard keeper, think bigger than that.'

Felix spoke with genuine respect, but it still wasn't clear to me how a yard keeper, even a head yard keeper, could solve our accommodation problem.

'Oh, he can,' Felix said offhandedly. 'He can, if he takes a shine to you.'

He told me everything he knew about this genuinely unusual man. By profession Dmitrich really was a yard keeper and a registered employee of the district housing committee. Only he was no ordinary yard keeper, but a clever one, well ahead of the times in some respects. Like most of his colleagues, Dmitrich had found the broom and shovel that were the main instruments of his gainful labour an onerous burden and dreamed of being liberated from them. But while other yard keepers limited themselves to dreaming, he had found a solution to the problem. Having acknowledged his own aversion to physical labour, Dmitrich quite sensibly reasoned that he needed to get others to perform this labour for him. Not a very cunning idea, but surprising for a yard keeper. The only question remaining was where to find fools who were willing to swing the broom for Dmitrich. They were found.

Dmitrich didn't really have to look far to find his fools. The point was that half of the neighbourhood entrusted to his care consisted of buildings scheduled for demolition. It's not true that old Moscow has all been torn down by greedy, grasping capitalists: the Soviet regime demolished just as eagerly, only it built slowly. So Dmitrich's neighbourhood included 'uninhabited' buildings. But you and I know there is no such thing as an uninhabited building in a city. Life carries on in every building until such time as its walls are crushed by the excavator and its dust is finally ground under the bulldozer's caterpillar tracks. Ghosts and abandoned cats linger in the flats with tattered wallpaper until their places are taken by homeless tramps and rats. Naturally, significant numbers of these creatures, the champions of urban sur-vival, had populated the supposedly uninhabited buildings of Dmitrich's domain. And these Individuals of No Fixed Abode were the reserve from which the clever yard keeper drew the workforce that he needed

The way he tamed them was brilliant in its simplicity. One fine day Dmitrich made the rounds of all the INFA lairs in his sector and put locks on their doors. He handed out the keys to the locks of these 'flats' to the inhabitants, on condi-tion that from now on the tramps would be subject to labour discipline, in other words, that they would do Dmitry's job as a yard keeper for him. Everyone likes to have the key to his own flat and so, apart from a few ideological hard cases, the tramps took up the broom with enthusiasm.

The scale of the operation increased when Dmitrich, having reaped the first fruits of this promising enterprise, made a secret proposal to his bosses: he asked them to entrust all the territory under their jurisdiction to himself and his illegal labour army. This bold innovator suggested that the other yard keepers should be sacked as superfluous, and the wages fund liberated by doing this should be divided up in a way that was fair. You can easily understand that his bosses did not spend too long thinking about it.

So Dmitrich began ruling his INFA colony on an almost legal basis. In time his housing association was even augmented by several needy or exceptionally greedy students. The students worked harder than the tramps, so Dmitrich set aside the VIP apartment for them: a large flat with glass in the windows, a functional electricity supply and electric coil heaters in the rooms.

This was the flat where my friend Felix was intending to accommodate Tamara and myself.

'You see,' he said, it's not free, it's in exchange for work.'

'But will they at least provide the grub?' I asked, laughing.

'No,' Felix replied seriously. 'You provide your own grub.'

I thought it over for another minute or two. Of course, I didn't much fancy the idea of labouring side by side with homeless tramps, but then, I was effectively one of them now.

'Oh, what the hell!' I exclaimed, slapping myself on the knees. 'Take me to this slave driver of yours.'

A little while later I was talking to Dmitrich in person. From the inscrutable expression on his face it was impossible to tell if he had taken a shine to me or not. But he probably must have done, since I received the key to a room and even a set of bed linen with the official stamp of some medical detoxification centre.

'Take your woman round, settle in, and tomorrow I'll show you what's what and where your patch is,' said Dmitrich, favouring me with a handshake.

In this way Tamara and I were granted the right of citizenship in a strange little state of non-citizens. Certainly, this state was almost completely lacking in creature comforts, it was undemocratic, unrecognised in law and condemned by history to demolition. But even so, after decades have passed, I still recall it with affection. The month we spent living illegally was an entire epoch in our life and, believe me, by no means the worst.

That month was December. Back in those days no one had heard of global warming yet; winters in Moscow were just as they were supposed to be: frosty and robust. In December an entire communal army waged a defensive war against the elements of snow and ice. And we, Dmitrich's partisans, were part of that army. Without any chemical agents, with just an ice pick and a shovel, we scraped and pounded the Moscow pavements, not even for grub, but just for the key to a room. As an apparently conscientious soldier, I was entrusted by the commander with an important sector of the front. I cleaned the area round a mysterious structure that Dmitrich assumed must belong to the Committee of State Security. Who else could a building like that possibly have belonged to, with no signs, brightly lit by streetlamps from the outside, but always dark on the inside?

'Give it a thorough scraping, especially the entrance,' the boss ordered me. 'You never know, what if some general shows up and his Chaika gets stuck on the ice? Then they'll shut down our little business.'

What general and what Chaika? There weren't even any footprints near the building … But nonetheless I scraped away with a will, in order to keep warm.

It was very cold. At nights, huddling under two coats and wrapped in the detoxification centre's sheets, Toma and I kept warm by making love. And as soon as we quietened down, the rats came. They wanted love and warmth too: inspired by our example, they started chasing each other across the floor, across the table, all around the room, squeaking and thumping their tails. The rats ran riot until morning came; they could afford to, they didn't have to take any end-of-semester exams or chip away any ice.

But I had to. Roused by the alarm clock or, more accurately, by my own incredible effort of will, I woke up, quietly freed myself from Toma's sleepy embrace and got out of our wretched but blissfully voluptuous conjugal bed. And then, having subdued the rats' bacchanalian tumult, I put my feet into the one-size-fits-all felt boots issued to me by Dmitrich, pulled on my municipal-issue padded jacket, set my weapons across my shoulder and sallied forth long before daylight to clean that passage into that yard for that non-existent general once again.

Tamara couldn't sleep after I went. When she discovered that I had gone and she was left alone with the rats, she couldn't close her eyes again. Before she lowered her feet onto the floor, Toma clapped her hands for a long time to frighten away the long-tailed monsters surrounding the bed. But the monsters were less afraid of her than she was of them. The rats merely withdrew reluctantly into the dark corners, from where they observed Toma with their glittering little eyes and laughed into their whiskers. Constantly gazing round and shuddering from fear and the cold, she set the icy kettle on the rusty three-legged electric cooker, huddled up in her coat and sat down to wait for me to get back. My poor, wonderful Toma! I don't think that this was exactly her idea of domestic bliss. But during that whole month I never heard a single complaint from her, and not once did she ask to go back to her mum.

We saw the New Year in at our slum, in a large unoccupied room. The role of hosts was played by Tamara and me and our flatmates, two rather strange students; I don't remember what college they were from. In a fit of employer's largesse, Dmitrich had brought a bald, crooked little fir tree, which we stuck in the housing committee's bucket of salty sand. And then Felix showed up, already drunk, with a whole jerry-can of rectified spirits from the printing works. The smell of the alcohol started attracting tramps and other inhabitants of the uninhabited building.

Never, before or after, have I ever seen in the New Year in such a malodorous and friendly atmosphere. The walls of the 'festive hall', warmed by our breath and two red-hot coil heaters, wept like holy icons. We were all blissfully relaxed, the ne'er-do-well students, the tramps and the wary criminal types, covered in their blue tattoos. Even Toma smiled timidly as she nestled against my shoulder.

Dmitrich surveyed our gathering with an uncensorious, paternal gaze. We thought he was fine and he thought we were fine, just as we were. At one point it seemed to me that our benefactor was about to burst into song, and he probably would have done, but his gaze stumbled across me, as Nikolai Stepanovich's used to do. Suddenly changing his mind, Dmitrich held out his glass.

'Come on son, clink glasses!' he said. 'Here's to the New Year and to you. Everything will be just hunky-dory, you take an old man's word for it.'

And then a tramp sitting nearby announced that everything was going to be hunky-dory for him and his Ninka too, because they loved each other and they were going to get married.

'Isn't that right, Ninka?' he said, nudging the woman beside him.

The other tramps laughed raucously and all started shouting that they were getting married soon too.

As time went on the festivities became more and more boisterous, but we weren't involved for very much longer. Without waiting for the culmination, Tamara led me off to our little room, where I immediately succumbed to the wine weakness, collapsed onto the bed and fell asleep. A little while later Felix knocked on our door.

'The tramps are already fighting,' he announced and collapsed into bed beside me

Toma didn't sleep a wink all night, not because she had nowhere to sleep, and not even because of the rats. Or, rather, precisely because of the rats, because there weren't any that night. She thought that if the rats had disappeared, it meant there was going to be a catastrophe.

But everything was all right after all. Our riotous neighbours never got around to setting the building on fire or starting a knife fight; thankfully, the rectified spirits felled them before that. The yard keepers' housing association saw in the New Year without any emergencies, thank God – if you disregard the fact that the snow wasn't cleared for an entire week. At the end of that week, just before the Orthodox Christmas, Dmitrich came running to see Tamara and me in our room. He looked badly frightened and spoke incoherently: the only thing we could understand from what he said was that some high-up had come to the housing committee and was pounding his fist on the table.

'Talk sense, will you,' I told him. 'What high-up, why's he pounding the table? Maybe it's because we haven't cleared the snow?'

'I don't know who this high-up is, but he's very high,' Dmitry answered feverishly. 'And he couldn't give a shit about the snow – it's you he wants.'

To make a long story short, this 'high-up' turned out to be my father-in-law, Nikolai Stepanovich. Somehow, I don't know how, he had figured out where Toma and I were and shown up at the housing committee in person. And he was pounding the table because he didn't know how to do anything else but pound the table.

That very evening a black ministerial Volga with gleaming bumpers came for us. Poor Dmitrich was totally fazed by this.

'If I'd known you were such a big shot, I'd never have let you in,' he lamented. 'Now I've got to answer for you.'

'Don't worry Dmitrich, I'll put in a word so they don't touch you.'

I handed back the room and its contents, the padded jacket, the felt boots and the official-issue bed sheets. We hugged each other in farewell and never saw each other again.

But I started seeing Nikolai Stepanovich regularly again. And I must say that while Toma and I had been on the run, my father-in-law had changed significantly. He had probably been doing a lot of thinking. The very first evening after our return Nikolai Stepanovich summoned me into the kitchen for a man-to-man talk, something he had never done before. When he closed the door behind us and took the vodka out of the cupboard, I knew the conversation was going to be serious, and so it was. Without any yelling or snide attacks, Nikolai Stepanovich informed me that although I was, of course, a villain and a scoundrel, now that he 'was convinced' that 'that little fool' Tomka was stuck on me in earnest, he also wanted to have a normal human relationship with me.

'How about you?' asked Nikolai Stepanovich, looking me in the face.

'Why not?' I muttered in confusion.

'Then we'll drink to that!' said my father-in-law, pouring vodka for both of us. 'You don't shake your own shit off the shovel, eh?' He laughed good-naturedly and added: 'Only don't call me dad.'

We drank as a sign of reconciliation, but then it turned out that wasn't all. To make sure that Toma and I wouldn't go traipsing round any more rat-infested slums, Nikolai Stepanovich promised to register us for a flat with a housing cooperative. This news really floored me.

'Thank you ...' I muttered, blushing. 'Thank you very much ...'

Nikolai Stepanovich enjoyed my embarrassment.

'No worries!' he said, slapping me on the shoulder. 'Make the most of it, lad, now it's turned out this way. Just make sure you never do anything to upset Tomka and stick to your studies. When you graduate from college, you can join the Party and I'll take you on as chief engineer. Eh? Would you like to be a chief engineer?'

We had another drink or two as we discussed my career prospects, then Nikolai Stepanovich looked at his watch and suddenly said in a conspiratorial tone of voice.

'Now let's have one for Christmas, but keep it quiet.'

Many, many years have passed since then. Tamara's parents are no longer with us. Fortunately, they died before we were divorced. I am writing these lines, sitting in the very same flat that Toma's father arranged for us to have and paid for, and to this day I am very grateful to him. Forgive me, Nikolai Stepanovich, for not keeping my promise never to upset your daughter. And you, Irina Borisovna, forgive me for reading at the table.

THE ENGLISH
TEACHER

If someone from the pre-mobile phone era was relocated to our time, he would be very surprised to see every second person in the city walking along holding his or her head. As if they have just all banged their skulls together while bending over at the same time to pick something up, or they have all received a collective smack round the ear from someone or other. We, of course, would start explaining to our visitor that no one has bumped heads with anyone and these people are simply talking on the phone. But our guest would not believe us. 'In the first place,' he would object, 'why on earth does half the city suddenly need to make a phone call at the same time? And in the second place, where are their phones? A telephone has to have a receiver for speaking into, but they're muttering into empty space.' The pre-mobile individual would think that Muscovites had gone insane or fallen into their second childhood, and he would not be entirely wrong. Remember the way many of us – practically all of us, in fact – when we used to play in the sand-pit with our young peers, would hold a stone or a clenched fist to our ear in just the same way, pretending to be talking on the phone? We imagined our adult future, eating imaginary food, concluding imaginary marriages and dandling imaginary or, in the best cases, plastic babies on our knees.

Recent research has now demonstrated that advances in IT and telecommunications are prolonging our childhood. The researchers are at a loss to say whether this is good or bad, but I would like to think it is good because in the imaginary world of childhood our potential is so much greater than in the real world. 'X per cent more' as the advertisers put it. For instance, at an early kindergarten age I was friends with a little girl by the name of Vera. She was about forty per cent older than me, so she liked to imagine that I was her little boy – perhaps she was already preparing for the role of a single mother. But I didn't like that role: I was my mother's little boy already, and what point was there in playing at being myself? I preferred the role of the Faithful Husband, and sometimes, indeed, I managed to persuade my little girlfriend into marriage. Then she and I became mum and dad and we had a child in the form of a doll, which Vera took out from under her skirt in a highly convincing fashion. That was the terrible kind of thing that used to happen in our sandpit, but it proves that in the child's world nothing is impossible.

In adult life, however, things are a bit more complicated.

Of course, thanks to the Internet revolution we can now carry on playing into old age, imagining ourselves ... well, it's shameful even to admit who we imagine ourselves as. Although, actually, it's not shameful anymore these days. But we can still only *imagine*. The moment we try to realise our fantasies in external reality, we run into all sorts of problems. Society is not yet ready to abandon its customary taboos.

By this I don't even mean excesses and perversions, which really should be left behind in the sandpit, and buried as deeply as possible. Ah, and now that mention of my games with little Vera has reminded me of another story that echoes some of the same themes, a rather more adult story, about something that happened to my classmate Slavik Korablin. He fell in love with our teacher of English at school, and the feeling was reciprocated.

And why, indeed, should he not fall in love with her? I suspect that apart from Slavik very many of our lads entertained secret fantasies about her. How could we possibly not have? The girls in our class had been specially handpicked, each more hideous than the last. There was no Internet with pictures yet and Maya Arkadievna (that was the teacher's name) really was a looker.

She was nothing at all like the other English teachers, who in our day fell into two categories. Some were fat, elderly authority figures who had learned the language fifty years earlier from gramophone records; the others were pale, of indefinite age and completely lacking in authority, but they held diplomas with distinction from faculties of foreign languages. In class the fat ones were heavy on discipline and, by and large, they managed to impose their will, but the pale ones came to our lessons as if they were about to be shot, although I don't understand why: we never shot a single one. In fact no one shot the pale teachers, but they never lingered at our school for long – God only knows where they all went. The result was that we had a perpetual problem with teachers of English, because there weren't enough fat ones to go round.

That was why no one was surprised when one day the class teacher announced that we were going to have a new English teacher. We were surprised later, when this teacher showed up in person for our lesson. She wasn't fat and she wasn't pale, in fact she was an extremely attractive young woman. At first we even thought she was yet another of the headmaster's dolly-bird secretaries who had got the wrong door. But all was made clear when this dolly-bird greeted us in English:

'Hello, friends! My name is Maya Arkadievna.'

'My, my, Arkadievna!' some stupid clown joked and immediately received a clip round the back of the head from Semyonov.

Semyonov was actually quite a hooligan in his own right; all of us boys were hooligans to a greater or lesser degree, but Maya Arkadievna's beauty had an ennobling effect on us. It wasn't even her beauty, it was a certain romantic femininity that she had – we sensed it straightaway.

The new teacher didn't have a diploma with distinction, nor did she possess any outstanding pedagogical skills.

I wouldn't say that when Maya Arkadievna arrived we suddenly started doing much better at English, but we loved her classes. For us they were classes in beauty: she sang to us about prefixes and we simply listened to her voice, watched the shapes formed by her lips and admired the grace of movement with which nature had endowed her. Even the girls – our poor, plain girls – devoured Maya Arkadievna with eyes that radiated envious rapture. In short, I don't know how things were in the other classes, but in 10B we developed a genuine cult of the beautiful English teacher. I think she realised something of the kind herself and, within reasonable limits, employed her charms for the good of the cause. Everything was just wonderful: in Maya Arkadievna's lessons we sat there as meek as lambs, and in gratitude for our good behaviour she gave us decent marks. Our girls tried to imitate the English teacher's manners and even her clothes, and the boys, as I have already mentioned, indulged in fantasies about her. In secret.

But not all of us. One boy – Slavik Korablin, that is – proved bolder than the others, or crazier, depending on your point of view. Or perhaps his fantasies simply filled him up to the brim and overflowed, so he decided to share them, as it were. In short, Slavik declared his love to Maya Arkadievna. When and how he did it, in written form or *viva voce*, we never found out. It was hard enough to believe that he could have done it at all. In our class Korablin did not have a reputation for conquering young maiden's hearts; he wasn't even an early developer. He looked like a typical secret fantasist – intellectual and introspective. It was only later, after the whole business came out, that our girls discovered how fanciable he was.

Be that as it may, the fact remains that Slavik confessed his love to the teacher. Of course, he was delicately rejected . . . and, of course, he repeated his confession. Following goodness knows how many confessions, made in goodness knows what form, the English teacher's heart began to falter. Otherwise how can we explain that instead of giving the boy a piece of her mind, summoning his parents to the school and raising the matter at a school staff meeting, Maya Arkadievna entered into a series of educational dialogues with him. The intended purpose of these clandestine extracurricular dialogues was, naturally, to cure Slavik of his fatal fascination and, naturally, they led to the teacher and the pupil becoming lovers.

I don't know about schools nowadays, but in pre-mobile times this kind of occurrence was considered rare and untypical. Sexual contact between a teacher and a pupil was regarded in a highly negative light and condemned unreservedly by the community of parents and teachers – if, of course, it came to light. And in our case the occurrence did come to light, because Slavik and Maya Arkadievna proved to be absolutely hopeless conspirators. Whether the community caught them at it red-handed or deduced the substance of the crime from the accumulated mass of circumstantial evidence, I don't remember now. I only remember that there was a full-blown scandal, Slavik's parents were summoned to the school several times, and extraordinary staff meetings and Komsomol meetings were convened. There was no stoning, but that was only because the school desperately needed a live English teacher. However, the concerned community apparently overdid things with the meetings anyway, because Maya Arkadievna, who had her pride after all, resigned and left us.

During the humiliating investigation, Slavik also felt insulted, but less for himself than his beloved. Her disappearance without leaving any address left him genuinely sick at heart. Although the pain of his grief for Maya was sweet, the sweetness could not compensate for the suffering. Gradually, however, the keen pain of his loss was blunted. Korablin finished school with quite respectable results, although he got 'unsatisfactory' for behaviour.

Nonetheless, you must agree that all this is rather sad. This is what happens or, rather, used to happen in pre-mobile times if someone gave free expression to his fantasies. But I must tell you that this is not yet the end of the story – either literally or metaphorically. Of course, many years have gone by since then: all the boys in our class – all the Slaviks, Toliks, and Voviks – have been scattered throughout life and lost sight of each other. But when you lose of sight of someone, he doesn't cease to exist. Here is what happened recently at a certain art exhibition. (By the way, I enjoy going to art exhibitions. With the exception of certain of its more ultra-modern forms, visual art has the advantage of being silent.)

Anyway, this is what happened. Just recently I was wandering round a certain rather conservative art exhibition. It was quiet – either the mobile phones had been silenced by this encounter with the beautiful or I was alone in the hall.

I moved from stand to stand, enjoying other people's art and thinking about my own . . . Suddenly my eye was caught by a small portrait of a woman. I took a closer look and couldn't believe my eyes: there was our English teacher, Maya Arkadievna, staring out at me from the canvas! The name of the artist meant nothing to me; the age of the model was impossible to guess. But it was her, there was no doubt about it. I backed away to the nearby bench, felt for it with my backside, sat down and became immersed in thought.

Exactly what I was thinking about is hard to say, but just then three other visitors arrived. The first was a man of my age, balding and cultured-looking. Like me, he fixed his gaze on the portrait . . . then he gasped, clutched at his heart and staggered back. He too would probably have been glad to sit down, but I had already occupied the bench. And then who do you think walked in? You'll never believe it! It was Maya Arkadievna herself. She wasn't alone, she was walking arm-in-arm with some gentleman, but that's not important. I must say that the former English teacher was looking superb. The balding man turned his gaze from the portrait to the original and . . . but here my pen fails me. Scenes like that have always been better portrayed by painters of the old school than by writers.

'Hello,' the balding man said in a faltering voice, 'don't you recognise me?'

'I beg your pardon?' she replied, raising one eyebrow.

'Never mind, it's nothing,' he said, embarrassed.

Maya Arkadievna and her impressive companion stood in front of her portrait for a short while and then withdrew, but the balding man carried on hanging about, looking lost. I felt sorry for him and was even ready to give up the bench, but I was afraid of offending him with the offer and, in addition, I was desperately keen not to reveal my presence. I really ought to have got up quietly and slipped out, but I must admit that my curiosity is a match for my modesty, and I like to be the last to leave. I somehow had an inkling that the action of this little play would be continued, and I was not mistaken.

About ten minutes later the silence of the hall was broken by a hasty clatter of woman's heels – Maya Arkadievna had come back. She walked quickly over to the balding man and thrust a scrap of paper into his hand. He held out his card with a trembling hand and she immediately tucked it away in her handbag. I realised that they had just exchanged telephone numbers. This was followed by an exchange of glances, the depth of which once again defies my powers of description. The whole scene lasted only a minute or two. Then Maya Arkadievna suddenly blushed, swung round and set off with an uncertain wave of her hand, almost at a run.

The high-heel drum tattoo faded away. The balding man mastered his agitation and took his spectacles out of the inside pocket of his jacket. Setting them on his nose, he took the little piece of paper that Maya Arkadievna had given him out of another pocket and read it attentively. After that he put the piece of paper back in his pocket, closed his eyes and moved his lips soundlessly, evidently repeating the telephone number to himself. Then he took the piece of paper out again to check himself . . .

At this point I got tired of spying on him. And apart from that, I sensed a certain vibration in my own inside pocket, on the left, close to my heart. I know, I know – talking on a mobile phone at art exhibitions is most discourteous, the same as in the theatre or at a funeral. But it was Tamara calling me. The day before she and I had agreed to meet at this very exhibition – what would I have been doing there otherwise?

Toma phoned to say that she was delayed. I sighed and went back to thinking about Maya Arkadievna and Slavik Korablin. After they met completely by chance at that art exhibition, their mutual feelings were resurrected. But once again any relationship between them lay beyond the bounds of the socially acceptable. Maya Arkadievna had been married for a long time to a member of the Union of Artists – the same gentleman I had seen arm-in-arm with her – and Slavik was married to someone as well. Fortunately, the years that had passed between their two meetings, those years that had carried away their youth, had left them and the whole of mankind something else in exchange. By which I mean mobile telecommunications and e-mail. Maya Arkadievna and Slavik Korablin now stay in touch with each other via the Internet and meet surreptitiously at art exhibitions, and no one in the whole wide world knows about their affair.

So that is what happened in front of my very eyes at an exhibition of rather uncontemporary art. Or perhaps it didn't happen, and I imagined it all. That happens to me sometimes, and probably to you too, if you're the same age as me. We like to fantasise; we keep hoping that something unusual can still happen to us, when in actual fact everything has been decided long ago and all that's left for us to do is live out our lives reminiscing about the past and growing old to the music of our memories.

CAUCASIAN CUISINE

'Well, what do you think?'

'About what?' I ask, pretending not to understand.

'Don't act stupid,' says Dmitry Pavlovich, narrowing his eyes. 'I'm talking about Mary.'

'Mary?' I shrug my shoulders. 'Well, Mary's lovely . . . Only she carries a lot of gold around.'

'Yes, she likes that,' he laughs. 'Only that's not what I'm asking you about.'

'But I don't know about anything else apart from that.'

We fall silent, each engrossed in his own thoughts. We can hear dishes rattling in the kitchen; no doubt the women are whispering in there too. 'How do you like him?' Toma asks. 'But is he really a writer?' Mary counters, question for question.

Mary Kerimovna is their neighbour. Dmitry Pavlovich and Tamara arranged this dinner especially to introduce us to each other, although I think Tamara's involvement is merely incidental and he was the instigator of the entire occasion. Dmitry Pavlovich has obviously sensed a suspicious warming of relations between Toma and myself and decided to place me *hors de combat*. All his recent conversations with me have revolved round the idea that it is time to settle 'the woman question', and for some reason he has narrowed the woman question down to his neighbour Mary, lavishing enough praise on her to give the impression that he himself is by no means indifferent to her charms.

Well, now I have seen for myself that Mary Kerimovna is a woman of no mean quality, in corporeal terms and in all sorts of other areas. Our dinner today was her benefit performance, an assortment of dishes from her own native Caucasus. Everything was quite delicious, but now I feel like a fire-eater after a performance.

'She's a theatre critic by education . . .' Dmitry Pavlovich says, as if he's talking to himself.

'There you go again . . .'

'Yes, and that bust! Did you see that bust?'

This is beginning to annoy me: he can marry her himself, if her bust is that good. And give Tamara back to me. Out loud, though, I simply play along.

'Yes, an interesting woman. But with too much gold on her.'

'That's true,' Dmitry Pavlovich agrees. 'Gold, trinkets – they like all that. Only she is a theatre critic by education . . .'

'So what?'

'Well, it means that she has cultural needs to satisfy.

In fact, that was the reason she left her husband. Do you know who her husband was? The most famous orthodontist in the whole of Moscow!'

'You don't say!'

'I do say. Only he's one of them too, from the diaspora, so, you understand, he's a bit of a despot. But this woman's a theatre specialist, she has her needs. So she emancipated herself from him.'

'Good for her . . . But where does she get her gold from now?'

'He still gives it to her. And he bought the flat here for her too. That's the Eastern mentality, they don't abandon their women. He satisfies her material needs, and she satisfies her cultural ones herself.'

'That's amusing . . .' I mutter under my breath. 'So they're half-divorced, like me and Toma . . .'

'What was that?' asks Dmitry Pavlovich, who didn't quite catch what I said.

'Oh, nothing . . . So what are these cultural needs that you say she has?'

He opens his mouth to answer or to avoid answering my question, but just at that moment the women walk into the room.

'There they are, our little bunnies!' Mary Kerimovna warbles. 'We've brought you coffee.'

'Bunnies'! The term doesn't really suit me and Dmitry Pavlovich, but this, as I have already realised, is her style. The standard kind of thing: a woman laying the charm on thick, so certain she is irresistible that all men are 'bunnies' to her.

I wonder who it was that raised her self-esteem to that level. Could it have been the orthodontist?

The coffee's good, though – Toma clearly didn't brew it – and the conversation over the coffee is cultured and agreeable. Mary Kerimovna (you can just *tell* that she's a specialist on theatre) holds forth on cultural topics, in particular show business. But all good things in moderation: Dmitry Pavlovich has yawned twice already. I think it's time for us to wind everything up.

Then come the goodbyes.

'Goodbye, my little sweetheart!' says Mary Kerimovna, giving Tamara a thorough kissing.

'See you soon, kitten!' she says, presenting her cheek to Dmitry Pavlovich.

'I'll read you, I'll definitely read you!' – that's to me.

'Liar,' I think.

As always I go home from their place in a taxi, for which Dmitry Pavlovich, as always, has thrust five hundred roubles into my pocket. He doesn't know (how could he!) that for driving from their home to mine a taxi driver always takes at least six hundred and fifty. My heart is heavy, and not only at the thought of the hundred and fifty roubles I shall have to shell out from my own pocket. I am still dazed by the jangle of gold in my ears, and the Caucasus is still ablaze in my mouth.

'I'll read you,' she said. I rather think not.

She's arriving home right now – in fact, she's already there, because the flat bought with the orthodontist's money is less than a stone's throw away. She has already arrived, taken off her earrings, pendants and rings, and now she's standing there, examining herself in the mirror. I was wrong to think that she adored herself so greatly. There's no denying that the bust really is magnificent – the reader has already heard about that detail from Dmitry Pavlovich. Her bum's not bad either, although it used to be better. But below that . . . Actually the mirror only shows Mary down to the waist, but she knows. A woman knows when her legs are not up to the mark, and that's why she sighs. No, no one can be absolutely perfect, especially if that someone is already well past forty. And those wrinkles there on her forehead . . .

The standard schedule of pre-sleep procedures is performed with deliberate thoroughness. After removing her makeup, she looks at herself in the mirror again. Things have not improved . . . The news from the mirror could definitely be better, but that is not the only or, rather, the real reason for the lack of joy in Mary Kerimovna's heart. The fact is that she didn't like today's writer. She's no fool and she knows why the dinner was arranged. But the writer . . . how can she put it? He turned out to be an arrogant namby-pamby. He didn't express any clear opinions and always seemed to be trying to joke – at her expense. It's a good thing Mary was brought up properly, or she would have put in her *kopeck's* worth too.

'I khaven't read khim and I never will!' she concludes out loud as she moves the toothbrush around in her mouth

But her thoughts run on. Dmitry Pavlovich now, he's quite a different matter . . . Dmitry Pavlovich is a real bunny.

Of course, he's got Tamara . . . Tamara's impossible to understand too. She says she and this namby-pamby writer loved each other quite insanely. Then why did she leave him? What does she want with Dmitry Pavlovich? And what does he see in her, anyway? She can't cook . . . Next time he invites me round, I'll make *dolma* for him.

The idea of *dolma* comes to Mary Kerimovna when she's already in bed. She falls asleep with it in her mind.

Meanwhile I'm already approaching my home.

'Turn left here, then left again,' I tell the taxi driver.

'I know that, my dear man!' he replies with dignity. 'It's my bread.'

Fine bread it is too – six hundred and fifty roubles! My driver has a distinctive accent and nose – the Caucasian theme runs right through the evening . . .

We say goodbye in the dim light from the taxi's interior.

'Good luck to you.'

Thank you, friend, only good luck with what? It's too late now . . . If I were in your place, then, yes, I could use some good luck. I'd have the entire night ahead of me, the entire exuberant, ebullient Moscow night that promises such rich pickings to a taxi driver. After leaving me at home, that is, after offloading this namby-pamby, I'd go . . . where would I go? To the railway station, for instance.

The railway station is a risky place for a private cabby. The railway station is mafia territory. But on the other hand, the passenger at the station is amenable to persuasion. Newly arrived, he doesn't know our rates, but well-intentioned people have told him, of course, that taxis in Moscow are an incredible rip-off. They were right – I'm certainly going to rip him off.

'Where to, guv'nor?'

'Me? I don't know ... The address is here on this piece of paper.'

'Clear enough. We'll get you there fine, no worries. You just relax, comrade, light up – that's okay by me. The worst is all behind you now. You're lucky to have found me – the Caucasians drive all the cabs in Moscow these days. Don't even know the city, and they make out they're taxi drivers. By the way, how do you like our little town now, a long time since you were here last, is it?'

The passenger gazes out of the window in confusion.

'I don't even recognise it ...'

Yes, the capital is changing. Moscow of the welcomes, city of the golden domes – where is she now? Where is the enduring, red-brick, Kremlin-museum city of the Soviet TV logo?

Our provincial compatriots are not very fond of Moscow these days. Just recently one tried to tell me that the city's sucking all the juice out of Mother Russia. Swelling up as it draws the blood out of her white body, like some huge tick that will have to burst some time soon. Maybe so, I won't argue with that, but have you ever thought, comrades from the hinterland, that the substance swelling up this tick – or whoever it is – is you? You just keep on pouring in, and that's the problem: Moscow's wheeling-dealing big noises are ex-provincials like you. And two-thirds of our *beau monde* – pardon my French – that flits from one cultural event to the next, is also you. Some come for the cheap goods at the markets, some for the Vanity Fair of Moscow's intelligentsia, but the result is the same: the capital just keeps on getting fatter and it really is almost fit to burst. We can only thank all the swindlers and conmen for helping Moscow slim down a bit.

And the foreigners! The city's infested with them nowadays. Look at that lady over there, for instance, trying to stop a cab – she raises her hand and the diamonds on the fingers blaze like cat's eyes. There's an obvious . . . Ah, no, sorry, she's one of ours.

'What a surprise, Mary Kerimovna! Where are you going at this time of the night? According to my information, you're sound asleep at the moment.'

'You may have decided that I'm asleep, but I have cultural needs to satisfy.'

'I beg your pardon. But tell me, aren't you afraid to be out at night in all that gold?'

'Why should I be afraid? My husband's an extremely famous orthodontist.'

'Ah, so that's all right . . . In that case, that will be six hundred and fifty roubles.'

No, I don't really think she's like a tick (I'm talking about Moscow again). She's not really like anything at all, nothing but a blurred sequence of flickering images. Armeno-Azerbaijanis, Arbat Streets (Old and New), Alfa Romeos, assassins, authors, apricots, attorneys, avocados . . . Turn the corner onto the letter B and there are boutiques, BMWs, Bentleys, bums, bimbos in boots, bootleg taxis, bedlam, bandits, buffoons, boulevards, bistros, babel . . . Maybe Moscow is basically an open concept, like those kindergarten barges that we used to load up with nouns when we were children? We just keep on loading them in without giving a thought to the fact that the barge settled on the bottom ages ago.

It seems to me that that the image of Moscow only exists in the minds of the provincials. It's the same with a whale, for example: look at it from the outside and you see a certain image, but when it swallows you and you end up in its belly, the image disappears.

Moscow is faceless, but sly. Let your guard down for moment and she'll creep up, blow in your ear and break into raucous laughter. The suddenness of it stirs up a blizzard in your head, leaving your thoughts hopelessly tangled, and she thinks that's just great. Moscow is very fond of confusing things. For instance, have you ever tried travelling round her using the map? On paper everything's clear: Such-and-Such Street runs into Such-and-Such Square. But once you wind up on that square, you're done for: where's the street, where's the junction? Nothing but the sound of Moscow's derisive laughter on all sides.

But don't you worry, I know the capital all right. I know it every bit as well as our Soviet agent Stirlitz knew Berlin. It's my *brot*, after all. So just hand over that six hundred and fifty, dear non-resident, and good luck to you. Although I think you've already been lucky – you arrived in Moscow at night, didn't you? Everything you've seen, this seething confusion of lights, people and cars, was only her dream. But she'll start waking up any time now, and then you and I won't have time to spin any more stories. The foundations will quake, the bilges will be flung open and all the nouns, from A-Z, will come gushing up to conjugate with verbs.

Only I won't be there to see it. As fortune's own nocturnal favourite, I turn my steed back towards its stable at the first glimmerings of dawn. My glove compartment is stuffed full of hundred-rouble notes and my one remaining ambition is to get home. At the last moment Moscow realises what's going on and arranges for traffic jams along my route, but she can't catch me now. I swerve in and out of courtyards with two exits, I'm as tricky as Stirlitz and I'll get back in time: I'll get back before my Tamara wakes up. Back at home, after taking a shower, I'll rouse her with my body and she'll smile at me through her sleep.

'Raked in the loot?'

'Oodles of it.'

'That's my boy!' says Toma, wrapping her legs round me. 'You're no namby-pamby man, a real breadwinner, that's you . . . Would you believe, I dreamed you were a writer and you were sponging off me!'

THE DOGS' AREA

As a citizen I'm a pretty peaceful individual, not a persistent troublemaker or inveterate picketer, but I can no longer remain silent. If I knew how to write complaints and which official offices to send them to, I swear I'd sit down and write one now. Unfortunately, from the vast range of municipal institutions, the only one with which I am familiar is our own local housing office (which is just inside the next entrance of this building); and I don't know how to write anything except books. The only adjudicating authority to which I am in the habit of appealing is eternity, and the wheels of that administration, unfortunately, grind extremely slow. So far it has only filed my applications but not got around to examining their substance.

I hope, however, that *you* will accept my representations: I hereby denounce the local authorities or, to be more precise, our district council, for the wanton destruction of the dogs' area in the courtyard of our flats. Yes, I realise against whom

I am raising my voice; yes, the very sound of that phrase, 'district council', sets me trembling with fear. But after all, I am not alone. I am sure that apart from Phil and me there are hundreds and hundreds of other victims. Even if we take our unit of account as dog plus master (in bureaucratic terms – the 'dog-man'), there will still be very many of us. But apparently that is the very nub of the catastrophe. For a long time the district council, assuming that there was no canine problem in our neighbourhood, didn't bother to count us in any way at all and occupied itself with more important business. But then one morning, some council member or other, glancing out of his kitchen window, found the sight that met his eyes quite intolerable. The designated canine defecation area was crowded with such large numbers of dogs that there was no space remaining even for said designated activity. In addition, canines and their masters were milling about outside the designated area, engaging in verbal conflict with those who were inside and had locked the gate against them.

Overwhelmed by what he saw, the district council member convened a meeting at which he raised point-blank the issue of overcrowding at the dogs' area. Naturally, neither he nor his fellow council members felt that they were in any way responsible for the situation that had arisen, because it was not the present district council that established the area, it had been established by the preceding authority, which had a different name. The council members then had a brainstorming session that produced what I can only describe as a paradoxical result. For the purposes of achieving an equal distribution of social opportunity and obviating further conflicts in relation to the dogs' area, the district council ruled that the barrier around the dogs' area should be removed forthwith and that henceforth citizens with companions of non-human origin should meet the needs of nature as and when they felt inclined.

A source close to the district council commented on this revolutionary decision as follows.

'Let them shit where they want, but no hard feelings.'

No sooner said than done. Naturally, to facilitate universal social equality, together with the fence they also pulled up the benches, the garbage cans into which the more socially aware dog-owners placed the excrement of their own and other peoples' pets and the wooden beam along which the more socially aware of those pets used to trot.

It is hard to describe the depths of despondency into which our dog-man community has been plunged. We have only one consolation – that the council didn't liquidate us along with the designated area: it would, after all, be quite capable of doing that. For me as a writer there is another, more personal reason for mortification in all this. The point is that I have been nursing the concept for a short work in which our dogs' area would have been the central scene of action. Unfortunately, all this has happened before my concept came together, and I can report to all who are interested that this work will not now materialise.

I should also mention that since the dogs' area ceased to figure in the listing of municipal facilities, it has not actually disappeared and continues to serve in its former capacity. We have not yet learned how to relieve ourselves as and when we feel inclined and still visit the old spot, loitering within the limits of a non-existent fence. Dogs running at full pelt brake to a sudden halt at an invisible line and turned puzzled little faces towards their masters. Ah, if only the masters themselves knew the answer . . .

The sad fate of the dogs' area gives pause for thought. It begs the question: Is a similar fate in store for our entire overpopulated city? If it is, then writers should make haste with their works about Moscow.

The first warning signs are already here. For instance, there are discussions in the capital's mass media of certain plans to do away with the administrative boundaries of the city of Moscow and amalgamate it with the Moscow region. Well, if that should happen, just wait for a while and the levelling-down will begin. In their dreams, some people see the city throwing off the shackles of the MOH (Moscow Orbital Highway), squaring its shoulders and striding ineluctably into the surrounding area, trampling the squalid hovels of the sons of the soil under its elegant high-rise feet . . . But somehow I don't think so! On the contrary, it is the Moscow region that will invade the confines of the city, crushing under its calloused peasant heel all that we urbanites hold dear. Farewell civilisation, farewell Armani and Gucci, boulevards and city squares. Cleanliness and culture will become things of the past, the dogs' areas will disappear from all the city's yards and carrots and potatoes will grow in their place.

The peasant gene is aggressive and possesses great creeping power. Just look at what is happening even now, before any merger of territory. My housing district is still pretty much okay, but further out on the perimeter, where there are no Individuals of No Fixed Abode or yuppies, and people walk to the shop in their slippers, the lifestyle is downright rural – I've seen it with my own eyes. Women plant parsley in the forecourts, chickens live in the citizens' loggias, and sometimes you can even find a horse in the garages.

The vegetative gene is very powerful! Even now in my courtyard the indefatigable Tajik yard keepers can't trim the grass fast enough, and that's in a place where it has been trampled by thousands of shoes and poisoned by smog. What will happen when invaders from the region bring in fresh, wild seeds and spores on their boots? We'll simply be lost in the tall grass, creepers will wind themselves round our legs and our lungs will choke on the oxygen.

We, pale urbanites, raised in hydroponic style on the shelves of the high-rises, will lose out in the battle for survival to creatures who draw their strength from the earth. We will be eliminated, and art and fundamental science will follow us into oblivion.

Such is the prospect that we face. But it's interesting to wonder what will come after us, how Moscow's new masters will behave. We know from the history of centuries past that when barbarians captured a city, they faced a dilemma: whether to burn it and carry away the loot or stay and live in it. Over time, they did both. But the trouble is that you can't carry away any booty from a modern city like Moscow – there's simply no point. Everything valuable in the city, all those fancy trappings of civilisation, only have value and power within its boundaries, within its own energy field, so to speak. Out in the region, where the barbarians are encamped, you can't even pick up FM radio. So the invaders will have no choice: they'll have to settle down on the asphalt. Of course, they'll defile the asphalt of Moscow and spit their sunflower seed husks all over it. But as for digging it up to plant vegetable patches – no way, they'll never manage that. And in addition, they'll have to get used to living in large agglomerations, and that's a really hard thing for regional savages to do. For all their genetic energy, they still lack what we have: an exoskeleton, a shell that provides protection against collisions with others of your own kind. They'll have to learn a lot of new things in Moscow, for instance, feigning indifference at the sight of a corpse they come across in the metro, exclaiming 'wow!' when the occasion requires it and not gasping out loud at the sight of two men kissing passionately.

And that's not all. I must warn in particular all present and future female conquerors of the capital who may be hoping first to become a fully-fledged Muscovite, and then afterwards achieve a state of familial bliss that they must banish this idea from their head. Muscovites don't marry each other. You are supposed to catch your bridegroom immediately on arrival in the city, when you are still fresh tribal material from the provinces. Otherwise you can bid a fond farewell to your dreams of marriage, or simply of finding a good man. Those career ladies who claim to have made themselves must also accept responsibility for satisfying their own needs. I don't know why this happens, but it's a law you would do well to remember.

To give my argument some substance, let me take the example of my niece Lariska. Here you have an absolutely typical example of a successful self-made woman with an unsuccessful personal life. About ten years ago she turned up here in Moscow, young and fresh with ripe apple-cheeks. The moment Tamara laid eyes on her, she said:

'You're just right for marrying, my girl.'

But Lariska merely snorted.

'Nonsense, I could have got myself a husband back home in Vaskovo. That's not what I came to Moscow for.'

'And just what did you come to Moscow for, my dear?' I asked her.

'To do business,' Lariska replied imperturbably. 'First I'll earn a bit of money and buy a flat here, and then I'll choose a husband.'

Tamara and I smiled, exchanged glances and offered our visitor tea. Lariska drank the tea, slurping loudly. Tamara watched her until she couldn't hold back any more and asked:

'So what business are you planning to get into, Lariska?'

The slurping broke off.

'That makes no difference. People in the know say money's just lying around in the street here, but you Muscovites are simply too lazy to pick it up.'

Immediately after tea, before she had even finished chewing her last sweet, Lariska got up from the table.

'Well, I'll be off,' she said. 'You know what they say, time is money.'

'Off you run,' I said with a nod. 'Pick some up in the street.'

This visit from my niece was merely a matter of family courtesy. Tamara and I obviously did not impress Lariska as people in the know – useful people – so she didn't show up at our place again for the next few years. However, by various roundabout routes the amazing information reached us that Lariska really had become a businesswoman. How she had managed to do this and what kind of business she had was something that my sources (mostly in Vaskovo) were at a loss to explain. 'Damned if we know,' said the sources, with a shrug. 'She imports something, maybe mobile phones from China, maybe amber from the Baltic. It's buying and selling anyway.'

As the years passed Lariska's business flourished and grew strong, expanding many times over. Lariska acquired her own registered firm, a rented office in some business centre or other and several full-time employees – every last one of them from back home in Vaskovo – although it still remained a mystery what the firm actually did. But those matters are basically beyond my comprehension; there are plenty of firms like that in Moscow, and it's not what my story's about. Let us assume that the firm simply picked up money in the street. Naturally, Lariska had also acquired a flat in Moscow. I wasn't invited to the housewarming, but I heard about it from my sources.

I was, however, able to confirm with my own eyes that she drove a very stylish automobile, because I saw the car when Lariska came to visit me. I was very surprised, not by the car, but by the fact of Lariska's visit, only the second in several years. But then, perhaps the visit came as a surprise to

Lariska too – the point being that at that particular moment in time she was in a state of stress, and women in that kind of state, even Moscow businesswoman, are inclined to act impulsively. And it's when they start feeling the stress that they remember they have an uncle.

I won't attempt to conceal the fact that the passing years and the city had taken their toll on Lariska's appearance. The apple-cheeks were a thing of the past: she was now definitely a hundred-per-cent, forceful, rouged businesswoman who would never fall off her heels, no matter how high they were. Yet despite that it was obvious to me that she was emotionally tattered.

'I just dropped in to see you,' she declared. 'You're the only person in the whole of Moscow who's in any way close to me.'

How do you like that! Lariska and I had never been close, but her words melted my heart.

'Of course, of course . . .' I responded, flustered. 'Come in, let's sit and talk . . . unfortunately, Tamara's not here.'

'Why, where is she?' Lariska laughed.

'She left. We got divorced, you see.'

My visitor seemed strangely cheered by this news.

'Well, well,' she said. 'I come to see you and I feel better immediately. So even you're human, then!'

I tactfully didn't ask straight off what was weighing so heavily on her heart; I had guessed in any case that she wouldn't just blab the whole story straight out, and that proved to be right. Lariska happened to have a bottle of Hennessy and two large pomelos with her. Before we had even polished off half the bottle and decimated one of the fruits, I had already been briefed on Lariska's sad circumstances and, in particular, what had brought her to me.

It turned out that my niece's woes were all of an intimate nature. As a potential advisor that suited me just fine, because I would have been pretty useless as far as business matters were concerned. Lariska's problem was basically that, despite her business success, she had had no luck at all when it came to her 'boyfriends' (as she called them in English) who behaved like macho slobs. Every man who was offered refuge at her brand-new, far-from-cheap flat soon started wandering round the place in his underpants and even breaking wind without the slightest embarrassment. It was quite impossible to bring these boyfriends down a peg, because at the first expression of dissatisfaction from Lariska, they simply gathered up their bits and pieces and disappeared. The latest of then, to whom I was indebted for the Hennessy, had even called Lariska a stupid fool as he left, which could not really be taken as anything but an insult.

In principle, Lariska's situation seemed quite typical and rather ordinary to me but, as someone close to her, who also happened to be drinking her Hennessy, I felt duty-bound to express sympathy.

'You're such an interesting woman,' I remarked, 'and he actually called you that ... By the way, who is he, this boyfriend of yours?'

'You mean, what does he do?' she asked with a casual wave of her hand. 'He's a supplier, what else?'

'No, what I meant was: Is he a Muscovite?'

Lariska nodded.

'Of course he is. All my suppliers are Muscovites.'

'There, you see, Larochka!' I said, raising my finger. 'Now you listen to me, I know about these things. You'll never click with a Muscovite.'

She raised her eyebrows sharply.

'And why's that?'

'Because . . . because there's a force of mutual repulsion that exists between Muscovites. It's hard to explain, but trust me on this.'

Lariska sipped thoughtfully on her cognac.

'So what can I do? All my suppliers are locals . . .'

I felt sorry for her.

'I don't even know what advice to give you . . .' I said, shaking my head helplessly. 'You could try crying a bit, I suppose.'

But Lariska was too proud to cry.

'Moscow doesn't believe in tears!' she declared theatrically. 'I'd rather . . . I'd rather get drunk!'

My niece promptly demonstrated that she was a woman of her word. She got drunk right there in my kitchen, without even stirring from the spot. When Lariska felt like being sick, I took her to the bathroom and then put her to bed. In the morning she put on her makeup, got into her deluxe auto and drove off to do business.

After that Lariska started visiting regularly. She probably didn't have any close girlfriends. In any case, it's not every girlfriend that you can simply massacre a bottle with, and she felt at ease with me. We downed our cognac like two men and picked over the bones of personal life like two women.

Everything was just great, apart from the fact that Phil, a regular participant in all my kitchen chat sessions, believed that conversation over cognac could not take the place of personal life as such. He himself didn't drink any cognac and he kept mum – but only until his own personal requirements became too pressing. When that happened, we left Lariska to ponder the most recent tentative conclusions reached and went out to the dog's area in the yard. Generally speaking, the personal life of dogs takes place in a public forum.

Our own special little area was still intact then. What a truly significant symbol of public utility that fence was! How many times it had protected Phil from large, aggressive dogs – and protected small, decorative dogs from Phil! Bitches, of course, didn't count – they were protected against the teeth of the male dogs by nature herself. But only from the teeth: the space inside the fence was a no-go area for bitches on their more sensitive days.

Things went on like this for a year or even longer. Chat sessions over cognac became a regular habit for Lariska and me. On the one hand, this was no bad thing; people need to have habits – they create the illusion that life is stable. But not all habits lead to good outcomes, indeed, we know that some of our habits actually complicate and even shorten our lives. I believe that our joint cognac habit could have led Lariska to alcoholism; and then her business would have fallen into decay and all her suppliers would have abandoned her. That kind of career is fairly typical: driving over the capital's asphalt roads is so nerve-wracking that many, very many of those who thought they would conquer her end up taking to drink.

But our chats suddenly came to an end, and in the light of what I have already said, I can't really say that I regret it. In any case, Lariska disappeared again. She didn't come to see me for a week, then two, then three, and after that I stopped thinking about her, because my own problems were piling up.

It all started with the local authorities demolishing our dogs' area. There was no fence left to provide refuge and the result was that Phil, wandering round the yard as the fancy took him, found a girlfriend. Unfortunately, the girlfriend's master and I failed to realise that the relationship between our two pets was getting serious, and one evening we found ourselves running across the courtyard, uttering stupid cries of 'Phoo!' while Phil and his new flame consummated the act that renders all estates and classes equal. The degree of equalisation was significant in this case, because my canine friend was coupling with a pedigree Dalmatian.

I don't know if you're aware of this, but in its canine version the act concerned lasts for rather a long time and is quite impossible to interrupt at a late stage. So the Dalmatian's master and I had no option but to sort things out between ourselves while we waited for it to end. Basically, from the dogs' point of view (which I am inclined to share) there was nothing unnatural in the act of coition that was taking place, but my adversary did not agree. Our dialogue went something like this:

Bitch's Master: Do you realise what you've done? She's an exhibition dog.

I: I haven't done anything. You should take more care walking your prize exhibit.

B.M.: These bloody mongrels are all over the place now.

I: Would you rather she was covered by a Riesenschnauzer?

B.M.: You're a bloody Riesenschnauzer yourself.

I: Ha, look who's talking!

Fortunately we never got as far as fisticuffs, because the dogs concluded their business while we crossed swords. Their feelings on parting were most tender-hearted, which is more than can be said for their masters.

The occurrence described above had diametrically opposed consequences for me and Phil. Having cut loose in this fashion, Philip felt, quite naturally, that his stature had been substantially enhanced, while I experienced the opposite effect. That cry of 'You're a bloody Riesenschnauzer yourself' left a bitter residue in my soul. Sometimes, when I got the feeling that something had been left unsaid, I used to go out into the yard and look around for the Dalmatian's master. I don't know what I wanted from him, I wasn't even sure that I really wanted to meet him.

Nonetheless, the meeting did take place and, of course, it took place when I was absolutely unprepared for it. I didn't run into the Dalmatian's master in our communal yard or some other obvious spot, but in a crowded metro carriage. The metro is not really the right place for delving into canine genealogy, and I pretended not to notice the gentleman, but he spotted me and squeezed up close.

'Hello!' he shouted, smiling for some reason.

I raised one eyebrow in reply.

'Fancy meeting you here!' he continued chirpily.

'It's an abominably small world,' I muttered, but fortunately he didn't hear.

'What? Do you know that Vesta had six pups?'

It took me a moment to realise who Vesta was, then I roared in reply:

'Congratulations! Are you going to sue for alimony?'

At this point the train stopped at the station where the Dalmatian's master and I were both getting off.

'Alimony? Don't say that!' he exclaimed, taking me by the arm, 'They're so loveable. I tell you what . . . come over for the christening. With your . . . I'm sorry, I don't know what either of you are called.'

So the unexpected outcome of the stupid story of Phil's cutting loose was a happy ending.

In addition, it turned out that while we were engrossed in these events, the plot in my niece Lariska's life had taken another twist – a surprising one that also led to a happy ending. I read about it in an e-mail I received on the evening of the day I learned that Phil had become a father. The message, from Sweden, informed me that Lariska had got married and would soon become a mother. Omitting all the romantic details, since I am no great lover of such things, the gist of the message was that one fine day it had dawned on Lariska to change her supplier and, unlike the Moscow suppliers, the

Swedish model had met her requirements in every respect. He didn't wander about the place in his underpants, only farted in the designated areas and didn't think Lariska a stupid fool. So now the business partners were on their honeymoon, which they were spending gathering mushrooms under the pine trees on the shores of the Gulf of Bothnia.

Naturally, I was delighted by this message from my niece, but it also gave me pause for thought. Why shouldn't certain Moscow businesswomen take note of Lariska's experience? Although, of course, Sweden is a small country and its supply of suppliers is strictly limited.

As for me, for the first time in a long time, I retired to bed that evening in an optimistic frame of mind. Say what you will, but it's no bad thing when the world acquires six new half-Dalmatians and one new half-Swede.

GOODBYE
TO ZAMOISKY

Grisha Zamoisky is dead; I was informed of his death and the date of the funeral on the phone by his wife Mila. She told me in a grave, strangely detached kind of voice, as if she were speaking on behalf of the deceased. Exactly the kind of voice, with a slight hint of accusation, in which the surviving relatives of someone recently deceased usually communicate with the world around them. In fact, Grisha would never have spoken to me from the next world in that tone: he and Mila are old, close friends of mine, except that now he is in the past tense.

We were in the same student group at college. Grisha and Mila were the witnesses when Tamara and I got married in the third year, and a year later they employed our services in the same capacity. On graduating from college, our girls were free to seek employment wherever they wished and

Grisha and I found good jobs in a Moscow engineering office. He and I even ended up in the same department, which could have been cause for a certain rivalry between us – two young specialists at the very start of their career ... But no rivalry sprang up and it never have could have done. I heard somewhere that only one in ten of all graduates from technical colleges eventually becomes a half-decent engineer. Of the remaining third-raters, three make administrative careers, three leave to 'find themselves' in the sphere of the humanities and three swell the ranks of the good-for-nothings in white coats that abound in all engineering and design organisations and only display any kind of activity when leave and free holiday travel are being allocated. Well, you have probably already guessed that neither I nor Zamoisky demonstrated any talent as engineers, great or otherwise. What's more, we unfortunately lacked the essential low villainy and cunning required to suck up to the boss. Grisha and I very soon realised that we were in no danger of creative development or administrative advancement in the engineering office. But after that our ways parted, in accordance with the statistical pattern adduced above. I shifted the workload of my brain from the left hemisphere to the right and became a novelist, but Grisha continued to serve as an infantry private in the engineering ranks until the end of his days.

For many years our two families were friends. Although I must admit, with my hand on my heart, that only the Zamoiskys had a genuine family, because a genuine family is one in which there are children. Unfortunately, when it came to reproduction the score was two-nil in the Zamoiskys' favour, although Grisha was not entirely satisfied with the result of their productive efforts: both their children were of the female sex.

'I tried, I really did ...' he lamented after the birth of the second little girl, 'but it's the same again ... Just that much, that's all that was missing!' he said, showing me the tip of his little finger.

However, despite the lack of what Grisha had in mind, Liza and Nastya – that's what his daughters were called – were as lively and mischievous as boys. Their angelic little foreheads were frequently adorned with bumps and their plump extremities with scrapes and bruises. With only a year between them, the girls squabbled over anything at all, but the most frequent cause for a quarrel was who was going to ride on daddy's shoulders. Grisha carried them for a very long time, until Mila forbade it for reasons of decency. But even then almost every weekend dad and daughters set out on an excursion. These excursions, often quite long, were always educational in nature. Zamoisky might have been a hopeless engineer, but he had a passion for mechanisms, so he took his little girls to an exhibition of armoured vehicles, or an air show, or simply to the Polytechnical Museum. His daughters never objected to this programme of events; perhaps they felt guilty for not being born the boys that their daddy had wanted.

I hope you can pardon my excessively keen interest in the way that other people's children grow up. Let's just put it down to a writer's professional quirk.

The years passed and the little girls began developing as

individuals. Liza 'grew in the leg' which, according to Mila, guaranteed her the figure of a fashion model in the future; but Nastya grew a little bit everywhere, which soon guaranteed male interest. Apart from a polite interest in armoured vehicles, Liza demonstrated the usual inclinations of little girls and did well at school. Nastya's progress at school was erratic and Mila was frightened by her inclinations. At a very early age her parents started discovering in her room cigarettes and other artefacts which indicated that they needed to keep a close eye on the girl.

Be that as it may, Tamara and I loved them both. When we came to visit the Zamoiskys, the girls kissed us on the cheek. Then Liza went to her room 'to study', but Nastya hung about with the grown-ups and butted into our conversations until Mila drove her out. When this happened, Grisha sighed furtively; I think that, despite her difficult character, Nastya was his favourite and he especially regretted having failed to bestow on her that snippet the size of the tip of his little finger.

At that time we used to get together with the Zamoiskys three or four times a year, that is, quite often. General speaking, those were hard times, especially in financial terms and especially for lower echelon staff engineers. So on our way to see them Tamara and I tried as far as possible to buy everything necessary for the meal. And later, during that meal, we delicately avoided talking about money or Grisha's job. For their part, the Zamoiskys tried to avoid the subject of children with us. If Mila was careless enough to start chattering about the stresses of parenthood, Grisha stepped on her foot under the table. We and the Zamoiskys secretly regarded each other as unfortunate. Perhaps that was what made us close during those difficult years.

Later, when the state of society started to improve, we started seeing each other less often. I actually managed to conceal our divorce from the Zamoiskys for more than a year. They didn't even find out about it from me, but by chance from some acquaintances that we had in common. I remember the telephone call from Grisha.

'Listen, my friend, I heard that you and Tamara are . . . you know?' he enquired cautiously.

'Yes, indeed: our ways have parted.'

'Mmm, I see . . .' he sighed sadly after a pause. 'So now what?'

'Nothing. I'm writing.'

Poor Zamoisky! I'm sure he hadn't read a single one of my books. His intellectual spirit perished long before his body. Such, perhaps is the price of family happiness . . . Perhaps now, when he has also left his family, I ought to put a little volume in his grave. With an inscription: 'To my friend Grisha for his journey'. Only I don't have a volume with me and the priest would abuse me for it. But then who knows, the priests in Moscow turn a blind eye to many things. This one is performing the funeral service even though I think he realises the deceased was not baptised. And the priest certainly knows that afterwards we'll take him to an entirely non-Orthodox establishment: the crematorium.

'Poor Mila!' someone whispers right in my ear.

She came after all. Tamara takes my arm and presses herself against me, and I feel her trembling slightly.

'Are you on your own?'

'With Little Dima. He's outside.'

'And Palich?'

'Why would he come? He didn't know him.'

'Yes, that's right . . .'

The funeral is over. The priest extinguishes his censer and gives instructions, telling us 'dear ones' what to do at the cemetery when saying our final farewell to the deceased. Mila gazes intently at the priest, but I know she doesn't hear a word he's saying. It's okay, Tamara's with her. So are Liza and Nastya. I wouldn't have recognised them – they've become such grown-up ladies.

We carry Zamoisky to the hearse – myself and three other men, colleagues of his from work. It's heavy work.

We drive to the cemetery. Tamara has taken Mila and her daughters with her in the car and I, knowing that I will be needed again to help with the coffin, have taken a seat in the hearse with Grisha and his colleagues. The budget-class Moscow hearse is a refurbished minibus. A space has been freed up at the centre of it for the main passenger, and benches for those accompanying him have been set along the sides. We sit there, holding the lid of the coffin in place with our knees – the bumpy road keeps shaking it off. The hearse smells of petrol, damp wood and stale alcohol. Of course, Grisha's colleagues have taken a drink or two beforehand and they tell stories about work all the way. The point is for Zamoisky to figure as the central character in every story. I learn lots of new things about Grisha and as I listen I recall the corridor of the engineering office, the rubbish bins overflowing with cigarette butts and the same kind of storytellers, only twenty years ago.

The potholes jolt us up into the air and again a storyteller loses his thread. He gazes in confusion at Zamoisky's coffin.

'Yes,' says one colleague, filling in the gap. 'Grisha went early, all right.'

'Yes he did,' say the others, nodding, 'he should have lived a bit longer.'

The potholes indicate that we are already approaching the cemetery. Wiping the steamy window, I see a large open area packed with minibus hearses just like ours. The queue for the next world. After squeezing into a free space, the driver switches off the engine and sets off to reconnoitre. Well, if that's how things are, we can get out too, for a smoke and a breath of fresh air. We clamber out of the hearse, everybody except Zamoisky; he doesn't smoke any more.

Not far away I spot the Geländewagen, which arrived before us. The women are probably sitting inside, concealing their tears behind the tinted windows, but Little Dima is striding up and down outside with a cigarette.

'Hi!' I say, walking over to him.

'Hi . . .'

'Did you find the way to the cemetery okay?'

Dima laughs.

'I could find that road with my eyes closed. The number of our lads I drove here . . .'

'I see . . .'

In previous times Little Dima was a member of what he calls 'an unofficial trade union'.

The queue for the crematorium moves more quickly than we could have expected. In less than an hour we are already carrying Zamoisky into the leave-taking hall or, rather, pushing him in, because there's a trolley here for the convenience of clients. As we push the trolley over to the special plinth at the back of the hall, the female attendant switches on the sad music; she puts it on quietly, so as not to interfere with the funeral orations. There will be orations, have no doubt about that. Grisha's colleagues are already whispering among themselves, evidently identifying the most eloquent of their number. Now the coffin has been installed on the plinth and opened again. The eloquent colleague steps up to its foot and . . . mutters something unintelligible. He looks as if he has been summoned to the boss's office for a dressing-down. With the threads of his report thoroughly tangled together he looks round for support from his colleagues and one of them comes to his rescue. With an effort, the two of them formulate some kind of statement in their engineering-office language about Grisha's professional and social achievements. It sounds as if they are reading a Diploma of Honour in chorus, only instead of wishes for continued success, their address concludes with the words 'rest in peace'.

The crematorium attendant keeps glancing at her watch. It's time for us to get on with kissing the deceased and carrying out the priest's instructions. We line up and take turns to kiss. It's not a pleasant procedure; some of us shirk it.

It's over. The deceased has been sprinkled with earth from a paper bag, the coffin has been closed and nailed shut and is now moving into the opening in the wall. There are no flames raging in the opening, it's not the furnace just yet, but soon . . . I was probably right not to put my little book in Grisha's coffin, it would have burned up.

As soon as the opening in the wall closes, the attendant turns off the music. For a few seconds a faint whisper runs round the hall and the sound of noses being blown with restraint can be heard from various corners . . . Then suddenly in the middle of the silence a loud sobbing breaks out – the first during the entire ceremony. Liza is weeping on Mila's breast like a little girl. Nastya looks at her sister, biting her lip.

'Silly fool!' she whispers angrily . . . and faints.

Tamara, standing beside her, barely manages to catch her in time, but the crematorium attendant is there in a flash with the smelling salts.

'It's all right, it's all right,' she says, 'just the usual procedure.'

Probably. She ought to know.

The funeral is over, and our next stop as part of 'the usual procedure' is the wake, which takes place at the Zamoiskys' flat in rather crowded conditions, but is generally well up to the mark. I'll omit any descriptions in order to avoid the appalling monologues from Grisha's colleagues.

The evening is already dark when we make our way

back from the wake. I sit on the back seat of the Geländewagen with Tamara and listen to her telling me how Mila came home from work to find Grisha dead. 'Mila comes home and he's sitting there at the table. And the soup in front of him is already cold . . .'

'Calm down . . .' I say and pull her close.

We drive on for a while in silence, but I feel Toma's body start trembling slightly. She's crying.

'You're much too . . .' I mutter. 'You shouldn't take it so much to heart . . .'

Toma raises her tearstained face.

'I'm sorry . . . I suddenly felt afraid: what if I come to see you, and you're sitting there like that . . . sitting with your soup in front of you.'

I conceal my ironic smile in the dark.

'Why me, and not your Dmitry Pavlovich?'

'I don't know,' she says, moving away almost angrily. 'I just thought about you now.'

Assuming a vertical position, Tamara looks at Little Dima's broad back.

'Dima!' she says.

'Yeah?'

'You won't tell Dmitry Pavlovich, will you?'

'About what?' he asks and shrugs his mighty shoulders. 'Telling tales isn't done in our line of work.'

'It isn't done? That's good then,' says Toma, and her voice sounds determined. 'Then turn round – we're going somewhere else.'

Dima looks at us in the rear-view mirror.

'Where?' he asks dispassionately.

'His place,' she says, looking at me, and I think I see a smile on her wet face. That dear, forgotten, smile of Toma's from the past, a smile filled with tenderness. All right, so let's go to my place, we'll remember our friend Zamoisky again, and lots and lots of other things as well . . .

A GELÄNDEWAGEN TRAP

Do you remember how they used to shoot car-rides in the old movies? Somewhere in the studio they set up a model of the interior of a car and sat the actors in it. Projected on a screen in the windows of the model, the road slipped back and away, telegraph poles flickered past, and the actors swayed about as if they were riding over a bumpy surface. Meanwhile, the actor playing the driver looked straight ahead all the time, swinging the wheel vigorously to and fro ... But now imagine that shooting is over. The driver has let go of the wheel, the passengers have stopped bouncing up and down over non-existent potholes; everyone is relaxing, drinking coffee and chatting about something or other. Only outside the windows of the model car the forgotten road is still running along on the screen, it hasn't been switched off yet ... Copses of trees ripple across cloud-dappled blue sky; fields of pasture open out like fans; Caucasians at the roadside go flying past, wreathed in shish-kebab smoke; a village spurts out from behind a hill in a lava-flood of houses: peasant women with jars, peasant women with buckets, flickering past, dazzling your eyes . . . Then it's clear again, with just the open country rising and falling in long, smooth movements, as if it's breathing with its large stomach. Ahead, drawn up in close formation, the perpendicular trunks of a pine forest advance into sight: a tight-packed, bronze organ-pipe colonnade, the forest trees drone, breathing out their solemn liturgical dampness at the windows of the cars flashing past. The windows of the cars, however, are tightly closed.

Sitting inside our model, we don't smell the aroma of the freshly mown grass or the breath of the forest, and if we imagine that we catch the scent of pine needles, it comes from the little cardboard deodorant tree dangling under the mirror on the windscreen.

'We'll miss our turn, Palich. You could at least give the road an occasional glance.'

'Don't teach your grandmother to suck eggs,' Dmitry Pavlovich replies.

He's sitting half-turned towards me with a little cardboard cup of coffee in his right hand. The plump fingers of his left hand are resting on the steering wheel. Resting and nothing more, because the Geländewagen, blasting along the federal highway at a speed of a hundred and sixty kilometres an hour, needs no steering. That's what it's like to drive a good car! Every little corner inside it is upholstered with something soft and non-traumatising. The interior is like a case for some precious item and a person sitting in it can't help feeling that he is that item. There's nothing so surprising about those weirdos who leave wills with instructions to bury them in their own cars. I wouldn't mind being buried in the Geländewagen myself, as long as it doesn't happen too soon.

But to ensure that our burial doesn't take place ahead of schedule, Dmitry Pavlovich needs to hold the driving wheel with both hands. I take away his cup of coffee and try to make him concentrate on his driving. It's not easy, though, the highway feels so wide and open after the automotive clutter of Moscow . . . Dmitry Pavlovich dropped the reins the moment we got past the ring road, and I have a very uneasy feeling that the drivers of the cars we overtake and the cars that overtake us have all done the same.

A road sign comes darting up and I read it: 'R. Volya'. I heard somewhere that the names of all the rivers around Moscow have Sanskrit roots. I wonder what the word 'Volya' means in Sanskrit? In Russian it usually means 'will' or 'freedom', but in this case it means that we've almost missed our turn!

'Palich, we're here already,' I shout. 'Look for the turn-off!'

'I see, stop yelling,' he burbles.

In actual fact he doesn't see anything, or he wouldn't be travelling in the third lane from the shoulder. Scaring all the drivers dozing at their wheels, we cut hard to the right across two lanes of traffic going in our direction and brake so hard that Phil, who is dozing on the back seat, tumbles off onto the floor.

The Geländewagen's moment of truth has arrived. It's time for our German to prove that he's a genuine all-terrain model, that those big wheels and that cavalry army under his bonnet are there for more than just insolent swagger. Our German replies confidently: 'Kein problem! Only plis explain me, ver going are ve?' No, he's not afraid of being tested, he's a jeep, he's rugged and powerful and the finest engineers have designed him to conquer impassable roads. But the Geländewagen is slightly puzzled: Why have we turned off a perfectly decent *autobahn* onto this nominal road that is a mere dusty earth track – sinewy, twisted and shrivelled, like some old anatomical specimen. God only knows where this track leads. The Geländewagen has heard that Russians call this sort of thing a 'cross-country road'. But what do we want with it, we almost-European inhabitants of the megalopolis? Or have we decided to have some fun, go for . . . what's it called now? – a joyride? If that's it, then he understands.

'Hold on, brothers, it's going to get bouncy!' our driver warns us excitedly.

With a roar of its mighty diesel engine, the Geländewagen plunges into the waves of Russian off-the-road terrain. Its broad tyres splat the fresh, damp cowpats and leave a clear track across hoof-prints and tractor herringbones. Its suspension handles the numerous tussocks and ruts confidently, with no banging or creaking. And, as it happens, no bouncing either: a modern jeep is not your old Soviet collective-farm bone-shaker!

The Geländewagen has no more questions, but Phil does. Behind us he runs from one window to the other with his tail tucked away, squatting down on it every now and then and whining agitatedly. Calm down my friend! You don't really think Dmitry Pavlovich and I have decided to go joyriding in our old age, do you? We're simply . . . we're simply going on a fishing trip, that's all. Drink a little vodka, breathe the river mist and feed the mosquitoes. Also an extreme sport of a kind, but rather more in keeping with our advanced years. And you, my friend. have your own amusements to look forward to: you'll be able to run around to your heart's content, wallow in dung and, if you're lucky, catch a water rat.

The track runs alongside the high bank of the river, alternately moving closer and further away.

'Where's the way down?' Dmitry Pavlovich asks anxiously.

'Coming up soon,' I promise him firmly.

To tell the truth, though, I'm bluffing, because I don't remember this area any longer. I used to come here once upon a time, but that time was so very long ago . . . The memories surface in my mind like fragments of dreams that carry no real credence . . . And, by the way . . . Ah, there, of course! That's it, the way down!

'Palich!' I screech in delight.

'I see . . .' he replies, scowling.

Dmitry Pavlovich is scowling because the way down looks too steep to him. But then, what exactly was he expecting? Out in the wild, with no conveniences . . . Like a horse poised above a river, the Geländewagen is halted, motionless, at the top of the descent, which is more like a sheer cliff ... Right then, boldly does it! A stone spurts out from under a wheel and goes tumbling downwards. The Geländewagen follows it cautiously, snuffling intently and skidding first on one wheel, then another.

There now, fantastic, and you were afraid! Just look at that wonderful little green riverbank – this is a heavenly spot! True, as you walk through the grass here you have to watch your step, or else ... Ah! There, I warned you ... As he scours the dung off his trainer, Dmitry Pavlovich mutters something about anti-personnel mines.

'What did you think we'd find!' I reply with a smirk. 'This isn't Gorky Park.'

Now I feel my superiority over him, the archetypal urbanite, and there's a certain satisfaction in it. How could I not feel it: these are my native parts, I remember them from my childhood ... Aagh! Now I've put my foot in it too.

Never mind. In the great outdoors the most important thing is never to let anything get you down. After a brief period of wandering along the bank, I find a relatively clear spot and we start setting out our camp. We, that is, Phil and I; Dmitry Pavlovich would be only too glad to give us a hand, but he can't, because he is engrossed in doing battle with the horse flies. As he lashes at his neck, his forehead and his legs below his shorts, he looks like someone doing a wild gipsy dance, and the longer he dances, the more horseflies are attracted to him, less by hunger than by curiosity.

Gradually, however we get the upper hand and, despite

the resistance offered by enemy air power, we establish a bridgehead on the riverbank. Our tent has been erected, our campfire is raking the heavens above with scattered volleys and our limbs have been securely protected with a coating of salve that could frighten off even a large predator. Half-glassfuls of vodka have been downed.

An initial glance at our base might suggest to the unobservant outsider that we are a group of city folk who have simply driven out into the country for a banal picnic. But only to the unobservant outsider. Unlike those lovers of picnics who drive out into the country merely to have a drink and a bite to eat, we have arrived at this spot with serious intentions. This is already obvious from the fact that we have a tent with us, but no women. Not to mention the strange manipulations with which Dmitry Pavlovich has been occupied for the last half hour. On closer inspection it is possible to guess that he is assembling American fishing rods out of components that we have brought with us. He has already caught himself on a hook several times, but in general he's doing just fine and the job will only take him another forty minutes or so. Of course, it would have been quicker and simpler to go into the nearest bushes and cut two good, stout rods there, but then what is technological progress for?

There is another achievement of progress that has definitely proved useless to us. I mean the American electric pump that Dmitry Pavlovich bought to inflate the rubber dinghy. The trouble is that the pump and my old boat, which was acquired by my father at an army surplus sale in a previous historical era, do not mate together in any form or fashion. The two products represent not only different systems, but also technological generations that are very far apart. This, however, is no disaster, because for inflating the boat we still have the standard hand bellows, which look like the leg of one of those boots that people used for pumping up samovars in times gone by. The hose runs between my clasped thighs, against which the bellows are braced. The boat's valve produces a loud, indecent sound; as I pump, the healthy sweat of honest labour drips from my nose.

At last our flotation and angling equipment is all in working order. Now, even from the most superficial glance, it is obvious that Dmitry Pavlovich and I intend to engage in one of the most ancient of human arts, that is, fishing. Naturally, neither my companion nor I are under any illusion that this is a simple business. That's why Dmitry Pavlovich laid in the American rods, the electric pump and a jar of some repulsive and extremely expensive caterpillars, which according to the adverts simply drive fish crazy. To be honest, I can't imagine myself eating a fish that eats crud like that: the mere thought of picking up that caterpillar and impaling it on the hook makes me shudder.

Here too, however, my memory comes to the rescue or, perhaps, not even my memory but some kind of instinct or atavistic intuition. I pick up a stick and rummage in the bushes, where the earth is damper. After about a quarter of an hour I grub up a dozen or so wonderful, fat, moist, shiny, appetising earthworms. They will be my bait, and Dmitry Pavlovich can use his foul caterpillars, if he really doesn't find them too disgusting.

So, everything's ready. All that's left is to down another half-glassful apiece, launch the boat and ... And decide what to do about Phil. As soon as he realises that he's not being taken sailing, he has a fit of hysterics. While Dmitry Pavlovich and I load ourselves into the dinghy (which is no easy task, in view of our overall dimensions) Phil dashes backwards and forwards along the bank, howling despairingly. He even makes an attempt to throw himself in and swim after us but, fortunately, he's a hopeless swimmer and his fear forces him, wet and miserable, back to the dry land. His barking gradually merges into a plaintive ululation; hysteria is replaced by melancholy. And then Phil's attention is distracted by a frog hopping into the grass. In the face of this provocative challenge, all woes are immediately cast aside.

As happens with all of us, more urgent concerns help Phil to bear the separation. Especially since our separation is not so very great, in terms of distance. From the shore to the spot where Dmitry Pavlovich and I have dropped anchor is no more than fifteen metres. There's no point in sailing any further, because we are already at the midpoint of the river. In fact, it's not really clear why we had to do our fishing from a boat in the first place. Supposedly someone told Dmitry Pavlovich that the biggest fish lurk here, in the deep water. Maybe they do, but why would they be interested in us? The mere fact of sitting in the same boat helps fishermen develop chummier relations, though – if not with the fish, then at least with each other. And isn't that precisely why Dmitry Pavlovich and I have undertaken this outing?

Each of us threads his bait on a hook and we toss them

into the water to give the big fish pause for thought. Now, it would seem, we can socialise a bit. My companion has apparently been wanting that to happen for a long time . . .

Only what are he and I going to talk about? Men in a boat usually talk about politics or women. The problem is that my Dmitry Pavlovich is an ideological Westerniser. He holds such liberal views and is so doctrinaire in the way he holds them that if we start talking about politics, we'll frighten all the fish away. It's even more awkward for us to talk about women because, after all, we are husbands to the same one. Never mind that I am the deserted husband: I know Dmitry Pavlovich is jealous of my relationship with Tamara, and I know he has good reason to be.

To put it scientifically, his attitude to me is ambivalent. On the one hand, I can tell that I often irritate Dmitry Pavlovich, but on the other, he is attracted to me in certain ways. Perhaps he simply doesn't understand me as a person and wants to figure me out. Well then, let him try; he's not likely to succeed, even sitting in the same boat with me. How could he understand an artist, with nothing but a westernising left hemisphere to rely on?

However, contrary to my expectations, Dmitry Pavlovich is in no hurry to make conversation. We've been sitting here for half an hour without saying a word, dangling our rods over opposite sides of the boat . . .

. . . My float has disappeared. I didn't notice it straight away, although I thought I'd never taken my eyes off it. Maybe it has simply sunk? No! The float surfaces again, pauses for a moment's thought and suddenly goes darting off to one side, listing lopsidedly and trailing whiskery wrinkles across the surface of the water. I observe its manoeuvres, entranced, for about three seconds . . . 'Hook it!' The voice from my distant childhood sounds entirely real to me. If I can just remember how it's done . . . I jerk my rod convulsively against the movement of the float and – oh, wonder of wonders! – suddenly weighed down, the rod tautens, transmitting a live, twitching pulse to my hands. The fish resists for as long as it remains in its own element and its jerking arouses exaggerated hopes in me. But, once hoisted out of the water, it proves much smaller than I was expecting. When I clutch it in my free left hand, its entire body, apart from the head and the tail, fits into my fist.

Inanely wise, round, goggling eyes and a drop of pale, fishy blood smeared across the lips. So that's you, my first fish. I'd put you back in the river, but there's another fisherman sitting here, and we're supposed to keep count. So you can swim in the bucket for the time being.

Dmitry Pavlovich, by the way, is rather reserved in his praise.

'That fish is bit on the small side,' he remarks, squinting sideways at the bucket. 'What species is it anyway?'

'How should I know?' I reply with a shrug.

In the next half hour I manage to catch another three little fish of the same species and Dmitry Pavlovich doesn't catch a single one. Having lost faith in his patented caterpillars, he has cadged a worm from me, but it hasn't done him any good. We've swapped places and rods, all to no avail: the fish continue to ignore him. For the last quarter of an hour a tense silence has prevailed in our boat; Dmitry Pavlovich is concealing the fury that is tearing him apart and I am concealing my exultation. Finally, unable to control himself, he explodes into coarse obscenity. His thunderous, aimless expletives hurtle along above the smooth surface of the river, echoing back from both banks.

'Don't shout, you'll frighten the fish away,' I say, trying to reason with Dmitry Pavlovich, but there's no stopping him now.

'How can I bloody well frighten them, when they're already afraid of me? I've sat this way and that way, and I spat on the worm the way you advised me to! No, there has to be some rational explanation for this . . .'

'It can't always be found,' I remark meekly, but Dmitry Pavlovich isn't listening.

'What I'd like to do . . .' he says, glaring with hatred into the murky riverine depths, 'what I'd like to do is blast them with dynamite!'

I shake my head reproachfully.

'That's what all you rationalists are like. If something doesn't submit to your explanation, you try to blast it into shape . . .'

This remark of mine could well serve as the prologue to a debate, and there's no telling what general conclusions we might reach in the course of that. Dmitry Pavlovich is clearly about to object to something . . . But he doesn't get a chance, the debate is interrupted before it has even begun, because Phil suddenly starts barking furiously back at base camp. Glancing round at the bank, we see the reason for all the commotion: a herd of cows is jostling at the top of the descent to the river, the one and only way down, which we used to get here. Ah, damn them! But we ought to have expected this . . .

With a cry of 'Save the camp!' Dmitry Pavlovich and I start paddling furiously for the bank, although we should have thought about it first. For instance, if this group of domesticated ruminants is under the watchful care of a bull, we would do better to sail away from the shoreline. Fortunately there's no bull to be seen; however, a human figure with a whip has appeared on the edge of the cliff. Dressed in a cloth jacket and tarpaulin boots, the cowherd looks a figure on a poster; the only thing that spoils the image is the baseball cap set on his head instead of a cloth one. Sizing up the situation, he swings his whip majestically and the air is split asunder by a clap as loud as a gunshot. The cows all shudder at once and start lumbering down to the riverbank, lowing as they go. Jostling and skidding on their splayed hoofed feet, they slither down the incline . . . and then stop again, as if something has frightened them. What bothers them so much? It's certainly not Phil, they've seen plenty of heroes like that back home in the village. It's the Geländewagen: the cows are definitely wary of it. They give it a wide berth on the way down to the water, eyeing its bright, shiny flanks, shaking their heads excitedly and fluttering their long lashes.

Fortunately for us, there aren't many cows, and Phil doesn't let them get near our camp in any case. He has unilaterally determined some invisible demarcation line between us and the new arrivals and now he's patrolling along it. Even so, we think it best not to do any more fishing while the cows are here. Dmitry Pavlovich and I wait for the herd to leave, and there's nothing else to do except down another half-glassful each, so we do that. However, this procedure does not pass unnoticed: the cowherd, who has so far appeared entirely indifferent to our presence, suddenly abandons his charges and moves in our direction, with a smile on his face that is pleasant, despite lacking several teeth.

'How-do, mates!' the cowherd greets us from a distance, showing Phil the whip at the same time, just in case.

'How-do, mate,' we respond. 'Fancy a drink?'

'Well now, I won't say no,' he says, blossoming even more brightly.

Who could ever have doubted it?

Another hour went by, or perhaps longer, before the cows finally sated their thirst. Paying no more attention to the Geländewagen, the ruminants, somnolent now after all the water they have drunk, start clambering up the incline one by one. After the vodka, their leader is also noticeably heavier on his feet, but a cowherd's duty obliges him to follow his herd.

'Well, good health . . .' he says with a sad expression on his face as he bids farewell to us or the unfinished bottle.

'And you keep well, too . . .' we reply in relief.

When he is already some distance away, the cowherd turns back towards us and says something, jabbing his great whip up at the sky.

'What?' we ask.

'There'll be rain, at'swot!'

We look up at the sky, but we can't see anything on it apart from a few wispy little clouds.

'Takes a drop or two and he starts seeing things,' Dmitry Pavlovich sums up.

After the departure of the cows, the remainder of the day passes without serious incident, unless you count Dmitry Pavlovich catching his first and only fish, a tiddler. With the advent of twilight, we return to the bank, down a half-glassful each and have supper. After supper we sit there in silence for a long time, gazing into the fire. Sparks fly up and hang in the sky like bright stars and little starlets. And when the generative power of the firewood is exhausted and the time comes for a beautiful death agony to scatter it into a multitude of little grey coals – by that time the sky is already densely populated. As if in mockery of the cowherd's drunken prophecy, the sky is populated by a multitude of tiny but clear, almost unblinking stars.

'I don't even remember the last time I saw them,' Dmitry Pavlovich says in a subdued voice. 'Probably at young pioneer camp.'

Our faces and stomachs are turned towards the night sky. We lie there in the grass, smoking, and our cigarette smoke hovers over us, thickening the Milky Way.

'Always work and more work,' Dmitry Pavlovich says with another sigh. 'No time even to take a look at the sky. The only thing I know is the Great Bear.'

His sadness wins me over.

'If you know the Great Bear,' I remark sympathetically, 'then I can show you the Pole Star.'

'The Pole Star?' he repeats, narrowing his eyes distrustfully. 'Go on then.'

'All right,' I say. 'So, you can see the Great Bear?'

'Yes.'

'Then take the two stars on the edge of its dipper and follow a line straight up from them. The first relatively bright star on that line will be the Pole Star.'

Dmitry Pavlovich peers tensely up at the sky for about a minute.

'Have you found it?' I ask him.

'Yes, I have,' he mutters. 'Only it's not bright.'

'I said relatively bright.'

'And the line's not straight.'

'Ah, what a hopeless misery you are, Palich!'

His petty quibbling annoys me. I don't want to contemplate the stars with him any longer: I yawn and creep into the tent to sleep.

Phil seems to have been waiting for just this moment. He also yawns as widely as he can and as soon as I settle down, collapses beside me with a groan, snuggling his side up against me. In the two-man tent Phil and I could have spent the rest of the night more or less comfortably, but before we can nod off a third, extranumerary figure squeezes in under the canvas with a grunt. Phil is displeased but, following a brief struggle for his place, accompanied by growling and swearing, he is forced to concede defeat. Dmitry Pavlovich doesn't stand on ceremony with me either, although the assault is less furious. All three of us squirm about for a while until Dmitry Pavlovich suddenly goes limp and ceases to offer resistance – he has apparently fallen asleep in the thick of the battle.

The tent shudders from Dmitry Pavlovich's snoring and I lie there, wondering what on earth Tamara could have seen in this coarse, egotistical individual.

Meanwhile, I am gradually overcome by slumber. Through my sleep I hear new sounds added to those produced by Dmitry Pavlovich. There is greater harmony in these other sounds, but their rhythm, which resembles the beating of distant tom-toms, carries a warning message. I struggle to decipher this message, but I cannot, because the tom-toms are already beating beyond the bounds of my consciousness . . .

Meanwhile, somewhere the waters are already raging. Turbulent rivers are washing away entire cities and bewildered people, soaked to the skin, are thrashing about in search of a rational explanation. But there are no newspapers or police and the elements have disrupted the Internet connection, snapped the cable. With no one to help the people, the lamentations in their midst are most great. . . I am woken by my compassion for humanity or, perhaps, by someone shaking me by the shoulder.

'Get up, brother! We're in a bad way . . .'

I see Dmitry Pavlovich leaning down over me. Soaking wet, like the whole of humanity, he shakes me, which makes him shake too, and water drips off him onto my face.

'What? What's happened?' I ask in fright, raising myself up on my elbows.

'Disaster, brother! That damned cowherd jinxed us.'

Now at last I realise I wasn't dreaming about the water. It really is raining. The rain patters densely on the roof of the tent and drums a noisy tattoo on everything out in the open. But the resonant clatter of raindrops on the flat, bald crown of the Geländewagen is especially derisive.

Evacuate! Without even eating breakfast, Dmitry Pavlovich and I hastily bundle together our bits and pieces and stuff them into the car, dumping kilograms of riverbank clay, if not worse, on the expensive rugs. 'Right, my German friend, take us out of here!' I pray silently, although I have a bad premonition.

With a powerful roar, our Geländewagen sets off up the incline. But going up an incline, especially after rain, is not the same as coming down it. We race up about ten metres and then get stuck. After that the Geländewagen slides down sideways, right back to our starting point, still spinning its wheels senselessly. Time after time we try to drive up the incline, but only reach the same spot, which can now be termed our point of reversal. Alas, a powerful engine and computerised transmission are no help to the Geländewagen: a bond with the earth, with the soil – that's what's lacking just at the moment.

After the fifth or sixth unsuccessful attempt Dmitry Pavlovich loses control of himself. Swearing shrilly, he curses the day and the hour when he agreed to come on this 'damned fishing trip' although, as I recall, it was his idea. Intending to wait until Dmitry Pavlovich stops banging his head against the steering wheel, I get out of the car, open the boot and extract the bottle of vodka from a heap of wet clutter.

I drink approximately one half-glassful from the mouth of the bottle, take a breath in, raise my eyes ... and what do I see? On top of the hill, right above the incline, a bell-shaped human figure has appeared. The man reminds me of a bell because he is encased in an army ground-sheet cloak, but the peak of the baseball cap protruding from under the hood and, more importantly, the smile, allow me to recognise him as our cowherd of the previous day. I wave the bottle in the air, inviting him to come down. He doesn't need much persuading.

As he gets closer, the cowherd starts babbling something cheerfully:

'See now, I toldya yesterday!'

'Yes, you told us all right!' says Dmitry Pavlovich, sticking his angry face out of the Geländewagen. 'So tell us what we can do now!'

Without answering, the cowherd takes the bottle from me and follows my example by taking a long swig. Only after he gets his breath back and wipes away the tears that have sprung to his eyes does he turn to Dmitry Pavlovich and say:

'I'll tellyallrite – I'm on the tractor.'

He utters the words so simply, so matter-of-factly ...

Tears spring to my eyes too, but the vodka's not to blame. Our dear, wise, Russian peasant! What would we do without you?

A MAN FROM
OFF THE STREET

When Tamara and I moved into our flat, the first thing I did, of course, was replace the standard, municipal-issue lock on the door with one exactly like it, bought in a shop. Immediately after that I took a piece of paper with my new address (in case I forgot it), went to the post office and subscribed to a newspaper. Both of these actions were, as I understand them, intended to assert my identity as a citizen, something I felt an acute need to do at the time. After all, the flat had been bought by Toma's dad, and I, as a student of merely average academic achievement, represented a social unit of a rather low order. The keys to my own flat and a newspaper that would now be delivered to me personally implicitly raised my status, even if only in my own eyes and also, perhaps, in the eyes of the local postwoman. I wanted to acquire greater respectability, and I can't see anything greatly wrong with that. In addition, when I was still little I had acquired the ineradicable habit of reading while I eat. But there was another reason for subscribing to the newspaper: I needed a regular source of information. After all, I was intending to become a dutiful philistine and, as a general rule, the philistine likes to snuggle down in a safe little refuge from which he can peep out unnoticed, observing what's going on in the world.

However, not many peepholes were available to us philistines of the totalitarian era. The hot and cold water taps functioned more or less adequately, but the information tap oozed only turbid sludge. The TV and most of the newspapers were not only brazen pedlars of political untruth, they also simply suppressed all the facts that interested us. I am not talking here, of course, about crimes, air crashes and the personal lives of celebrities: the philistine of the totalitarian era was interested in far loftier matters than that. Only two daily organs of the press could even come close to satisfying the philistine demand, one Moscow paper and one All-Union paper. I won't mention their names now because, with the arrival of freedom and democracy, they were both dumbed down and have deteriorated into tabloids.

My choice, therefore, was not wide. Of the two newspapers I, as a philistine with a relatively broad outlook, chose the All-Union one.

However, a few years later the winds of change began howling across the country. We greeted them enthusiastically, my newspaper and I. Everybody then was literally intoxicated with the advent of new freedoms. But, as everyone knows, intoxication loosens the tongue – and my newspaper's tongue was loosened to a positively indecent degree. My philistine nature sought objective yet reassuring information, but I had to read interviews with insane politologists, accounts of crimes and daily reports of various 'glamorous' binges. For a while I continued to subscribe to this newspaper out of sheer inertia, although I could feel it slipping down the ladder of evolution and dragging me with it. The paper got more expensive with every month that passed and grew fatter on my money, spawning all sorts of senseless inserts and supplements. My home began to resemble a collection point for waste paper.

Eventually my tolerance snapped and I decided to find myself a different, more respectable newspaper. However, despite the modern-day abundance of periodical publications or, perhaps, precisely because of this excessive abundance, my search dragged on and on. The philistine of the totalitarian era, leafing through today's newspapers would probably decide that he was being taken for an idiot. Today's newspapers are not actually intended for any normal kind of philistine. They are mostly read by what is euphemistically referred to as 'the people', but should really be called 'the herd'.

Even so, my obstinacy was eventually rewarded – I found exactly the newspaper that I was looking for. I won't say what it's called, to avoid providing it with free advertising, but it's a very good newspaper. Not left, not right, not pro-government or anti-government; not sensational, with no advertisements and no show-business faces. A sound, reliable philistine newspaper. Nonetheless, in the light of my previous experience, I decided not to register any official relationship with the newspaper in the form of a subscription. Instead of this I got my wife Tamara into the habit of buying it for me at the kiosk beside the metro station on her way home from work.

Some might perhaps say the only possible reason to read any kind of newspaper these days is for the ritual of it. Forty TV channels and the Internet provide us with information 24/7, so there isn't even any need to go downstairs to the post box to get it. I won't argue with that. I'm a philistine, which means that my existence is dependent on rituals. Without rituals, life starts to seem empty and pointless to me. As an example, let me tell you that when Tamara left me and there was no one to buy my newspaper at the kiosk by the metro, I fell into something like a state of depression. I drank my morning coffee, staring blankly at the fridge, ate lunch without any appetite and in the evenings I quaffed vodka, simply to get to sleep. I had developed such an entrenched aversion to the television and the inane consumerist optimism it touted that I never even went near it. I didn't switch the computer on either, so that it wouldn't remind me about work.

Without a newspaper I was going completely to seed, losing count of the days and losing track of international political developments. Naturally, things couldn't go on like that forever. I was already gathering myself to take the plunge and subscribe to that newspaper of mine. Or I could have walked to the kiosk at the metro every day to get it, which would, of course, have been stupid and irrational. The root of the problem was that every action taken to improve my conditions of life would have signified acceptance on my part that I had made the transition to the unmarried state. Such an admission would have signified the final collapse of all my philistine illusions, and I absolutely did not wish to part with them. It still seemed to me, especially in the evenings, that the door would open at any moment and Tamara would walk in, bringing me my newspaper.

Nonetheless, some decision had to be taken, and a decision had almost matured within me, but I can't remember what that decision was now, because I never took it at the time: external circumstances intervened. My thoughts concerning the newspaper and other matters were interrupted by an unexpected telephone call from a certain literary club: I was invited to a meeting with readers. I say the call was unexpected, but that was only because I was so engrossed in all these difficulties with newspapers and other non-literary problems. Generally speaking, all Moscow writers expect calls like that as a matter of course and respond to them enthusiastically, since they believe that meetings with readers increase their popularity. The writers preferred by clubs are poets, because poets have more charisma, and the clubs preferred by writers are the ones that offer decent hospitality. In this respect the club to which I had been invited was highly regarded and I was delighted to accept the invitation.

Forgetting all my philistine woes for the time being, I immersed myself in preparations for the literary evening. The first thing I had to do was find my best pair of trousers and remove the stains deposited on them at my last buffet reception. This proved far from easy, because previously my trousers had always been found and cleaned by Tamara. In addition, it was rather a long time since my previous buffet reception, so the stains were well dried in. After that it got easier; I knew how to wash my hair and shave for myself – I actually performed both these functions more often than I had meetings with readers. My appearance did not require any other cosmetic procedures; in this respect we male writers have an advantage over our colleagues of the female sex, who have to work hard and earn lots of money to pay the masseuses, facialists, etc.

The function had been arranged for seven in the evening, but since I don't use surface transport, I arrived ahead of time, as always, for this meeting with myself. In order not to cause the organisers any stress by making my appearance too early, I didn't go into the club immediately but stayed outside on the porch for a smoke. The public gradually began rolling up. Men and women of various ages – all, however of a readerly appearance – walked in through the door without taking the slightest notice of me. Only one gentleman, probably a regular at the club, came over, politely shouldered me aside and started reading a notice that I had apparently been obscuring.

'Who have we got today?' he muttered. 'Aha.'

The notice announced that today they had me. The gentleman paused doubtfully for a moment, but then proceeded into the club anyway.

Eventually, having smoked two cigarettes, I decided it was already acceptable for me to enter. To the organisers' great credit, they recognised me the moment I walked in and immediately led me off to a special little room to discuss the format of the evening in prospect.

'Do you smoke?' they asked, pouring me coffee. 'If you do, go ahead.'

In order not to offend the obliging organisers, I lit up a cigarette – my third in the last twenty minutes.

We exchanged ideas over coffee, first on a professional wavelength and then on a social one. Whatever I said, the organisers listened to it with interested expressions on their faces, although from time to time one or other of them would offer his excuses and absent himself from the room to see what was going on the hall. The burden of their reports was that the hall continued to fill up, a circumstance by which the organisers were clearly surprised.

'Generally speaking, not so many people show up for the prose writers,' they told me. 'But then, of course, you know that yourself.'

We started hypothesising, wondering what could be the reason for this unprecedented turn-out, and came to the conclusion that I had the French writer Houellebecq to thank for it. He had cancelled an appearance in Moscow that evening for reasons unknown, thereby unwittingly divert-ing the readers' attention to me.

Then my hour struck. I walked out into the hall, accom-panied by the organisers. There were fifteen, perhaps even twenty people out there. It wasn't possible to tell which of them were Houellebecq's admirers and which were mine. After the applause died down, the youth chairing the meet-ing introduced me and listed off my services to Russian literature, checking with his notepad as he did so. When he finished he handed me the microphone and I also said a few words about myself. Then, in accordance with the agreed format for the evening, I opened a small volume containing my latest work and started reading out loud to the readers. After that everything went as usual. At first the audience responded adequately to the text, that is, they laughed at the funny parts and sat quietly through the parts that weren't funny. But gradually the audience's attention started to flag; some were already whispering together, hiding their mouths behind their hands, others were searching for something in their handbags. Eventually, unable to take any more, one of the readers got up, hunching over as if he was in a cinema, and loped out of the hall on squeaking shoes. Taking this as a sign, I slammed the book shut and suggested that the remaining readers ask me questions. The audience brightened up a bit.

The first question, naturally, was what I thought about Houellebecq. That, though, was the only non-traditional question throughout the entire evening, apart from the very last one, which I'll tell you about later. In this respect, by the way, our reading public is not brilliantly original: whatever a novelist might write, the questions put to him will be the same. I don't think there's any point in listing them here – after all, since you are reading the present lines, you are a reader and you ask these questions yourself. That's the way these meetings with writers go, provided that some complete outsider doesn't blunder in from off the street. But my function happened to be graced with just such an individual.

This person had absolutely nothing to do with me or
Houellebecq. While I was reeling off stereotype answers to
stereotype questions, he kept his head well down. But when
our pleasant discussion had almost reached its conclusion,
when my ear had already caught the distant clinking of
glasses; that was when he raised his hand.

'Tell me, please,' the man from off the street asked,
'what do you think about the global financial crisis that has
broken out?'

After a momentary pause the audience broke into a
general chorus of laughter.

'This is not an economic forum,' the youthful chair-
man remarked with a withering glance at the man from off
the street. The man blushed and pulled his head down into
his shoulders.

'I only asked . . .' he muttered.

At that moment I felt the urge to pity him – a purely
philistine response. But, of course, I didn't give any sign of it.

'Well, sir,' I said with a condescending grin, 'you see,
this crisis that you ask about, for me it's as it if didn't exist.
The fact is . . . er . . . I don't read the newspapers.'

The audience giggled and craned its necks to see this
fellow-citizen of theirs who had made such a fool of himself.
The man from off the street had sat right through that boring evening to ask his one and only question, which might
have been agonisingly important to him. What if all his hard-
earned savings had gone up in flames in some bank or other,
and he had come here to ask a writer how he could carry on
with his life now? What had he heard in reply? An arrogant

'I don't read the newspapers'! Why hadn't I told him I didn't read the newspapers because my wife had left me and a crisis had broken out in my life as well, and the emotional capital I had accumulated over the years had gone up in flames too? If I hadn't spent all those days wallowing in my own tragedy, but read a newspaper and thought about the financial crisis, perhaps now I would have found something comforting to say to the man from off the street. And he might have found words of comfort and support for me.

The miracle didn't happen. The literary evening concluded as it was supposed to do. I signed about ten of my own books and when all the grateful readers eventually left, the organisers called me into that special room, where they regaled me at the expense of the establishment. We started with very hot, but rather weak mulled wine and concluded, of course, with vodka, accompanied by herring salad. Yet another minor event ticked off on the calendar of Moscow's cultural life.

Two years have gone by since then. Of course, I long ago took myself in hand and subscribed to a newspaper, which I now read every day. During the time that has elapsed I have had another two or three meetings with readers, but I haven't come across the man from off the street at any of them. Nonetheless, I follow the fluctuations of the stock markets regularly – just to be on the safe side.

Oleg Zaionchkovsky

DANCE, LELIK!

It's back in Moscow again, that unmistakable autumn rain. I'm not alerted by thunder and lightning or the roar of a torrential downpour: it's that quiet, mysterious whispering, that subtle rustling in the darkness outside the windows. As if thousands of spiders have crept into the city on slim, sensitive little legs and are probing and tickling at every last detail. But they'll never weave together a mist. Tomorrow morning will be colder than the night: there'll be nothing left of the rain but puddles and sluggish, half-frozen streamlets. And no one will launch toy boats on those streamlets, because all the children have grown up over the summer.

Our autumn is strict: it washes the city without soap, scrubbing it with a coarse sponge of dark clouds. And Moscow has no idea what fate lies in store for it after this wash – whether it will be put to bed in fine white sheets or thrown out naked into the frost.

I recognise this rain from the rhythm, that quiet, meditative tapping. What is it trying to do, put me into a trance or remind me of something? Some writers say they work well when it's raining. Others say they sleep well. I can't make up my mind which to choose.

The outside of the window is spattered with countless numbers of tiny, undersized droplets of water, too weak to launch themselves down the dusty surface of the glass. They will hang there, trembling in the wind, until they dry out, until they evaporate back into the atmosphere, leaving behind only a tiny pockmark of mineral deposits that will stay until spring arrives.

The roofs of the various buildings, the sheet-metal car-shelters, the pavements: everything down below shimmers as if it has been lacquered. The courtyard looks as if it has been sprayed with chrome-effect paint. On the lawn directly below me a scattering of empty bottles and multi-coloured tin cans glitters. Since time immemorial this lawn under my windows has been a kind of forum or meeting-place for our local youth. Boys and girls from the age of thirteen and up drink their energy drinks, chew nuts, smoke, swear and chat about their own business in their own amusing youth lingo. Every morning the Tajik yard keepers gather an incredible harvest of litter from the lawn and every evening the indefatigable teenagers sow it again. Only rain or hail can drive them away from their favourite spot. I called them teenagers, but this definition doesn't apply to all of them. Many of the regulars have grown up and even developed pot bellies in front of my eyes. The low metal fence surrounding the lawn was bent out of shape long ago under the backsides of these former teenagers.

How many nights, especially summer nights, I have fallen asleep to the pealing of their laughter and the obscene murmur of their talk. How many times when I couldn't sleep I have wanted to douse them with water from the balcony, to deal with them the same way my mother used to deal with the raucous tom cats in our front garden. But I'm not a strong enough character for that: the rain has dispersed the teenagers for me today, and I don't even know whether to be glad or not. The cocky, back-talking, rebellious younger generation has surrendered to the elements and scattered to spend the rest of the evening at home with its PC 'shooters'.

The young people's pitch has been left empty, apart from Lelik, our own courtyard halfwit, dancing at the very centre of it, all on his lonesome in the light of the yard-lamps. He dances on the wet lawn, stepping elegantly between the scattered bottles – and he dances well. His inspired solo performance feeds on music that only Lelik himself can hear. There are two little speakers in his ears and hidden somewhere under his jacket, close to his heart, is a music player from which Lelik is never parted anywhere.

Once upon a time this player was responsible for a great and joyful transformation that took place in both his heart and his social position. By buying Lelik this toy that was beyond his comprehension, his parents unwittingly performed a service for their son second only to the act of granting him life, which was also an accident.

When Lelik's father set the phones in his ears and then

pressed the sacred switch on the player, the outside world ceased to exist for the boy. The music completely filled his head, from ear to ear. In an attempt to express the rapturous delight that had overwhelmed him, Lelik started bellowing, but was cut short by a parental clip round the back of the head. Soon even he realised that his own voice did nothing to add harmony to the music. Something – but definitely not his parents – suggested a different way of expressing his feelings: in movement.

He began to dance and, like all half-wits, he abandoned himself to his passion totally and completely. Lelik danced at home, while his parents were at work, he danced on the way to the shop and back, he danced in the yard to the amusement of the other, normal teenagers. But the kids on the block didn't notice that in making fun of Lelik, they had accepted him as one of their own. Previously they had driven him away, as children drive away everyone who is smarter or more stupid than they are, but now that Lelik had started dancing, it turned out that he could be useful to them. With him around, it wasn't so boring for the teenagers whiling away the time when they occasionally ran out of subjects to yak about, or when the courier sent to the shop for beer was delayed. Lelik and his dancing even became a stand-out feature of their group: other groups in other yards didn't have a crazy weirdo like him. Now, whenever our teenagers went off anywhere for a wander, they took him along, the way gypsies take their bear.

Ever since then Lelik's life has been much more interesting – he has tried all sorts of different crisps and learned the taste of beer and gin-and-tonic. But most importantly of all, he now feels that, even though he isn't the same as everyone else, he's no longer an outcast – people need him. Those people no longer kick him casually or thump him on the ear for no reason at all. If they do thump him, it's to say 'Give us a dance, Lelik!' And Lelik dances. Even when the weather's bad or it's raining, like today, he dances – without any audience, without any thumps, just for himself.

I watch him and envy him. I envy him because I don't have a magical music player, but I've got to dance. Yesterday I got a good kick up the backside from the publishers – a hint that it's time to be finishing off my book. The problem is that I'm not Lelik and kicks do nothing to inspire me. And the rain, I must admit, makes me feel more like sleeping than working.

AN ENDING

Sound sleep is the best preventive measure against neurosis. I know this because I read my weekly TV programme magazine all the way through. Not everyone's prepared to admit it, but I think there are quite a few in-depth readers of these magazines like me. Though no longer current, these unassuming publications continue to share our morning or evening periods of enforced solitude for a certain time before they are thrown out. The TV week has been lived and forgotten, but they carry on silently providing us with a whole range of information that possesses more than ephemeral significance. In particular, between the recipes and the horoscopes, my magazine has a medical page that offers recommendations on what to do when you have a pain in your stomach, how to protect your feet against fungal infections and so forth. The head is not neglected in this section either: the compilers of the page always pay due attention to the struggle against dandruff and how to choose the right toothbrush.

The medical page contains many pieces of useful advice but, unfortunately, in my view it doesn't deal adequately with mental ailments. 'Sound sleep is the best preventive measure against neurosis.' And that's all. They might as well have added: 'Things will look better in the morning'.

All right then: let's talk about sound sleep. The good people who compile the page assert that sound sleep is correct sleep. And correct sleep, they say, is when a person goes to bed before midnight and wakes up naturally in the morning, that is, without the assistance of an alarm clock and not because he or she is dragged out of bed by the leg. So it turns out that if in the evening you deprive yourself of the pleasure of a good movie, which is always shown after midnight here, and in the morning you jump out of bed at the crack of dawn, that will be the correct sleep for you. Of course, the trilling of the alarm clock will catch up with you anyway, only you won't be able to shut it off, because it will surprise you in that little room where you spend time with the TV programme magazine.

Apart from that, the compilers of the medical page will help you choose the right pillow and give you tips on how to orientate your bed in relation to the points of the compass according to the practice of Feng Shui. If you apply all their simple recommendations, they guarantee you correct sleep and no neuroses. But these good people fail to take into account one other important consideration. I remember my dear departed mother used to say: 'He sleeps well whose conscience is clear'. Conscience. She put a clear conscience above clean hands. Whatever she did, she did it with a clear conscience – even pulling my ears. But then, the compilers of the TV magazine were never acquainted with my mother, or with the forgotten practice of 'living according to your conscience'.

As for me, I sleep long and soundly, and my conscience is as clear as is decent for any civilised individual. The reason I'm on the verge of neurosis is that I have to finish a book. I know the entire reading public is waiting impatiently for this book, but far more frightening to me is the fact that my publishers are waiting for it. One day some time ago those kind people paid me an advance and took a written undertaking from me that by a certain date of a certain month of this year I would write a book, even if it killed me. Can you imagine that? A book! I polished off the advance very successfully long ago, but somehow I can't quite manage to polish off the book. And a certain date is looming up very close already, so polishing myself off might be the only option. Only that still won't get the book written ...

Why is everything so different for me? A horse steps up the pace when it senses the end of the journey; the steamship blasts exultantly on its horn at the sight of its home port. But for me it's those final few metres of that long string of words that cost the greatest effort. It's not that I'm tired of writing; on the contrary, I'd be only too glad to receive advance after advance and start book after book. No, I like writing books, it's just that I have trouble finishing them: I am a horse that has picked up all the clay of the roads on its hoofs; I am a steamship that has wound the oceans around its propeller.

Meanwhile, however, from the little magazine's point

of view, there's absolutely nothing wrong with me. I get up by myself without an alarm clock. Then I take a healthy walk with Phil, but without straining myself at all. Life is beautiful until the moment I sit down at the computer. When I sit down at the computer, it's as if someone sits down beside me and grabs my elbow the moment my hand reaches out to the keyboard. 'Think,' this person whispers to me, 'think one more time. An ending is such a great responsibility.' I'm so sick of him! With a certain date already looming up, it's either think or write . . .

What do I really have to think about, anyway? Surely I know how books are written and how they're finished, don't I? If I want to, I can invent ten endings in ten minutes. The only thing that stops me is what I would call a strange authorial prejudice. You see, I believe that a good ending shouldn't be invented. A good ending should emerge of its own accord, naturally.

For a book, ending is like waking up for a person. That's my creative method: after churning out two hundred pages of disjointed jumble I await the ending like my redemption, like a happy awakening. It will pop up from somewhere (only not out of my head!), explain everything and set everything in its right place, and my pages will line up into a neat stack that will form a book. Then, with my burden eased, I can start another one.

Only when will this happen and where should I expect it from? Wan indeed is the face of my computer, pale and bloodless. In vain do I stare at the screen – it doesn't even reflect me. The machine waits impassively, hour after hour;

it is ready to suck every last line out of me, but it won't give me a single one. Looking out of the window is just as pointless: the sky today is that greyish, off-white colour, like a blank document in Word. The rat-voiced squeaking of two women rowing fiercely in the yard wafts in through the open window frame like damp rising from the basement . . . In conditions like these only a pathological optimist could hope for inspiration.

But then, I'm not hoping: it's only fear of my publishers that keeps me at my desk . . . In fact, instead of just sitting here, I could do something useful – for instance, boil up some porridge for Phil and some borscht for myself. You know, I have learned the right way to make borscht after all: Tamara's tried it and she said it was good. She comes to see me sometimes, although mostly in my dreams. When I dream about my ex-wife, it's a good dream, although it's sad too. There's probably nothing surprising about this, but since she left me, the exciting dreams of my youth have returned. Good dreams, only they fade rapidly, their aroma doesn't linger and it can't be captured in prose. I'm yawning so hard that my jaws cramp up. Really, though, why shouldn't I lie down and take a little snooze? At this unnatural hour of the day, after coffee, why not lose myself in sleep tinged with insanity? I get up from the desk and stretch, and at that moment, in my habitual fashion, I lose consciousness. My poor brain is suddenly drained of blood; I am blinded and deafened and yet I don't fall but remain on my feet, like a samurai with his head lopped off. A few seconds of blissful, mindless intoxication, and then consciousness returns, refreshed by its brief flight. However, during my short swoon, something has changed in surrounding reality . . . What? That sound – I recognise it. That's the way the phone rings.

'Hello-a . . .' the very word provokes a yawn.

The receiver responds with a sarcastic snicker.

'Sleeping as usual?'

'No, darling, I'm not sleeping. There's no time for sleep, you know I've got urgent work to do.'

But it's all the same to Tamara if I'm sleeping or doing urgent work. She needs to talk to me about something important, very important, and it's not telephone talk. She's calling to arrange to meet me – somewhere in town, naturally, close to her office, because she's a busy person and I'm not.

'Yes darling . . . all right, darling . . . Of course I'll come, although, as you know . . .'

In my heart I'm actually glad she's called, glad of the unexpected distraction. Now I can postpone the problem of the ending, because somewhere in the real world a real problem has come up, and when I think about real problems, my mind relaxes. The Word document window is minimised on the computer screen and a game of patience hangs in its place. I click on the cards and speculate on what could have happened to Tamara that isn't telephone talk. I really ought to be feeling worried and I am a bit alarmed, but my thoughts gambol freely after casting off the yoke of my over-riding scheduled priority. The plot lines swarm around in my head, each more stupid than the last. Dmitry Pavlovich has been ruined and put a bullet through his brain. Or he is under investigation for the dubious dealing that I'm sure is essential to the running of his business. Or he has simply got roaring drunk and given Tamara a beating. Who knows what goes on in these New Russian families? But then, Tamara must have known what she was getting into. 'Now do you see who you dumped me for? Didn't I tell you . . .' – I invent our imminent conversation without interrupting the game of patience. My reproaches, Toma's belated tears – I should get it down on paper, it's great! Time spent in this kind of creative activity slips by imperceptibly and now I need to set out for our appointment.

I try to take out the rubbish every time I leave home. Then, whatever might await me out there in the city, I have already done one small, useful thing. The rubbish, which only yesterday was not rubbish, rumbles and clatters as it somersaults down the chute. I will come back home again, but it will not. After that, it's the usual story: the lift and Nasir are the final milestones of stable normality.

The moment I set foot outside, normality comes to an abrupt end. Before I've even looked around properly, I spy an absolutely incredible machine advancing on me with a hiss. The asphalt-spreader – or whatever they call this unbeliev-ably complicated mechanism – is driven by a swarthy-faced Asiatic, perched on the tall superstructure with a haughty air. Ai, Shaitan! I jump to one side before he can roll me into the asphalt without even noticing.

It's a good jump – my legs are eager for action after a long period of inactivity. My step is light and springy. My gaze is keen. Mums are walking their babies in the children's playground that my route skirts. When they lean down over the baby carriages their breasts, full of milk, quiver alluringly. I should remember that . . . or have I already written about it somewhere?

It's still a long way to the metro, but I can already sense its gravitational pull. Within its field of influence, chaotic motion acquires a dominant vector. Clattering their heels or shuffling their worn soles, skipping lightly or breathing with difficulty, the people are all moving in the same direction, forming up into chains, jostling as they flow round each other. We are Muscovites, children of the metro, time and again we seek refuge in its maternal womb. We find solace and reassurance that only we can understand in this hubbub, in the perpetual, deafening peristalsis of these windy stone intestines. For us urbanites, brazen and timorous at the same time, suspicious of everything, there is only one thing we trust – the Moscow Metro, the most reliable in the world. Here under the ground is where we arrange our trysts and here, I am sure, is where we first conceive new little Muscovites in our minds. When the end of the world comes, we won't need to make a dash for the nearest caves and seal ourselves in: we'll ride down to our ready-made common grave on the escalators with no panic, with or without a prayer, and accept our fate here.

It's well worthwhile coming to meetings in the metro ahead of time. It's so fascinating to press yourself up against some column and spend minute after minute gazing patiently into people's faces as you wait for that incredible assortment of noses, ears, smiles and eyes to resolve itself into the unique image that is dear to your heart.

I like the way people in the metro talk to each other too: like mountain shepherds on opposite sides of a precipice, they choose the most important, crucial words and yell them with all the power of their lungs . . . There's a girl squeezed against the next pillar; her friend, with his slim, youthful arms wound round her, is shouting at her about his love.

'What?' the girl asks. 'What did you say?'

She can hear everything perfectly clearly, but she doesn't hear anymore, she read it all ages ago from his lips, from his eyes . . .

Yet another train comes bursting into the station and its lock-gate doors all open at once, releasing a new torrent of humanity onto the platform. And at last the long-awaited miracle happens: the torrent splashes out Tamara, straight into my arms. She holds out her cheek for a kiss and then straightens her little cap. The glance she gives me seems rather uncertain somehow . . . Come on, my darling, shout it out, what's all the fuss about? But Toma procrastinates, she can't do it just like that, it's as if she needs to summon up her courage, and there's still something wrong with her cap . . . It ends with the cap being pulled off her head altogether.

'I'm pregnant!' I hear through the rumbling of the train.

Well, that really is news! I'm in shock; I slump against the column for the support I need to stay on my feet. Toma, my Toma! I think I'm beginning to realise that I've lost you completely. This child that you and Dmitry Pavlovich have conceived, it will separate us forever . . .

I must look awful.

'What's wrong?' Tamara asks in alarm.

'It's nothing . . . It'll pass . . .'

'Well then, if it's nothing, listen to the rest. I'm pregnant by you.'

'There used to be a bench somewhere round here.'

Come on, my darling, let's sit down for a moment.

It's a good thing that I'm psychologically robust. What she says is quite inconceivable . . .

'Are you sure . . . sure that it's not from him?'

'In the first place, Dmitry Pavlovich can't have children – that's a medical fact. And in the second place . . .'

The first medical fact is enough, but Tamara details everything for me with female thoroughness. I'm not listening to her any more . . . I'm trying to understand: before she left me and we started meeting again later, behind Dmitry Pavlovich's back – before all that, we were married. The two of us lived together for many long years in a marriage that was sometimes happy but, alas, childless. There's good reason for the theme of fatherhood and motherhood never appearing in my prose. Well, maybe now . . .

I am overcome by a strange feeling of undeserved joy. What can I compare this feeling with? Imagine that all of a sudden, out of the blue, your book has written itself.

. . . Meanwhile the metro carries on pulsating indefatigably. Like capsules in a pneumatic post system, one after another the light-blue trains leap out of the tunnel on the right and pause briefly before being drawn into the tunnel on the left, leaving part of their living freight behind on the platform. The belly of the station alternately swells up with the human mass and then ejects it from itself. In this little underground world everything is in motion ... Everything except Tamara and me. For goodness only knows how long, we two are its sole invariable constant. The smoke-stained, whitewashed vaults above our heads are the colour of a December sky; the bench under us has been polished by an untold multitude of Moscow backsides. We ourselves are like two small sculptures incorporated into the decor. At the more sumptuous stations they cast the figures in bronze, so that people walking by can touch them for good luck.

October 2008

Dear readers,

With the right book we can all travel far. And yet British publishing is, with illustrious exceptions, often unwilling to risk telling these other stories.

Subscriptions from readers make our books possible. They also help us approach booksellers, because we can demonstrate that our books already have readers and fans. And they give us the security to publish in line with our values, which are collaborative, imaginative and 'shamelessly literary' (Stuart Evers, *Guardian*).

All subscribers to our upcoming titles

- are thanked by name in the books
- receive a numbered, first edition copy of each book (limited to 300 copies for our 2012 titles)
- are warmly invited to contribute to our plans and choice of future books

Subscriptions are:
£20 – 2 books (two books per year)
£35 – 4 books (four books per year)

To find out more about subscribing, and rates for outside Europe, please visit: http://www.andotherstories.org/subscribe/

Thank you!

Contact
To find out about upcoming events and reading groups (our foreign-language reading groups help us choose books to publish, for example) you can

- join the mailing list at: www.andotherstories.org
- follow us on twitter: @andothertweets
- join us on Facebook: And Other Stories

This book was made possible by our advance subscribers' support
– thank you so much!

Our Subscribers

Adam Elston
Adam Mars-Jones
Adrian Goodwin
Agnes Jaulent
Ajay Sharma
Alasdair Thomson
Alastair Dickson
Aldo Peternell
Alec Begley
Ali Smith
Alison Layland
Alison Macdonald
Amelia Ashton
Ana Amália Alves
Ana María Correa
Anca Fronescu
Andrew Tobler
Andrew Marston
Angela Thirlwell
Ann McAllister
Anna Athique
Anna Milsom
Annalise Pippard
Anne Withers
Anne Meadows
Anne Longmuir
Anne Marie Jackson
Annette Nugent
Apollo Libri Kft
Barbara Glen
Barbara Latham
Barry Wouldham
Ben Thornton
Brendan Franich
Bruce Millar
Bruce Ackers

Bruce and Maggie
    Holmes
Carlos Tamm
Caroline Rigby
Caroline Maldonado
Caroline Perry
Cecilia Rossi
Charles Boyle
Charles Day
Charlotte Ryland
Charlotte Holtam
Charlotte Whittle
Charlotte Williams
Chloe and Oli Diski
    Marlow
Chris Stevenson
Chris Watson
Chris Watson
Christina MacSweeney
Ciara Breen
Clare Bowerman
Clifford Posner
Colin Holmes
Dan Becker
Daniel Hahn
Daniel Gallimore
Daniel Barley
Daniel James Fraser
Dave Lander
David Johnson-Davies
David Roberts
Davida Murdoch
Debbie Pinfold
Deborah Smith
Deborah Smith
Deborah Bygrave

Deirdre Gage
Eddie Dick
Eileen Buttle
Elaine Rassaby
Eleanor Maier
Emily Evans
Eric Dickens
Erin Barnes
Fawzia Kane
Fiona Quinn
Gabrielle Morris
Gay O'Mahoney
George Sandison
George McCaig
Georgia Panteli
Geraldine Brodie
Gill Saunders
Gillian Stern
Gillian Spencer
Gillian Jondorf
Glynis Ellis
Graham Foster
Gregory August Raml
Hannes Heise
Helen Collins
Helen Weir
Henriette Heise
Henrike Lähnemann
Howdy Reisdorf
Iain Robinson
Ian McAlister
Isabelle Kaufeler
Jacques Testard
Jane Whiteley
Jane Whiteley
Jeffery Collins

Jennifer Hurstfield
Jenny Diski
Jerry Lynch
Jillian Jones
Jo Luloff
Joanne Hart
Joel Love
Jon Lindsay Miles
Jonathan Evans
Joseph Cooney
Joy Tobler
JP Sanders
Judith Unwin
Julian Duplain
Julian I. Phillippi
Julie Van Pelt
K L Ee
Karan Deep Singh
Kasia Boddy
Kataline and Said
  Labidi
Kate Griffin
Katherine Wootton
  Joyce
Kathryn Lewis
Keith Dunnett
Kevin Brockmeier
Kevin Acott
Kristin Djuve
Krystalli Glyniadakis
Larry Colbeck
Laura Watkinson
Laura Bennett
Laura Jenkins
Lesley Lawn
Liam O'Connor
Linda Harte
Liz Tunnicliffe
Lorna Scott Fox
Lorna Bleach
Lucy Greaves
Lucy Greaves
Lynda Graham

M. C. Hussey
Maggie Peel
Margaret E Briggs
Margaret Jull Costa
Marijke Du Toit
Marion Cole
Mark Ainsbury
Martin Conneely
Martin Brampton
Mary Nash
Matthew Bates
Matthew Francis
Michael Bagnell
Michael Harrison
Monika Olsen
Morgan Lyons
Murali Menon
N Jabinh
Natalie Rope
Natalie Smith
Natalie Wardle
Nichola Smalley
Nick Stevens
Nick Nelson and Rachel
  Eley
Nick Williams
Nuala Watt
Odhran Kelly
Owen Booth
Owen and Moira Fagan
P D Evans
Pamela Ritchie
Patrick Coyne
Paul Hannon
Paul Dowling
Paul Myatt
Peter Murray
Peter Blackstock
Philip Warren
Phyllis Reeve
Polly McLean
Quentin Webb

Rachel McNicholl
Rebecca K. Morrison
Richard Martin
Rob Fletcher
Robert Gillett
Robert Gillett
Robert Leadbetter
Robin Woodburn
Ros Schwartz
Ruth Bareau
Ruth Martin
Sean McGivern
Selin Kocagoz
Selin Kocagoz
Shaun Whiteside
Shazea Quraishi
Simon Pare
SLP
Sonia McLintock
Sophie Moreau Langlais
Steph Morris
Stephen Abbott
Stephen Abbott
Stewart MacDonald
Tamsin Ballard
Tania Hershman
Tess Lee
Tess Lewis
Thomas Fritz
Thomas Long
Thomas Reedy
Tien Do
Tim Warren
Tom Russell
Tom Long
Tomoko Yokoshima
Tony Crofts
Tracy Northup
Victoria Adams
Will Buck
William Buckingham
Zoe Brasier

Current and Upcoming Books by And Other Stories:

Juan Pablo Villalobos, *Down the Rabbit Hole*
translated from the Spanish by Rosalind Harvey

Clemens Meyer, *All the Lights*
translated from the German by Katy Derbyshire

Deborah Levy, *Swimming Home*

Iosi Havilio, *Open Door*
translated from the Spanish by Beth Fowler

Oleg Zaionchkovsky, *Happiness is Possible*
translated from the Russian by Andrew Bromfield

Carlos Gamerro, *The Islands*
translated from the Spanish by Ian Barnett

Christoph Simon, *Zbinden's Progress*
translated from the German by Donal McLaughlin

Helen DeWitt, *Lightning Rods*

Title: *Happiness is Possible*
Author: Oleg Zaionchkovsky
Translator: Andrew Bromfield
Editor: Bethan Ellis
Proofreader: Christopher Summerville
Typesetter: Marie Doherty
Series and Cover Design: Joseph Harries
Format: 210 × 138 mm
Paper: Munken Premium Cream 80gsm FSC
Printer: T. J. International Ltd, Padstow, Cornwall

The first 300 copies are individually numbered.

FSC
www.fsc.org
MIX
Paper from
responsible sources
FSC® C013056